# STAR CHILDREN

# Gary W. Babb

# STAR CHILDREN

DOUBLE DRAGON

# Chapter 1
## (The Escape)

As soon as the security shield deployed and the conference room was completely isolated from the outside world, President Thompson said, "Okay, what's so damn important that we had to meet here in the Top Secret, glass room with the fog for this briefing? I hate this room."

Mr. Canton, the president's National Security Advisor, said, "Something happened that needs to be reported that is classified far above Top Secret, involving matters only you and a select few are authorized to know."

The president's face wrinkled in frustration and he said, "For Pete's sake, Tom. What is the subject?" said the president.

"It involves the Star Children Project."

The president's face froze and his eyes bulged at the mention of the project name. He jumped to his feet and blurted, "Clear the room! I want only the directors of the CIA, FBI and NSA to remain. All others leave."

The president, normally intimidating anyway, but suddenly standing to his lean, straight 6' 3" height, combined with his obviously stressed demeanor, radiated the impression he was not to be fucked with, and they should comply immediately.

He continued, "This involves 'Need to Know', and you others don't need to know at this point." No one argued, although the Secretary of State seemed to pause slightly before getting up to leave.

But, one look at the president was all it took to know this was not the time to debate over protocol.

When only the five of them remained and the security shield re-established, President Thompson said, "Okay, Tom ... continue."

NSA Canton said, "There has been an accident reported at Area 51. The dormitory where the Star Children were being housed blew up, killing them all."

President Thompson personally picked and appointed NSA Canton to his position. Tom was not physically impressive in stature, being bald, short and plump; but the president trusted him implicitly. If NSA Canton said something was so, then he believed him.

"All of them?" asked the president.

"There are 151 confirmed dead out of 157. It seems four were scheduled to arrive but never showed up, and one had already left. No additional information is available."

The president's hands shook with obvious emotion as he said, "Damn, they were children! Most were around ten years old as I remember."

FBI Director Setliff coughed to gain their attention, then said, "Sir, I don't know anything about the Star Children Project Can I be brought up to speed?"

"Harry, ... sorry, I mean Dir. Setliff, we will get you up to speed. We will need some of that investigative intellect of yours I'm sure. That's why I want you involved."

Director Setliff's actual name was Jack. Harry was a nickname Dir. Setliff's ex-wife gave him years ago, because, according to her, he looked like Clint Eastwood, tall and lean. She called him "Dirty Harry", and the name stuck among those who knew him well, which is one reason she became his Ex.

Tom said, "With your permission, Sir." The president nodded. "Well, where to start? I'm sure you know about Area 51, the secret, government facility that everyone seems to know about. Yes, there is a recovered alien flying saucer there, and we have been reverse engineering their technology for decades. What you may not know is that we are also supporting a colony of live aliens there as well. We call them 'Greys' for obvious reasons if you ever saw one. Well, these Greys are, we believe, the same aliens from the crashed ship. They are supposed to be helping us with that technology. Anyway, the Greys convinced those in control at the time that they had also been doing genetic engineering on humans and asked for our help in finding them and housing them at Area 51 so the Greys could educate the modified humans in their new abilities. The last administration agreed and named the project 'Star Children'. You are more involved than you know. The mandatory DNA database for school children, which you administer, has been locating these genetically modified children for years and delivering them to Area 51."

The president's tight expression refocused and he interrupted and asked, "How many Greys were killed in this, so-called, accident?"

"None were reported, Sir."

The president continued, "I smell a rat!" The presidents bear paws clinched and slammed down on the conference table, startling all. "I think we have been duped. I never trusted the skinny bastards. They give us some technology, but it is like pulling teeth to get it. So far every administration has been afraid of them, because of their advanced technology. But, that ends with them killing children under our watch. Of course, we probably won't be able to prove that, and we don't want to start a war with an alien race we know nothing about. Still, it's becoming obvious we have done their work for them by gathering the children together where they could be eliminated."

"The question we should be asking ourselves is: WHY? What mysterious abilities do these Star Children have that frightens the Greys enough to execute them, which is apparently what they did? But, if the Greys didn't modify the human genes, who did ... and why? There are a lot of questions that need to be answered, but our first priority is to save those surviving Star Children we know about and any others that may exist. We need to know more about them. Director Setliff, you're charged with finding those yet to be identified. Director Jones, NSA is charged with finding, saving and protecting those missing children. Director

Martinez, the CIA will help the others and house and protect any Star Children found at Langley."

***

At the age of sixteen armed government agents seized Tom Bradley from an Oklahoma orphanage where he lived for as long as he could remember. Terrified, he didn't know what he had done to be treated like a criminal, and after three year he still had no idea. The agents thrust him into what they called a school for Star Children, a name that was never explained. But in reality, the school felt like a prison would probably feel, the worst kind. The children were confined, and there were armed guards everywhere. The complex itself had many layers of locked fences and state-of-the-art security. School? Right.

There were other children there, but they were much younger. He was the oldest by far, and he had no real peer friends. He felt alone and isolated and without hope. His life at the orphanage had been bad enough, but forced imprisonment at the school was far worse.

Living without parents and love had taught Tom to be self-reliant and to depend upon himself. He had to grow up fast. Still, when he was plucked from an already bad life and thrown into something totally alien, he depended upon himself and his own judgment.

To make matters worse, many of his instructors *were* actually aliens, which he knew nothing about. He didn't know where they came from or why they were there, and no one would tell him. Tom had to

9

fight the fears that gripped him and rely upon himself even more to survive.

At nineteen now, Tom had survived at the school for three years. He simply endured the first two years, but this last year he had grown increasingly uncomfortable, due to his escalating ability to sense thoughts and images from those around him, especially the aliens.

Tom Bradley saw the disaster coming. To be more precise, he sensed it in the minds of the aliens interfacing and instructing the children. The aliens' hostility toward the children was not visible to anyone else, especially to the adult human supervisors and attendants, but it was there, and he alone sensed it. It hovered just under the surface and was reaching a dangerous level.

He began to sense more from the aliens. Hostility and hate radiated out from the aliens' minds and invaded his. His ability to sense the underlining emotions of the aliens was increasing, and it was disturbing.

The aliens instructed the Star Children, but he sensed their real purpose was to observe the children and discourage any abstract thought. They taught the children to resist abstract thought as if it was something bad. They wanted the children molded into fixed patterns of behavior, and he sensed the purpose was to stifle their mental growth. He didn't know why.

As he began to understand their hidden purpose, he became determined to do the opposite ... secretly. When the Greys instructed the children

10

not to allow their minds to control their bodies, he sought to search his mind to discover how to let it loose to control his body. When they told him to resist his mind's control, he opened it. Of course, he experimented in silence and secretly, mostly during the sleeping hours. The startling discoveries came slowly. He had already accepted the fact that his ability to feel the alien's emotions was one such ability, but his second discovery came suddenly and surprising.

One late night he let his mind free to search itself. He felt unusually calm and let his mind take him soaring into the sky. This fantasy of defying gravity and floating and flying comes to most children, and it now came to Tom. He allowed this abstract thought to grow and willed his body to ignore the force of gravity and rise up. When his face hit the ceiling, he jerked awake. With his concentration broken, he fell back to his bed with a hard thump and a sharp pain, which he ignored. The impossibility of this action made his mind reel, but he could not control the grin that spread across his face with the realization of what he had done. His mind overcame gravity!

Over the next month, he continued to experiment. He learned how to become weightless and float at will. When his body became free of gravity's control, he felt intoxicated and his mind whirled as he explored the fantasy that was now real. He had no restraint or pressure on his body. Being weightless was almost like floating in a pool of water but better. He never felt so free.

In water he would have been able to pull, push and kick against the water to move through it. Moving through weightlessness required altering gravity's direction to push his weightless body in any direction he wished. With practice it got easier and soon he began to master the ability. When all were sleeping he would experiment and quickly realized that his discovery was much more than just ignoring gravity, it was redirecting gravity. Gravity became a tool for him to use to lift, push, pull and manipulate. He could float through it, rise and fall with it and even direct gravity of other objects. He became gravity and its master.

With this discovery Tom's excitement soared like those eagles he fantasied, realizing that he had found his way to escape the prison. He could simply fly over the barricades and security.

Now a decision needed to be made when to escape and what to do once he did. Tom grew up in an orphanage, effectively without anyone close. He had always been alone and depended on himself. So, he had no family to help him financially. The only thing he had to offer was his newfound ability or gift. He had never heard of anyone having this ability. Maybe this might be useful to a scientist, maybe at a university. He thought they would want to study him and maybe help him to understand it better. Possibly they would even pay to study him.

Once he had this tentative plan of action, all that was left to do was decide when to escape. The aliens made that decision for him.

Through his increasingly heightened ability to interpret the aliens' emotions, images began to emerge. When they spoke together in their guttural language he began to understand some of their communication through these radiated and intercepted images. The hatred and, yes, fear became more pronounced, but he also saw their intent to destroy the children after the next Star Children delivery, which would apparently be in two days. His escape must be before this delivery. So, his escape must be tomorrow night.

There was nothing he could do to save the other children and couldn't bring himself to see or be around them. Every time he did, tears formed in his eyes. He was the oldest of the group, with most being far younger, too young and innocent to teach them how to fly and heavily indoctrinated by the Aliens. It was just him, and he could not fight the aliens and guards. Sadly, the others must be abandoned if he hoped to survive, and his self-preservation instincts were undeniably strong. He must survive, that rule was chiseled into his DNA. But, maybe, just maybe, he could save those Star Children en route.

*\*\**

The last few days of Sue Chamber's life seemed like a nightmare. Nothing had gone well. In fact, everything went wrong. Sue was with her third set of foster care parents and reasonably happy, considering, when a knock at the door abruptly changed her life.

A man introduced himself as Agent Black with the National Security Agency. He never spoke to her, only to her guardians, "Sue Chambers needs to come with me. It is a matter of national security." Additional conversations with her foster guardians ensued, but little information was forthcoming. She could detect little from his demeanor or thoughts, and she had always been good at that. She realized that the agent probably knew nothing more, he was simply sent to get her. Agent Black presented all the right credentials and necessary paperwork, and her foster guardians weren't about to jeopardize their income. They helped her pack, wished her well and turned her over to the agent.

Sue shook with rage. She hoped her foster parents would fight for her, but no effort surfaced to look after her. As they were leaving Sue anger got the best of her. She turned and said, "That's it? Bye and good luck? After two years and that's what I get? Well, you can kiss my ass." They hung their heads in shame but said nothing further. The release of the built up tension soothed her stress. Oh well, they weren't that helpful, anyway.

Sue's body shook and quivered but fought back her tears. She was only seventeen and not of legal age. She felt like a grown, mature woman, but she had no legal rights. The State of Arizona was her official legal guardian, and they gave her over to the federal government. She still had no idea why, and those few she met afterward would only say that it would all be explained to her soon.

She was transported to, the road sign said, Phoenix, to a dormitory facility without windows. Her room had no inside knobs on the door, only key slots on the inside, with no way to leave. Sue sensed no hostility nor friendship either. All she could do was wait ... alone. Sue hugged her shaking body and tried to understand, without success, what was happening to her.

After two days of living with silence and fear, four more children joined her. They were younger, but they were like her, at least they seemed as lost and frightened, and they were also all blond with green eyes ... like her. It didn't seem to add up how they could all look so much alike physically, it felt like they were somehow related. Also like her they all carried their life's possessions in a suitcase. There were two boys and one girl all about fifteen or sixteen years old, and one frightened little girl of about ten. Sue's heart went out to the tearful, little girl and beckoned her and took charge of her immediately. The little girl clutched her in a tight, bear hug.

After a moment of comfort, Sue asked, "What's your name?"

The little girl kept her arms tightly wrapped around Sue but looked up at her and said, "My name is Tina." Her voice quivered but came out clearly.

Sue said, "Tina, don't be afraid. I will take care of you. I don't know what is going on either, but you just stick with me. We'll face it together." In response Tina hugged her tighter.

The older children were named Fred, Jerry and Mary. Jerry and Mary looked typical for growing teenagers. They both had short hair, just as white as hers, but Fred's hair was longer and somewhat spiked in a goth style. White hair? Well, some of it was, but each side was dyed or painted. One side was orange and the other side blue. Sue assumed he was what was referred to as a punk rocker. He even had gothic spikes in his earlobes, the kind that required stretching a hole for them. Sue wondered why someone would endure the pain required.

They talked and none of them knew why they were here. Strangely, all came from various orphanages across the country with no memory of their parents.

As they continued to talk and learn about each other, an elderly lady, maybe sixty, entered, pushing a cart loaded down with food and drinks. The lady was of medium height and weight, with large, bouncy breasts and a slightly protruding butt. Her short, brown hair was liberally laced with grey. Sue sensed her friendly attitude and liked her immediately.

The lady cheerfully said, "Hello children. I'm Mrs. Wilks, and I will be your attendant until you reach your final destination. I'm sure you have no idea what is happening to you. I don't know a lot about your situation either, but I will try to help."

Being the oldest and practically grown, Sue assumed the spokesperson's role and asked, "Can you tell us why we are here?"

Mrs. Wilks proceeded to set the food and drinks on a table and motioned them to begin eating as she spoke, "As I understand, this is temporary. I was just assigned, so that's why no one has spoken to you. In fact, we will be leaving in the morning going to another location, a special school, as I understand. I will be traveling with you to take care of your needs."

Sue interrupted saying, "What do you mean by 'Special School'?"

"It has something to do with the mandatory DNA test administered through the school health program." When she received blank stares she continued, "A DNA test comes with the mandatory immunization shots you received in school. It's a test to identify certain genes that might indicate a future health problem or exceptional skills, which you all evidently have. At any rate, the special school is set up to teach those with these special genes."

Sue asked, "What will they be teaching us?"

"Sweetie, I have no idea. I'm sure the school can better explain it when we get there, but the genes you kids apparently have are extremely rare. I expect what you will be taught must also be rare and probably very important to the government."

"Where will we be going?"

"Again, I have no idea. The location is secret. They won't even tell me."

"Why are we locked in?"

Mrs. Wilks smiled and said, "Honey, this is a guarded government detention center. It wasn't designed for the likes of you children. You need to remain inside for your own protection. There are undesirables here. Sorry, if you feel like prisoners, but we will be out of here tomorrow."

Sue detected no deceit and believed her, and, for the first time since this nightmare began, the tenseness of her muscles began to relax, and she began to feel hopeful, even somewhat excited about the future possibilities.

They each had a room in this section, but Tina wasn't about to be separated from Sue. Tina eventually calmed and cuddled against her through the night. Feeling Tina's warm body pressed against her in need, helped Sue to also remain calm.

After the morning meal, Mrs. Wilks escorted them into a huge parking lot to a small, yellow school bus. The fact that they were going to a special school in a school bus gave credence to what she had heard. There were packed lunches, water and drinks in a cooler on the bus, so Sue assumed the trip would be a long one.

For some reason, she wanted to know their destination and decided to memorize the route. The driver, also an armed guard, took Hwy. 60 NW out of Phoenix straight out into the desert. The density of towns dwindled the farther they went until there was nothing, absolutely nothing, to see but flat sandy land dotted with sparse and scrub sage bushes. The road was straight as an arrow and narrowed into a barely visible line in the far distance that finely disappeared into a churning sea of hot air. The never-ending road seemed hypnotic, but Sue forced herself to remain awake, so she wouldn't miss any of the route.

They continued on Hwy. 93 all the way to Las Vegas, at least the sign read, "Welcome to Las Vegas". Sue welcomed the change of scenery, hoping the trip was over. She thought Las Vegas would be a great location for a specialized school, but they didn't stop there. They continued on Hwy. 93 out into the middle of nowhere and back to the boring view and heat.

The bus had air-conditioning, but it failed to lower the temperature enough and the driver's body odor permeated the enclosed air. The kids early on reverted to opening the windows, finding the outside air easier to tolerate.

There were many more miles of nothing to see, but eventually they turned west on Hwy. 375 into an even more remote and desolate area. She didn't think that was possible, but she was mistaken. Wherever this school was, it was certainly isolated and remote, and she was becoming concerned. This was not good, and she didn't like it one bit.

***

Tom had been planning. He knew that the children had all been delivered to Area 51 on a plainly marked school bus. What could be more inconspicuous? He felt sure this practice would continue. So, once he completed his escape he would fly outside the fences and wait to intercept a school bus. It had to be outside the security fences of the base, because security was intense within their security area. He remembered the signs they had passed upon entering had read, Government Property. Keep Out! "Deadly Force" would be used. He remembered the sign vividly, because of the near panic attack it generated at the time, but the signs indicated the level of security he would encounter. If he freed the new children inside the fences he would never be able to get them out. This made the task more difficult, but he remembered the route they had taken. He imagined it would be the same.

Waiting was the hardest. He had a backpack ready with bottled water and food, but he must wait until well after dark when the guards were more relaxed and potentially negligent. He wanted to be long gone before he was missed, hopefully not until the morning headcount. Tom believed he would have a full day before security exhausted their search within the facility and vast grounds of Area 51. Initially, they would not even consider the possibility of him being able to evade all the security measures such as infrared, motion detectors, cameras, guards, dogs and the like, but they would not consider flying out over the security as an option.

Finally, the time was right. He quietly got dressed, donned his backpack and slipped out the back door of his dormitory. Once he saw the stars he leaped into the air and kept rising higher. It was like floating to the surface in a swimming pool, weightless, except he went faster and higher. The buildings shrank in view, as he continued to rise. Tom had never experienced this level of elevation or expected the nauseous flutter in his stomach from an apparent phobia of the view from this heights, but he had no choice. He swallowed his fear and turned to the north and soared free. His speed increased, and he was quickly past the borders of Area 51. He heard no alarms … so far, so good. Then the small town of Rachel came into view. Once he saw the town he knew he was well past the borders and security of all government facilities. Freedom achieved, and the first phase of his plan complete.

The city of Rachel was the exit off of Hwy. 375 leading toward Area 51. This was the route his bus had taken and would be the likely route the bus would take to deliver the new Star Children. He floated lower until he identified the road going south out of the town. He followed the route and found a likely secluded spot on a slight hill to hide and observe the road. He settled to the ground not far from the road, found a ridge that overlooked the road in both directions, and began his wait. He would have to watch both directions in case the security decided to look outside sooner than he expected. It would likely take most of the day, as he didn't expect the bus to arrive until close to nightfall.

\*\*\*

Tina shook Sue's arm and said, "He is coming. He will be here soon."

Sue said, "What do you mean, he is coming? Who is coming?"

"A friend," Tina said, "I just know he *will* be a friend. He will help us. He is near."

Sue didn't know what to think about Tina's statement and asked, "Do any of you other children sense anything or feel something or that someone is near?"

Fred, Jerry and Mary looked at her, then each other. Jerry nodded and said, "I do sense something is about to happen, but I don't know what. It's just a feeling."

Sue had continued to memorize their travel route. Her anxiety had greatly increased when their bus passed a small town and turned off on an even more desolate road that wasn't even marked. Still, she had felt anxiety, but she didn't feel what Tina seemed to know.

Suddenly, a man walked out into the road in front of them and held his arms and clenched fists out toward the bus. He looked young, but he was big, certainly big enough to be a large man. What stood out to her, however, was the color of his hair. His hair was short, almost butch, but it was long enough to see the color. It was blond, almost platinum, like theirs.

Tina shouted, "See! That's him."

Tom had been right. The school bus arrived at his chosen location just before dark. There had hardly been any traffic, much less any school buses, and he was able to take short naps. It had been a long day, however, and he was thankful that he had brought plenty of water and some food. The bright yellow of the bus shone brightly in the evening sun and was visible miles away. The road was clear in both directions, so he climbed down from his vantage spot and waited by the side of the road. As the bus approached, he stepped into the road.

During his wait, he developed a plan. The plan was simple, he would control the gravity and reduce the bus's weight, even lift it if necessary. With the reduced weight, the bus lost its traction on the road. The rear wheels began to spin and the engine roared. The driver let the bus coast to a stop right in front of Tom with only a slight gravity push from Tom. The driver was armed with a .45 cal. military pistol. As the driver exited the bus and attempted to pull his weapon, he found it too heavy to hold, and it plunged to the ground generating a plume of dust. The startled driver/guard quickly followed his gun to the ground under extreme weight. Tom calmly walked over and picked up the weapon and slipped it into his pocket, as the driver struggled, unsuccessfully, to overcome his increased weight.

Sue and the others watched in amazement as the events occurred, but she was not frightened. This seemed right, and the man radiated comfort, no hostility.

Tom entered the bus and looked at all of them, giving Mrs. Wilks the longest stare, like he wasn't expecting her, or didn't know what to do with her.

Sue said, "You are one of us." It was a statement and not a question.

Tom said, "Yes." He smiled. "Yes, I am one of you. My name is Tom Bradley. I am here to rescue you. You are in danger, and if you had gone to the school you would die. They will all die today, and I couldn't save them." His ruggedly handsome face tightened, his jaw clenched and a tear leaked from his green eye. His face quickly relaxed into a smile and continued, "I can save you, however, and that's what I'm doing."

Sue said, "We believe and trust you. In fact, Tina here," pointing, "told us you were coming and that you were a friend." She then proceeded to introduce the other Star Children to Tom.

Tom said, "It is very nice to meet all of you, but we can't spend time in long discussions. It is much easier just to show you, so you will believe what I'm going to tell you. Please step out of the bus."

When they had all followed him outside he simply floated up in the air and stayed there, while they all stared with wide-open eyes. Once they got over their shock, Tom floated back down to stand in front of them.

Tom said, "You are called Star Children. I don't know where the name came from, but it must have something to do with the stars. Make of that what you will. As you can see, I have certain powers, and I believe you older ones do as well. As far as I know, I am the oldest. I discovered my first power completely by accident without any help. The special school tried to contain me, and I had to explore in secret. The school is controlled by aliens called Greys. They are fearful of us, possibly we are a threat. I sensed strong hostility and fear from them and believe that is why they hope to destroy

24

us. I don't think they want us to learn and develop our powers."

"The facility security will be looking for us soon, so we must go. If you trust me and want to go with me, get back on the bus. Remain outside if you don't want to go. They *will* find you, and they will kill you."

Sue noticed Tom stare again at Mrs. Wilks and said, "This lady is Mrs. Wilks. She is our attendant. We detect no hostility from her, only friendliness. She has been nice to us."

Tom said, "I detect no hostility, either. Mrs. Wilks, you are welcome to go with us if you like. If you don't wish to, remain outside with the guard."

Mrs. Wilks laughed and said, "You damn skippy I'll go with you kids. I was hired to take care of these kids, but I can tell there is a hell of a lot more going on here. I definitely want to be a part of it. It sounds exciting."

Tom said, "It could get very dangerous." Mrs. Wilks simply shrugged, as if to say "So?" "You are welcome to come. Can you drive this bus?"

Mrs. Wilks said, "Of course I can drive it, and danger at my age is exciting."

"Mrs. Wilks, please take the drivers wallet, IDs and any money he may have. Without ID it will take the Area 51 security time to check him out. That will give us a little more time." When Mrs. Wilks hesitated at the guard's side, he said, "Don't worry about the guard, he can't stop you. I have him weighted down."

Surprisingly, it was Tina that spoke first, "I'm going with you." For the first time she left Sue's side and bounced up the steps into the bus, but she was quickly followed by Sue, then the others. He waited until Mrs. Wilks entered the bus before saying, "We need to reach California as soon as possible."

After all were aboard he passed his hand over the guard, releasing him from his crushing weight. The guard struggled, staggered and finally stood. Tom made him strip off his gun belt, uniform shirt and pants, leaving him in his boxers and t-shirt. He handed the shaking guard a bottle of water and said, "Just wait here or continue to walk, it's up to you. Security will find you ... eventually." Tom got on the bus and they turned around in the road and headed back the way the bus had come.

Mrs. Wilks asked, "What route do you want to take to California?"

Tom laughed and said, "We aren't going to California. I just said that for the benefit of the guard. It was misdirection. They will be searching all over California for us, but we are going back to Las Vegas."

Sue stood and got behind Mrs. Wilks and said, "I memorized the route here. I can guide you back to Las Vegas." Mrs. Wilks just nodded. After a moment of thought, Sue asked, "What are we going to do now, Tom? Why Las Vegas?

"Well, we are going to have to get some quick cash, and Las Vegas is the best place for that. After we get funds we will find a place to hide and live, while we discover what talents we have. I'm positive I can teach you what I have learned about gravity, and I'm sure other powers will emerge."

"Possibly, we can go to Phoenix and talk to some scientists at the University of Arizona. Maybe they can help us explore our abilities, maybe even fund us. At least it's a thought."

Mary said, "How are we going to get funds in Las Vegas?

Tom said, "We will find a way to win them in the casinos. I can control gravity. What can the rest of you do?"

Fred shocked everyone when he said, "I think Tina can see into the future, at least she saw you coming. Maybe she can tell us when a slot machine is about to pay off."

Everyone laughed out loud at Fred's comment, but it was Mrs. Wilks that clicked on that suggestion and said, "If Tina can look into the future, even a short distance, the lottery is the way to go for the really big bucks. I suggest we pick up some operating capital on the slots. Once we get settled in a hiding place we can practice with Tina and perfect her gift. All you have to do is win one lottery to fund anything you want to do."

Tom said, "I'm glad you are with us. Can I assume you are going to stay with us for the long term?"

Mrs. Wilks said, "You bet your ass I am! I'm going to get rich hanging out with you kids, and as I said, this is exciting. Besides, I don't have anything better to do." She laughed, but she turned serious and continued, "It really pisses me off that you kids would have been killed after I delivered you. I was hired to take care of you, and I take that seriously."

Sue patted her on the shoulder and said, "Thanks." Nothing more was said, and nothing more needed to be said.

Sue remembered every turn and highway back to Las Vegas, and the trip became routine … slow and again, boring. Tom went back to visit with the other kids. As they talked, the subject of just how Tom could use gravity to win on the slots.

Tom had given it a lot of thought and explained, "Well, if I stick to the simple machine of three cherries, or oranges, etc., I think I can make it stop on whatever I pick. Unfortunately, I'm not sure I'm fast enough, since they roll past very fast. I will just have to try until I get it."

It remained silent for a long time as if they were all imagining the dilemma.

Jerry, the quiet one, broke the silence and said, "I think maybe I can help. I had never considered it a special power before, but after what you told us I've been thinking that maybe it is. I can make myself speed up my reaction time. It makes everything around me look like it is moving in slow motion, and I think my body is faster, too. I learned it in sports. I never miss a baseball pitch or a tennis serve, because they come at me in slow motion. I thought it was something anyone could do, but maybe not. That would help you, right?"

"You bet it would. It would help a lot. Can you describe how you do it?"

Jerry said, "Well, I'm not sure if I can describe it, I just do it. I was always getting struck out by this one pitcher. He pitched fast. I remember thinking and wishing his pitches were slower and the next one came in slow motion. I blasted the ball over the fence and have been doing it ever since. It feels great to be a winner and not a loser. All I have to do now is think about slow. It just clicks in."

Tom said, "That is very much the way I discovered how to manipulate gravity. I was thinking and willing myself to float up. I had my eyes shut and hit the ceiling. The aliens at the school discouraged that kind of thinking. They didn't want abstract thought or imagining. They wanted all thinking based upon a fixed scientific reality, their reality. I think our power comes from our minds, and we physically can do what our minds imagine."

Mrs. Wilks said from the front, "I used to be a schoolteacher. The word to describe that is 'metaphysical.' It loosely means that if your mind can conceive of an idea, it can become a physical reality in your body, if you truly believe it. I think maybe you kids have that ability."

It got quiet in the bus as each one turned into himself or herself and started the process of abstract thought. It was a simple process for Tom, since he had mastered one power already. It didn't take long to master this one. Just like Mrs. Wilks had said, it was as simple as imagining the concept, believe it to be possible, and it became a reality. At first, the cars in the opposing traffic lane zipped past. Now they seemed to be creeping along at a snail's pace. It was pleasing to be the master of two magical abilities. He was deep in thought and concentration when he was startled back to reality by Mrs. Wilks.

Mrs. Wilks said from the driver's seat, "Don't any of you float out of a window."

Tom looked around to see the other children floating around in the bus, even Tina. He laughed and was quickly joined by the others. For sure they were all Star Children.

By the time they reached Las Vegas, he had mastered the reaction time power, and it was fantastic. He was somewhat surprised that Jerry hadn't continued its development in himself once he discovered it, but then standard wisdom taught that normal people can't do this. Standard wisdom would have told him it was impossible; therefore he wouldn't have believed it possible. Well, things had definitely changed, and they were *not* normal people.

They parked in a back lot of a large casino, well away from traffic, but he was concerned and said, "Mrs. Wilks and I will go inside. I don't think it will take long, but if something happens, and you are found, fly away. We'll meet you at the last Denny's going out of town on the road we came in on." They all nodded.

Tom and Mrs. Wilks walked around inside the casino looking for the right machine and finally found one with a jackpot sign that read $1,000,000. The oversized slot machine, positioned on a main through fair, attracted attention. Most every casino has at least one such slot to advertise and excite players, but they never pay out. To win on this slot required four specially marked symbols to fall in a row.

Mrs. Wilks changed the $200 she got from the guard into twenties and fed one into the slot. She looked at Tom, and he nodded. She pulled the large, garish handle. Tom watched the wheels turn slowly, very slowly. He mentally tapped the first symbol, and it fell into place, followed by number two, then three. Easily, number four clicked in line on the row.

All manner of loud bells, whistles and sirens blared, along with bright flashing light. All in the casino heard the ruckus, and many came running to see. Tom quickly backed away, because he didn't have any ID and didn't want in any pictures. Tom grinned, but not so much from winning, since it was a sure thing. His excitement came because they succeeded in funding the group, one less worry. Mrs. Wilks, unlike Tom, was extremely happy. Her face lit up with a huge grin, as she jumped up and down. Tom also smiled, watching her abundant breasts bounce. She played her role perfectly, but then she really wasn't playing. A jubilant Mrs. Wilks posed eagerly for the cameras, as her smiles stretched her face and filled the pictures. True to her prediction, she would get rich hanging with them, and she definitely received her first installment of excitement.

Several casino officials surrounded Mrs. Wilks and congratulated her, probably begrudgingly, and after the publicity pictures, led her off to get her winnings. They were evidently followed closely by an IRS agent, because when she eventually came out she only had a cashier's check for $500,000 and $100,000 in cash. It crossed his mind to do it again just for spite, but that would really be taking a chance, and this amount would certainly take care of them for quite a while.

It had only taken them less than two hours by the time they got back to the bus. The others hadn't been found, but then he really hadn't expected it. He figured they had at least another day before the search for them got serious, and they would no doubt spend a day or two looking in the California direction. Just to be safe, they quickly returned to their route toward Phoenix, but they did stop at the last Denny's to eat a hearty meal and wait for a bank and car dealer to open. They weren't about to cash the check in Phoenix. That would be a dead giveaway as to their location or direction of escape. They also had to ditch the bus somewhere it wouldn't be found, but they needed another form of transportation first. He felt they could buy something here. If the purchase was found, it would only lead back to Las Vegas.

The time was late or early, depending on how you looked at it, and even later after their meal. They took a consensus and decided to get some motel rooms and rest. Sue, however, insisted on going shopping first for clothing and hair dye. Sue suggested they all needed to alter their appearance, especially Fred's blue and orange streaks needed to be cut or dyed. At a minimum, they all needed to eliminate their platinum blond hair. All agreed with her, so that is what they did. They also hid the bus as best they could in a different parking lot and walked back to the motel.

All tended to sleep later after their busy day and night, but they gathered mid-morning, retrieved the bus and returned to the same Denny's where they ate the night before.

A totally different looking group entered this time. With their hair color change and new clothing, they looked considerably changed. Except for Fred with a buzz haircut, Tom was the most changed.

Sue's eyes lingered on Tom in appraisal. Where before he wore a wrinkled, school uniform, now he wore Levis and a polo shirt. Where he had blond hair, almost white, now it was brown. Tom was still big, huge actually, but they couldn't do anything about changing that. He had to be well over six feet tall, because she was almost that herself and had to look up at him. His eyes shown emerald green and intense. She had seen those eyes and look before in the mirror every morning, but in Tom the look was somehow different ... erotic. No, she didn't just think that. He wasn't what she would consider handsome, maybe appealing in a rugged way. Well, maybe he was handsome.

Tom thought Sue keenly savvy, not to mention, shapely. Sue had suggested they only mask their hair color, that if they used a dark color the blond would more easily show at the roots when it started

33

growing out. At Sue's suggestion the others also colored their hair in varying shades of brown or darker, blond colors, none the same. Even Mrs. Wilks dyed her grey hair to a shade of red and groomed it differently. They all looked completely different.

They finished their meals and began their errands. The bank was first, and they knew it would take a large bank to carry that much cash readily available. But, that wasn't much of a problem in Las Vegas. Tom and Mrs. Wilks went in together, but he held back, knowing the bank would take pictures of this transaction. The bank didn't want to give out cash in those quantities, but Mrs. Wilks was insistent. Even then they called the casino to verify the check and force a cash transfer. Finally, they left with the cash in a bank bag.

The car dealer was next. Mrs. Wilks said, "This could get tricky. I suggest you let me do the dealing. We will have to get them to do some illegal acts if we want to remain invisible." Tom agreed.

The group settled on an eight-passenger, silver GMC full-sized Yukon. It was used, but it had a tag on it, which is what Mrs. Wilks wanted. The salesman took them into an office to close the deal. He presented the sales price at $30,000, which Tom thought was kind of high for a year old, used vehicle. Mrs. Wilks opened her purse, counted out and stacked $30,000 on the desk and said, "Go get the owner. We need to negotiate a deal."

The salesman's eyes bulged as she counted out the money and immediately left to get the owner. Very soon the salesman returned with a portly gentleman. The owner quickly spotted the stack of cash, and determination to get it shown in his eyes. He introduced himself, but no one cared about him, only the deal. He asked, "How may I help you. Mr. Jones said you wanted to negotiate. What will it take to close this deal?"

Mrs. Wilks said, "It's simple. I will pay your price up front, but I don't want anything in my name or any questions. I want it to remain in the dealership's name on the title, tag and insurance; however, I will require a blank Bill of Sale and receipt. Consider it a long-term rental, even though we are paying your price." Mrs. Wilks kept an expressionless face as she dictated her terms, like an experienced poker player might look. Certainly, she showed no doubt or give in her demeanor.

The owner studied her face, thought deeply, calculating, and finally said, "This is not exactly legal, but I can do it for a year, but you will have to pay for the insurance up front. After a year the tag will need to be registered. If that is acceptable, we can do your deal."

Tom thought Mrs. Wilks worked a great deal, even though she agreed to pay more for the insurance. No one could trace the vehicle back to them, at least for a year. By that time it probably wouldn't matter anymore. They closed the deal and passed over the money, and Mrs. Wilks got all the documents she required without having to sign anything.

Now they had two vehicles, which posed a problem. He had no driver's license and had never learned how to drive, the others were too young, all but Sue. He hoped she could drive, and luckily, she could.

Sue and Tina, since she would still not be separated from Sue, drove the Yukon and followed the rest leading in the bus. They traveled a new route toward Phoenix on the Nevada side on Hwy. 95, which was just as desolate as the other, maybe more so. When they reached a small town named Searchlite in the middle of nowhere, they left the road and found a secluded spot at the foot of the mountains next to a deep ravine. It was time to ditch the bus, so they transferred their gear over to the Yukon.

Tom said, "Let's practice our skills on the bus. I want all of you to concentrate some of the massive gravity of the earth toward the center of the bus. If we do it right the bus will collapse inward under the weight. We should be able to crush and compress it into a ball, then we can bury it in the ravine. But, before we start we need to remove the tag, just in case it's found. Jerry, can you remove the tag?"

Jerry said, "Sure. Do we have a screwdriver?"

Mary, being more vocal and outgoing, laughed and said, "Not that way you dumb shit. Use your mind." The others laughed at a blushing Jerry. "Oh, never mind, I'll do it." She concentrated and pointed a finger at the tag. At first, nothing happened, then a noticeable red glow began to encompass the tag and grow in intensity until molten metal began to drip. Soon there was nothing left of the tag. She smiled and said, "I learned that last night. The room was too cold, and I wished it was warmer, and it got warmer. I guess that makes me the master of temperature control."

Sue said, "That's incredible, another power." They all marveled at a new power to explore.

Mrs. Wilks surprised them when she said, "You're not finished. Nevada is a two tag state. You have another one on the front."

Mary chuckled and went to the front of the bus and removed that one as well.

After the tags evaporated they gathered in a circle around the bus and began the exercise. This exercise demonstrated a new way to manipulate gravity, that Tom wanted them to master. The bus began to groan and pop and slowly shrink on all sides, crushing toward the center. Some areas of the bus were slower to compress than others, but they eventually managed to compress the bus into an oblong ball.

Tom said, "Jerry, redeem yourself and open up a hole at the bottom of the ravine using gravity." Jerry quickly nodded.

They watched as rocks and dirt began to float up in the air and hover, leaving a gaping hole at the bottom. Fred, acting on his own initiative, seized the ball and floated it over the edge and down into the hole. Once the crushed bus was cradled in the hole, Jerry released the dirt and rocks to cover it. Problem solved: no more bus.

Tina said, "Wow! That was so cool. Tom, can we fly now? I have been wanting to fly."

Tom said, "Well, I don't see why not. Just make sure you are comfortable with your control of gravity. If you panic you might lose concentration and fall."

Actually, Tom had not done a lot of flying, just in his escape. He floated up and hovered, while the others did likewise. They all looked confident in their ability. Soon all the smiling Star Children floated a hundred feet in the air. None looked uncomfortable, it was like a fun game to them, and they were smiling and laughing. Tom redirected gravity to move him forward, feeling the air against his face. He moved faster, and as he did, he held his arms out like airplane wings or Superman. It seemed like a natural thing to do, but in reality it didn't matter. He could have flown on his back just as easily using gravity. He looked back and noticed that they all mimicked him. He guessed they would look to him as the master, which pleased him. He got braver and soared, dove and turned in intricate patterns, which they all duplicated. He needn't have worried about Tina. He could hear her giggling and laughing as she flew, and she was good at it, a natural.

They spent too much time flying, but it was actually fun. The stress seemed to evaporate. Nevertheless, they returned to the Yukon and resumed their trip to Phoenix. They continued south on Hwy. 95 and came to Laughlin, Nevada, and since Laughlin was the last casino town before Arizona, they stopped for a late lunch at one of the casinos and left with another $200,000 in cash for their kitty. They crossed the Colorado River at Laughlin and rejoined Hwy. 93 headed toward Phoenix.

# Chapter 2
## (Discovery)

FBI Director Jack Setliff, rushed out of the president's briefing, taking the National Security Advisor Tom Canton in tow. They went directly to the high security Top Secret documents room deep in a sub-level of the White House. Security demanded they take nothing in and certainly nothing out, and were searched to make sure. Under the presidential order, Jack's security clearance advanced a level, allowing access to the Star Children Project and alien contacts. Tom had been here before and seemed to take the intense scrutiny in stride, but this was all new for him. Armed security watched intently, and he couldn't shake the feeling that he was somewhere he didn't belong. They were taken to an empty room with a single clear table with two chairs in the center and cameras on all four walls. They would obviously be closely monitored for security compliance. Dir. Setliff brought Dir. Canton so he could refresh himself, advise him and corroborate on the tasks they had been charged with.

The archive supervisor brought the requested files and put them on the table, with instructions to buzz him when they were finished and he would come and retrieve the files. The files were thick and smelled like old parchment, but, except for various details required, Jack concentrated on the summaries.

The Star Children Project was pretty much what NSA Canton had described. It was based upon information the Greys had provided; although obviously fabricated. About ten years ago they came to their handlers at Area 51 claiming that they had done experiments in genetic research on humans, several hundred. They said they didn't know what the outcome would be and for our own protection, they needed to supervise them. They admitted that the results would generate a far more intelligent human, but they weren't sure if the children would be benevolent or aggressive and would need monitoring. The last administration, being fearful of the Greys and the children, agreed to the recommendation and set up the Special School to be able to monitor them. The Greys provided the genetic marker to be searched for and the FBI initiated the program. Jack Setliff wasn't the director at that point, but he remembered the project. He had even helped set it up and administer parts of it.

It had actually been simple. They just added a line item in the mandatory school immunization program that required a mouth swab for DNA testing. The problem was the actual DNA testing of the hundreds of thousands tested. It took almost a year to identify the genetic markers in over two hundred children. Once the children were identified, the NAS took over and delivered them to the school at Area 51.

Dir. Setliff said, "Hey, Tom. This file says over 200, 215 to be exact, children with the genetic markers were found, but there were only 157 at the school. Where are the others?"

Dir. Canton said, "Good damn question, and I have no idea."

Dir. Setliff knew he had that information available at the FBI, and that would be his next project.

In reading the file, what surprised him most about the project was the amount of discussion, or more precisely, lack of discussion. They hadn't even asked the Greys why they experimented with our genetics. It was as if the government was afraid of the Greys and simply accepted what they had to say and complied. In all fairness, though, who else might have done the genetic manipulation? Additionally, maybe the Star Children *were* dangerous and were destroyed by the Greys to protect us. Maybe they were right, and we were wrong to try and save the children.

Dir. Setliff said, "Will we be allowed to interview the Greys?"

Dir. Canton said, "I doubt the Greys will allow it. They live autonomously as our guest, and after many years we still know little about them. They want to remain hidden as much as the government wants to keep their existence a secret from the public."

With that tidbit of information, Dir, Setliff opened the file on alien contacts and found the section on the Greys. It was shocking that there were numerous files on aliens, most without direct contact. The file on the Greys was by far the most voluminous, but very little could be gained from it. Basically, they had contacted our government about thirty years ago to request asylum. They claimed to be the small remains (100) of their dying race and wanted to live here in peace. An NSA brief strongly recommended we agree to keep them from going to Russia for asylum. The brief warned against not cooperating, because of the Greys' highly advanced technology and the threat it imposed. The brief suggested this technology should be in the United States and not Russia. They suggested the government might benefit. It was a logical conclusion but totally political bull shit. Our government offered to allow them to use part of the secret facility in Area 51. They have been there ever since.

Another file offered a description of them. They were tall, averaging well over seven feet but skinny and grey in color. Their eyes were also grey and slightly enlarged. They were humanoid in that they had two eyes and ears, one mouth, a single nose, two arms and legs, although only three fingers on each hand. We learned these physical features only by observation, since the Greys never allowed a more detailed examination.

The Greys worked with our scientists with the engineering of the technology of the recovered crashed UFO, their technology. This had been beneficial, but some argued that the Greys helped only to gain new technology for themselves, since they had given up little of their technology to the scientists.

After several hours of research and due to other pressing requirements back in their respective offices, they left the secure documents area. Dir. Setliff immediately mobilized his department to investigate the accident at Area 51 and, more importantly, find the missing children as tasked. He also put some of his staff to research the DNA testing project to identify the discrepancy in numbers.

***

The trip to Phoenix was long, and Sue and Mrs. Wilks took turns driving, while Tom and the others napped. The drivers had just switched again, and Sue was sitting in the front passenger's seat. Sue said, "Hey, Tom. Do you have a plan for when we get to Phoenix?"

Tom jumped awake when he heard his name and said, "Well, not really. I haven't thought that far ahead, but I think we need to find a scientist at a university that can help us discover who and what we are and help us develop these powers of ours. I'm quite sure we are not normal humans."

Sue said, "We have gone to great lengths to become invisible, and we will have to tell him/her or them our story. Isn't that dangerous?"

"Yeah, it is very dangerous for us to trust in someone, but I'm hoping they will be excited at the possibility of studying us. Think about it. They could win the Nobel Peace Prize for this study. I don't think they will jeopardize the opportunity. Besides, eventually, we will have to trust someone. We can't run and hide forever."

Mrs. Wilks said, "Is there any particular reason you chose Phoenix?"

"Not really. I know the University of Arizona is there. Why? Do you have another idea?"

Mrs. Wilks said, "Well, yes I do. If you aren't hung up on Phoenix for any other reason, I might suggest Tucson. The University of Arizona is also at Tucson. In fact, it started there and is a world-class science research facility. I think they would be better able to help with what you kids need."

Tom said, "I didn't know that. What do the rest of you think? Want to go to Tucson?" Everyone nodded. "Tucson it is then."

Mrs. Wilks said, "Tucson it is. It's only a couple of hours more driving time."

Sue had been looking at the map and said, "There's an additional benefit. It's close to the Mexican border if we have to quickly evade the US government."

With the new plan formulated, they continued on through Phoenix without a stop and reached the outskirts of Tucson two hours later, where they found a 24-hour restaurant, another Denny's, next to a motel. They would initiate their plan at the university in the morning.

***

As soon as the security shield was engaged President Thompson said, "Okay, catch me up."

The others looked immediately to Dir. Setliff. They knew the FBI would be first on the scene, and they were. Dir. Setliff had agents from Las Vegas there almost immediately once the accident occurred. They would have investigated the incident anyway, but he had made it known that this investigation ranked extremely high in his priorities, and the agents, many of them, had converged on Area 51 carrying presidential authorization. In other words, there was no way they could be slowed down. Since they arrived, Dir. Setliff had been getting continuous reports, and he had been up all night reading and processing the information. He seized the leadership role.

Dir. Setliff said, "Well, Mr. President my agents have no doubt that this was no accident. It was deliberate. It gets strange after that. Area 51 security is, without doubt, some of the most advanced there is, and they can't explain how one of the children got out. We have a guess, which I will come back to."

"The missing child is Tom Bradly. He was the oldest one on the campus at nineteen. Even though not fully grown, he is reported to be big, at 6' 4" and 250 lbs. We have his photo out everywhere, the other children that didn't make it to Area 51also."

"It took the security many hours before they extended their search beyond their security fences, because they couldn't accept the fact that he had circumvented their vast security network. When they started searching outside, however, they found the security guard and driver of the other five children. He was walking toward Area 51 in his boxer shorts and T-shirt. My agents took him into immediate custody and interviewed him. He had the most bizarre story to tell, which we are analyzing."

"He reported that as he was driving down the access road a big man, that he positively identified as Tom Bradly, stepped into the road and stopped his bus. He didn't know how, it just stopped moving. According to him, he jumped out of the bus with his weapon pulled, but the weapon grew extremely heavy and slapped to the ground, and he followed right behind it. He reports that he became so heavy he couldn't move. This Tom emptied the bus and told the other children that he was rescuing them from being killed later that day. That of course was the so-called accident. We have no idea how he knew, but he obviously did and escaped. It gets really strange from here. The driver said Tom Bradly floated off the ground, saying it was somehow proof that he was telling the truth. At any rate, the other children got back on the bus, and the children's attendant, Mrs. Wilks went with them voluntarily. Tom made the driver strip and took all his IDs and $200. After that, they turned around and headed back the way they had come, but he heard Tom tell Mrs. Wilks that they were going to California."

"The Area 51 security believe the guard actually did see Tom Bradley float. They claim floating or flying over their security and out would have been the only way he could have evaded their security."

NSA Dir. Jones jumped into the conversation and said, "We have satellites searching all over California for the bus, it has a number painted on the roof, but we have nothing to report yet. It's just not there."

Dir. Setliff, aggravated at the interruption, said, "That's because it's not in California you stupid bastard. Tom Bradley would not have been stupid enough to let us know what direction he was going. It was an obvious misdirection. They went in the opposite direction."

The president said, "You think this Tom Bradley is that smart? I mean he is only 19 years old."

"I read the file, Mr. President. The Greys said increased IQ was one of the genetic traits being enhanced. Yes, Mr. President, I think this Tom Bradley is that smart. He wants to be lost, and he is."

The president said, "Okay group. As of right now Dir. Setliff, Dirty Harry, is in charge of this project." Laughs rang out around the conference table, even Jack smiled. "Now, let me ask. Do you think the Star Children pose a threat to us?"

"Well, Sir, I can't say they have done anything to indicate they are a threat, it's quite the contrary so far. They are obviously being exterminated, and all they seem to be doing is trying to stay alive. Tom didn't hurt anyone in his escape, and he didn't

48

hurt the driver/guard. It is apparent that the Star Children pose a potential threat to the Greys. There is a lot we don't yet know."

"I learned quite a bit from the secret files. One major question concerning the Star Children is that according to our DNA records and in recorded comments of the Greys they modified 215, and 151 died in the accident. Only 157 were assigned to the school. The question I had was, 'What happened to the other 58?' I had my staff working on it last night. The children in the easy categories of being in an orphanage or foster care encompassed all those children at the school. We discovered that those that had been adopted fell into a more difficult category. Those parents would fight back in the courts and the program would become public. That's where we found the other 58, but of those, at least 25 have died from various accidents or diseases. I'm hoping we can find some still living, but our research isn't complete."

"I also have to wonder why the Greys did the gene modification in the first place if the modified children would pose a major threat. Still, if the Greys didn't do it, who did?"

"From this research two facts are clear. Someone is exterminating the Star Children, and someone within our government is helping, or at least giving them access to our secret files and databases. If we assume the Greys are doing it, which I believe they are for some reason, then who is doing the actual killing? It certainly can't be the Greys. They would be too easy to notice in public."

The president asked, "Well, who is the enemy here, and who is the threat? We have to know which side to be on. As I see it, if the Star Children are the threat the Greys might be doing us a favor. If the Greys are the threat then the Star Children might be our solution, which means the Star Children must be protected from extermination until we know for sure. So how do we know what to do?"

Dir. Setliff said, "We must continue our research, next we must find the children and talk to them. We need to find out why the children pose such a threat to the Greys or potentially to us. It's too soon to know for sure."

The president said, "Very well. Continue your investigations and we'll meet again tomorrow." The president abruptly stood and walk out, leaving them to continue their meeting.

\*\*\*

This was now the third day of almost continuous contact, but Tom had been preoccupied with survival. Being somewhat less stressed now, Tom and the others were enjoying breakfast. He began to appraise the other children. Fred and Jerry were typical teenagers, tall and slim, and constantly giggling. Mary was about the same age but more serious and mature. She was a beauty already, and it was obvious she would grow into a stunningly beautiful woman. Tina was young and still scared, but calmer when next to Sue, and Tina remained constantly at her side. It was Sue that captured Tom's attention. She was tall, almost six feet tall, and perfectly proportioned, and quite stunning in appearance. Ok, OK, beautiful. Tom was torn between staring at her beautiful face and those emerald green eyes or her large breasts.

Tom also sensed her emotions. Sensing others emotions was a trait they all seemed to have, and they would have to deal with and learn to live with. Right now he sensed Sue's appraisal of him, and it was embarrassing. He felt her sexual desire for him and looked up into her eyes. She smiled a knowing smile, because he knew she felt his desire for her. Oh well. No secrets between them, any of them. The other children began to stare at the two of them, knowing. Sue laughed out loud, and so did he.

They managed to get their minds back on track for the coming meeting at the university. Mrs. Wilks accomplished that when she said, "Would you allow me to do the talking when we get to the university? I think I told you already. I used to be a schoolteacher, college professor actually, and I understand the academia mindset. They do actually tend to think differently. They operate under different motivations and goals."

Sue said, "I think that is a wonderful suggestion. Of course, we can break in at any time we feel hostility or threatened. I guess you have realized that we sense emotions in others, even among ourselves." As she spoke Sue looked directly at Tom and winked. Tom smiled and actually blushed, while the other children giggled. Mrs. Wilks' eyes stared blankly but remained silent.

51

After they finished their meal Sue drove to the university. After several administrative stops, Mrs. Wilks found a starting point. She had asked only two questions, "Who is the oldest scientist on campus?" and "Who is the smartest scientist?" She found Dr. Wisscroff fit both questions. He was the oldest at 80 years old, and his list of credits and accolades filled a page. From his picture, he even looked like Albert Einstein, complete with the white, unruly hair.

They found him sitting at a desk in his small office. No appointment was attempted, figuring that would be impossible. All of them just barged into his office. Dr. Wisscroff jumped when they entered and stuttered, "M...m...m may I help you?"

Dr. Wisscroff was much like his picture hanging on the hall wall. His hair was white, long and unruly. His smallish frame was obviously bent, even though he remained sitting. The many age wrinkles covered his face, and none of them appeared to be smile wrinkles.

Mrs. Wilks said, "It is us that can help you win the Nobel Peace Prize. Are you interested?"

Dr. Wisscroff's expression didn't change at all and said, "I've already won it once, but I'm listening."

Mrs. Wilks was not put off by his statement and said, "Children, show him what you can do."

In unison they floated up in his office and remained, as Dr. Wisscroff's eyes widened and stared at them. He got up slowly and closed the door to his office. He then came back and started inspecting them and feeling for wires. Finding none, he looked at Mrs. Wilks and said, "Yes, I'm interested. What else can you do?"

Tom said, "We can do other things and probably a whole lot more, but we need a friend and scientist to help us learn about our powers. We need someone that can keep our secret, because we are being hunted."

"Who is hunting you?"

Tom said, "Well, the US government and possibly aliens. We escaped from a top-secret facility at Area 51, where they wanted to exterminate us. About 150 of us were killed. Can you help us, or should we just keep going?"

Dr. Wisscroff said, "Yes, I can and will help, and I would love working with you. Please, kids, settle back down in the chairs. I don't want anyone else to see you doing that." They floated back down in their chairs. The Dr. continued, "You have already told me enough top secret information that I am glued to you forever, even though I have a Top Secret clearance. They will never let me go now. I know too much. For that reason alone I am committed to you, but I don't care about that. I'm 80 years old, so there is little they can do to me. I will keep your secret. The main reason I will help is this might be the most exciting project I have ever encountered."

"But, there are some questions I must ask before we go further. Why are they trying to exterminate you, and are you a threat to humanity?"

Tom sensed no hostility and was happy to answer the Dr.'s question, "Well, Sir, let me answer the last question first. We have not hurt anyone, nor do we wish to, but we can and will defend ourselves. We are not a threat to anyone, we are just trying to survive. As to who is trying to eliminate us. We are able to read the emotions and images of others, and I began to detect strong hostility and fear in the aliens monitoring the children at Area 51. That is how I learned of their plan to destroy us, and I escaped and intercepted these other en route. So, I have to believe it must be the aliens trying to kill us. I don't think the US government is trying to kill us, but I'm sure they are searching for us. We don't know why they feel threatened by us. Hell doc, we don't even know who we are or where we came from."

Doc said, "Let's start at the beginning, and let me hear your stories."

Sue and Tom actually exchanged thoughts this time. Neither sensed any deception or hostility and proceeded to tell their story, followed by the others. They left nothing out, even Mrs. Wilks contributed her own version. Dr. Wisscroff asked many questions to clarify different points in their stories. He focused his full attention and seemed to understand it all, maybe more than they themselves did. The full briefing took a full two hours, but at the end, they felt the doctor knew everything they did.

After long moments of thought Doc Said, "That is an amazing story, and I believe it all. I've heard of several powers that are indeed interesting. Obviously, the control of gravity was the first to manifest itself, which in itself suggest many areas of use and study. Just thinking about being able to fly is a fantasy come true. Still, controlling temperature with your mind is a completely different study and just as interesting. But, Jerry mentioned being able to alter his reaction time. I don't think this is the case. I believe he was altering time itself, again this would be a fantastic ability. Tina's ability to see the near future is an incredible power that I look forward to exploring. I also heard of several instances of reading minds, in lack of a better term. Unbelievable. I will have to live several lifetimes to study these powers in depth."

"The powers you kids possess are fantastic, and I agree that you probably have many others. But, the real miracle is the power itself. We need to discuss how you came to have this ability and how you got it. Mrs. Wilks said, according to her briefing, that the Greys did genetic research and manipulation. This sounds like gene splicing, and it makes me wonder whose DNA they spliced from. Tom, did you ever notice any of these powers in the Greys?"

Tom thought and said, "No. I never noticed any of these traits. In fact, it appeared they had no idea they were possible. They would certainly have been more guarded in their thoughts and speech if they even thought it possible."

"That's what I thought. I don't think the Greys did the gene splicing, nor do I think U.S. scientists did it either. If they had, no one would have believed the Greys did the genetic engineering. So, the big question is who took on this project and why? This is what we need to find out. Let me take it a step further. I don't think the DNA donor and benefactor was from Earth. Earth doesn't have that level of technology." The group began to fidget and squirm around in their chairs, obviously agitated but said nothing.

Dr. Wisscroff continued, "Let's make some scientific assumptions for a hypothesis. The Greys must be your enemy, since they are trying to exterminate you. Whatever you are, your existence poses a serious threat to them. So, whoever did the DNA manipulation must also be enemies of the Greys. Since the DNA manipulation obviously was done, it must have been done for a reason, and that reason must be to resist some nefarious threat to humans. I believe this means that you must have been created to help humans. This is going around the block to prove that you are a friend and ally to humans and thus our government."

"Now if this hypothesis is correct, and I believe it is, these mysterious aliens should have provided a plan. Since they are not here to protect you, they are probably dead or gone, but I would expect them to have devised a plan, explanation or information … something for you that only you could access through your powers. Someone must know where it is. Think about it."

Tina shocked everyone when she said, "I didn't know that I knew, but I think now that I do know.

It's been a dream, the same dream, I've always had. Now I know it's directions to them."

Dr. Wisscroff smiled and said, "I love it when I'm right."

Sue said, "That's great, Tina. Can you tell us?"

"It's a dream I've had for as long as I can remember. I travel, I fly actually, south to the ice. I see miles and miles of ice as far as I can see. When I turn around I see the sun traveling fast, and it comes out above the horizon at its highest point just above the snow, not quite touching the Earth, then sinks back under the snow as it travels. In my dream I am not cold. I look through the ice and see something deep. It is glowing red. I then somehow melt a deep tunnel down a long way through the ice and enter a cavern. Inside is a round ship that talks. That's all the dream, and it is always the same."

The doctor said, "That is another power you must develop. We'll work on it. You have already described the other powers you will need: flying and temperature control. How clever your donors were. Only you kids with these powers could find and reach the ship, and you can't be tracked the way you fly. This way no one but a Star Child could get to it. It was also very clever to give you the view of the sun on the low horizon. Just from that information alone, I can say the location is in Antarctica and probably within only a few degrees of the South Pole."

Dr. Wisscroff looked serious then asked, "Are you staying in a local motel?" They nodded. He continued, "I have a lot of pull here on the campus.

Go get your gear and by the time you get back, I will have an isolated place for you all to bunk with security. We have a lot of work to do, and we need to get started."

As they drove back to the motel Tom said, "That Dr. Wisscroff is a very smart man. He wiggled through all our ramblings and went straight to the heart of the problem. I like him a lot, and think he will help us a great deal." They all agreed.

When they returned Dr. Wisscroff took them to an isolated building that looked like a gym with dorm rooms inside. They had a completely open area inside for anything they might want to do. There were also balls and nets and various other equipment in the open area. In addition to a conference room and a small kitchen, there were about twenty sleeping apartments. It was quite cozy. On the way into the gym they also noticed security guards at several locations.

Doc said, "We've put up special, secret guests here before, and our security guards are classified as federal agents. We do a lot of government research here. This is not our first rodeo. This place is secure and private, and I might mention that at the top of the building is a hatch that can be opened only from the inside. It would be perfect for escaping out of, that is if you have a tall ladder or can fly. Meals will be brought to the door and left at 9:00am, 1:00pm and 6:00pm. You won't have to leave unless you want to."

Mrs. Wilks asked, "What if the FBI comes to get us? Will the campus security keep them out?"

"Good question. To be honest, I'm not sure, but they will certainly resist and stall them long enough for you to escape if you think it necessary. I will also intercede on your behalf. Hopefully, evasion won't be required. Keep in mind that the government doesn't know you are here. We have some time. Hell, if we're lucky they will never know. But, we have determined that Star Children and the government aren't enemies. At some point, we may want them as friends. We may even want to contact them, well the right ones knowledgeable of your plight. Another hypothesis: eventually the right ones will come to us."

Tom said, "Yeah, they aren't stupid, and we have probably left a footprint somewhere along the line.

***

Dir. Setliff had been totally unsuccessful in finding any leads on the children. They had no cell phones or any credit cards at all to track, so they were concentrating on the attendant, Mrs. Wilks. There had been no activity on her name. Her cell phone was turned off. She was as invisible as a person could be.

Once Dir. Setliff was put in charge of the investigation and operation, he redirected the NSA to alter its satellite surveillance for the school bus in the opposite direction, but too much time had passed. The search coverage area was now vast, and the results so far were all negative. He wasn't very hopeful at this point that they would find them via the satellite surveillance.

He had been somewhat successful in his other investigation for the security leak. It was a short list of agents or high-level politicians that had access to the whole DNA files. Any average level technician would only have limited access narrowed to a single function, which would be heavily supervised. None of them would have had access to enough of the functions to piece anything together. The president got him the warrants, and his agents quickly began their investigation. Dir. Setliff didn't trust politicians anyway. They can't keep secrets, but as it turned out it was one of the FBI's high-level agents, a deputy director ... sadly. The investigation found him out almost immediately. Thankfully, he was the only one that didn't check out. The agent had an influx of large payments from a D.C. law firm going back almost ten years. But, the telling evidence was his work history. The agent had previously worked in security at Area 51 as a high-level supervisor, where he originally got his Top Secret clearance. His knowledge of the Greys and the opportunity became the wind in the red flag. Little doubt remained where the leak came from. It would, however, take time to build a case and track down the evidence, but this case would never go to trial ... too much sensitive and Top Secret information. At this point it was more important to plug up any additional leaks, so they arrested him under national security issues and the "Patriot Act". They would keep him locked away for quite a while. He would probably be isolated and hidden away at Gitmo with the other terrorist and milked for information ... forever. That was the only sure way to keep it secret, short of executing him.

Having found the source of the funds paid to the FBI agent opened the law firm up for criminal investigation. A good forensic Audit should identify others, hopefully, the killers of the children. It would take some time, but Jack was comfortable they would be found, eventually. Jack remained suspicious, however, of other government operatives, not the FBI but possibly the CIA, since they had black operations agents.

The investigation of the Star Children was completed, and, sadly, they found another twenty-one assassinated children. There were only twelve children remaining alive, not counting the six they were currently looking for, but at least they found some. Right now his agents were rounding the other twelve up and delivering them to the CIA facilities at Langley. At least they would be safe there from the assassins until they figured out what to do with them.

Dir. Setliff had hardly slept at all since the explosion, working around the clock. His body and mind were waning from lack of sleep. He told his administrative assistant, secretary, he was taking a short nap and to wake him immediately if he got a call from the NSA.

It seemed like he had just gone to sleep when he jerked awake to his phone buzzing, but when he glanced at his watch through blurry eyes, three hours had passed. It was NSA Dir. Jones saying, "We have a lead in Las Vegas!"

"So Tell me."

"Mrs. Wilks, the attendant to the children, came up on our surveillance watch list. It seems she won a million dollars on a slot machine in Vegas, and the IRS' internal report put it out on the Internet, and we picked it up."

"Fantastic work. Please continue your watch and call me in Los Vegas if you hear anything more."

Dir. Setliff immediately called the National Security Advisor, "Mr. Canton, we got a lead on Mrs. Wilks, and I'm headed to Las Vegas. Please tell the president."

He grabbed his emergency bag he always had packed, and as he raced passed his secretary, said, "Call my driver and plane and have it ready. I'm going to Vegas." He wasn't quite sure if she heard him say "Thanks", as he raced down the hall.

His driver was out of breath, but his FBI limo was there in the front of the FBI building with the door open. Jack jumped in the back seat saying, "Get me to my plane and use the siren and lights. I'm in a big hurry." When they got there his plane's ramp was down and the engines warming on his Gulfstream V. They had all done a great job, and he was soon in the air.

He called his FBI Field Office in Las Vegas from the car going to their private field. He put them on alert that their targets had been there and to find them and interview the casino about Mrs. Wilks' big win.

Jack slept most of the way to Las Vegas, and when he woke he was refreshed and thinking clearly again. The investigation drained his energy, but he was back in stride. The pieces began to fit together. Tom Bradly had no funds, and he would need plenty on the run, especially since he gained five more, plus Mrs. Wilks. She wouldn't have much. Of course, that is why they took the driver's money. Where would be the best place to find money? Las Vegas of course. That's why they traveled there.

No one really expects to win big, gambling. A person could hope, but apparently, Tom had more than hope, he apparently knew how. It had to be because of his mysterious powers. Jack didn't know what those powers were, but they must have worked, and they walked away with a million dollars, well, less a substantial deduction of taxes. His first problem was solved.

Tom's next problem would be to ditch the bus and find another vehicle. Well, he had the money to do that now, but casinos don't just give out cash. Tom and apparently Mrs. Wilks would have to cash the casino's check. That means finding a bank large enough to carry that much cash. That would narrow the search.

Dir. Setliff was positive they were in a different vehicle by now, but they apparently hadn't left a paper trail that they had found. They would not want that, but you could do a lot of invisible deals with cash. They had thought it through thoroughly and accomplished it without names reaching the terrorist watch list, but they had a problem. The casino would know who cashed the check and where. There was his starting point, and once they located the bank they should be able to locate the car dealer, possibly in the same area. He smiled, knowing they would be able to find their invisible path soon.

# Chapter 3
## (Finally, they Meet)

Dr. Wisscroff returned while they were eating. He sniffed the air and licked his lips and said, "Is there more food? I'm hungry now." When it was offered he sat down and began stuffing himself, while they watched four technicians in white lab coats come in and begin setting up a thick lead plate on pulleys. Doc saw us looking and said, "That's for vision training. We'll start when we finish eating. I will also need to calculate your stamina." When he saw the lack of understanding on their faces, he continued, "How long you can maintain those powers? As an example, you don't want to run out of energy while you fly. You'll fall or freeze, etc. We don't even know how your powers work or what they use for energy. Maybe you will need some energy bars. See what I mean? We have a lot of work to do."

Tom said, "I've thought about that also, but I really don't think we are using our own energy. I think we are just redirecting Earth's own energy. But, maybe there is more to it. We'll see I guess."

Dr. Wisscroff said, "Yes, we will see. Are you kids ready to get started?" When they all nodded he continued, "I'm going to bring some technicians in to set up monitoring equipment, then we can begin stressing you in different powers. We will see if there are any reactions. Oh, by the way, I want to call in the head of our genetics research department to draw your blood. Once we analyze your DNA maybe we will learn something additional. As for Tom and Sue, let's start with you to learn how to turn on the X-Ray vision. Sorry for the Superman analogy, but from Tina's dream you will need enhanced vision to see deep into the ice to reach your goal. So, let's see if we can activate this power in you."

The technicians had the lead screen hanging in place and beside it was a black curtain, evidently hiding various objects. Dr. Wisscroff positioned Tom and Sue in chairs well back in front of the curtain and lead plate. The technicians got busy attaching equipment to them to measure brain waves, heartbeat, blood pressure and various other devises. The technicians nodded their readiness.

Before they started Dr. Wisscroff asked, "How did you learn some of the other powers?"

Tom said, "Well, when I learned I wasn't thinking about gravity. I just willed myself to float up, and I just did it. It wasn't until later that I figured out I was manipulating gravity. I was able to do a lot using gravity after I realized what the power was. With altering time, as you called it, I just willed myself to move and react faster."

Doc said, "Alright. I don't see this being different. As you said, you think you use the Earth's own energy. I don't think Earth's energy could necessarily do anything to actually improve your eyesight, but it might be able to alter the atomic structure of actual material to make anything you're trying to look through become invisible to you. Let's start off thinking that way. Now tell me what is behind the black curtain."

Tom looked up, thinking, then slightly rocked his head back and forth as if to say, "That made sense." He stared at the black curtain and willed himself to see through the black curtain. It worked immediately, and he said, "There are several things behind the curtain. There is a red ball, a purple cup, a black horseshoe, a silver spoon and a white golf tee with 'made in China' printed on it."

Doc said, "You can read that fine print from all the way over there?"

"Yes."

"I guess I was wrong. That seldom happens. Obviously, you can also alter your focus as well. Your mind must have created a focal lens somewhere in your line of sight, probably past the curtain. I guess you can tell how many fingers I'm holding up behind the lead slab?"

"Three" was echoed from all over the room, since the others were already also operational in the visual enhancement power.

Dr. Wisscroff said, "Wow! This is impressive. Okay, let's turn on your super hearing the same way, all of you. Imagine any obstacle in the direction of a sound you want to hear is nonexistent to sound waves and focused. You might as well imagine it amplified." He got behind the lead plate and started whispering the Gettysburg Address."

Almost in unison, "Gettysburg Address" came flying back to him.

Dr. Wisscroff said, "Damn, kids. Is there anything you can't do? Oh, I know something. Make me twenty-five years younger."

They concentrated and watched Dr. Wisscroff's hunched back slowly straighten, his posture significantly improve, his white hair return to mostly black and his wrinkles soften. He was one surprised looking man and obviously twenty-five years younger.

Dr. Wisscroff screamed in shock and said, "Damn, I was just kidding. There is no way in God's green earth I thought that possible. I don't even know what this power is." He began walking around in a bouncing step testing his renewed strength, shaking his arms around. He even hopped up and down. He said, "I can't believe that just happened. Crap! Now I'm wondering how I'm going to deal with this change. Hell, the people I work with might not recognize me. We can't let them know how this happened. I'm serious. Humans can't know you have this power. They will all want what you just did to me. I really should ask you to take it back, but I'm not. This is incredible. I haven't felt this good in ... well, twenty-five years. I will have to come up with an imaginary concoction and tell them it's one of our inventions. Hell, I might get rich selling it to the public. Hey, one of you look to see if dinner is here. I'm hungry as hell."

Mary had already heard the cart approach with her improved hearing and was walking toward the door. Once the monitoring equipment was all disconnected, Tom and Sue joined the others in the conference room. Soon they began dishing out food and laughing at a jubilant Dr. Wisscroff.

As they began to eat Fred stopped and stared. He suddenly said, "Mrs. Wilks, were you close to Dr. Wisscroff? You must have been, because you got some of it, too."

Mrs. Wilks said, "Got some of what? What are you talking about?"

Mary said, "The rejuvenating energy we sent to Dr. Wisscroff. You definitely look younger." Everyone around the table looked and nodded, including the doc.

Doc said, "They are correct. You look at least ten years younger, and you look good, too. Strange, I haven't had thoughts like that in years." Mrs. Wilks blushed and rushed off to her room to look in the mirror, and the others broke out in laughter.

Dr. Wisscroff said, "I'm too excited to keep working. I need to go back to my office and take the heat for my regained youth. Don't tell anyone what you kids did. We definitely need to keep that a secret. Even though I'm excited, I'm still giving you homework. I want you to work on your mental communications among yourselves (Telepathy). I'm sure you have resisted trying, because of the confusion it causes; but you will need it. Not only must you communicate with each other as a group, but you also need to practice one on one. Learn how to also block each other. Master that or telepathic communications will get confusingly jumbled, not to mention embarrassing, since you can't control what you think."

After a while, Mrs. Wilks returned with a big smile on her face and said, "Thank you, kids." She looked around and said, "Where did Dr. Wisscroff go? I hope he comes back before he loses that urge he referred to." They broke out in hysterical laughter that lasted for many long minutes.

*** 

Dir. Setliff was awake and thinking when the plane began to descend into Las Vegas. The pilot announced they were landing at Nellis AFB. They had made fantastic time, but he had still managed to get four hours of restful sleep. Apart from the rumpled suit he had lived in for two days, he was ready to get engaged.

The Special Agent in Charge, Bob Woodall, was waiting when the plane's ramp dropped. Bob was a capable and sturdy man with a shaved head and big ears. Dir. Setliff had been so rushed that he had outrun his mandatory security bodyguards, and it was just him. He quickly shook Bob's hand and they got in the black Yukon and headed toward town.

Dir. Setliff said, "What do you have for me, Bob?"

Special Agent Woodall said, "Well, quite a lot, actually. We realize how important this is, so we put as many agents on this as we could break loose."

Dir. Setliff was quick to recognize the brown nosing and interrupted, "Please, Bob, cut the BS. Just give me what you have."

"Sorry Director. Mrs. Wilks and Tom Bradly were recorded on surveillance tapes walking through the Mandalay Bay casino together. She didn't appear to be under any duress and seemed a willing participant. They appeared to be surveying and analyzing the machines. Evidently, they found one they liked and simply walked up and slipped a bill into the machine, and on the first play they hit the jackpot for $1,000,000. Can you believe it? One play! There was no evidence on the tape of any tampering, but Tom Bradley did seem to be intently watching the wheels turn. We did notice that neither seemed overly surprised to win, and Tom backed away into the distance as quickly as he could. Mrs. Wilks remained to deal with the winning attention and paperwork. She wanted all cash, but Las Vegas casinos just don't give out that volume of cash. Nevada doesn't have a state income tax, but after federal taxes, she was able to convince them to give her $200,000 in cash, but had to take a certified check in the amount of $500,000."

"The Mandalay Bay verified that the check was cashed the next morning at around 10:00 am at a branch of Nevada State Bank on Southern Highland. That's in south Las Vegas near Interstate 15, which goes toward Las Angeles. Maybe they *are* headed to California after all. I've got agents looking for the bus in that direction, and I notified the NSA."

The bank also has surveillance tapes, but Mrs. Wilks was the only one in the bank. The bank provided us with a list of the serial numbers of the bills, so if they spend any we can determine where they are."

"I have agents searching the motels in the general area of the bank, but I suspect that might be a while coming. There are hundreds, if not thousands, of motels/hotels to canvas in that area."

Dir. Setliff said, "That's very good work Special Agent Woodall for only a few hours. Do we have any leads on a vehicle? I'm sure they must have ditched the bus by now. It's too hard to hide. They must have new transportation. They certainly have the money to buy one."

Agent Woodall said, "We started canvassing car dealers in the area, and just before I picked you up one of my agents reported a hot lead. My agent said he was not very cooperative, and he was going to have to pressure him some. They are inventorying his cash for any of the bank issued money and also interviewing the owner now. Hopefully, we will hear from him soon."

Dir. Setliff said. "Bob, if you haven't already, have the casino and bank remain silent and report any others that might be inquiring about Mrs. Wilks and the kids. There may be others searching for these kids, and I want to know who. Our job is to find them first and protect them. That order comes from the president, personally."

"Yes, Sir. I will get right on that."

Bob Woodall's phone rang and he answered immediately. He listened for a while and shot his thumb up and smiled. When he hung up he said, "We've got their vehicle identified. It's a year old silver Yukon. The description and tag number are already out on the wire with instruction to notify the FBI immediately for instructions."

Dir. Setliff said, "Excellent! Now we have something to concentrate on."

No sooner than he said that, his phone rang. It was an encoded texted message from Dir. Jones that read, *"Mrs. Wilks won another $200,000 at the Tropicana in Laughlin, Nevada."*

He showed the text to Bob and said, "Now we have a direction, too! It looks like they crossed over the Colorado River at Laughlin. Take me back to my plane. I'm in the wrong spot. I need to be in Phoenix."

"I don't think you will be able to pick up anything new at Laughlin but send some agents anyway. Let me know if you turn up anything new."

He called his secretary back in D.C. to tell the plane to be ready to go to Phoenix. This way she could track his progress and maintain all the BS reporting and clearances required in the FBI and political arenas. He knew the plane would be refueled and the Special Agent in Charge at the Phoenix FBI would be notified and would meet him when he landed. For sure the FBI was a very organized bureaucracy, that's why he adored his secretary. He would be hard pressed to do without her.

When they returned to the plane the ramp was down and the engines were roaring. As Jack was getting on board and settled, the pilot informed him that their flight plan to Luke AFB at Phoenix was filed. It would be a short trip, but he was confident that they would be ready for him.

They had only been in the air for a few moments when his phone rang. It was NSA Director Jones saying, "Hey Jack, we have a location for you. Tucson. Head for Tucson. We picked up on a phrase on our watch list. There is a scientist at the University of Arizona, Tucson named Dr. Gene Wisscroff. He is a world-renowned scientist. He even does work for us, well the university. Anyway, he tried to Google 'Star Children' and that put up a flag. Of course, he got nothing on the search, but it gave us a place to look. We sent a drone there and found the Yukon, so they are there now, probably with Dr. Wisscroff. What can we do to help?"

Dir. Setliff said, "Nothing at this point. Thank you for nailing this down. I will call if I need anything. I will go there personally. I'm already in the air."

When he disconnected he went directly to the pilot and said, "Forget Phoenix. There has been a change of plan. Take us to Tucson."

The pilot said, "I'll call the change of flight plan in, and we will land at Davis Monthan AFB instead. It will only add about an hour to our travel time."

Jack's next call was to his secretary, well Executive Assistant. He still had trouble calling her anything but his secretary, but they both knew she was the boss when it came to the bureaucratic BS. He was only fifty-five, but he was old school, and she knew it.

With the last minute change in landing sites, Jack had to wait for his Special Agent to arrive, but he didn't mind. He was feeling much more comfortable now. His target was in sight.

As he waited he analyzed Tom Bradley's move to find a scientist. It was a logical move for Tom and the others to find help identifying their powers, and after having flown over the security at Area 51 and won on the slot machine … twice, there was no doubt he and maybe all of them had powers. Jack didn't know what to do about that. It had been an unexpected occurrence, which could be a benefit or a major problem. He would know better after he interviewed them.

Jack heard the sirens first then saw the flashing lights that announced his Bureau Chief's arrival. They had actually made good time. Janet Welch was a fortyish agent and very competent, not to mention very appealing. She was one of the few females that had made Special Agent in Charge of an operation as large as Phoenix. In the FBI her good looks had probably been a detriment to her advancement, since it might be considered an impropriety to promote her. This meant her abilities

75

and competence excelled to counter her good looks. When she got out of the vehicle, Jack was surprised and at the same time appalled to see that Agent Welch dressed down to mask her beauty. Her long, blonde hair was pulled back in a tight ponytail and she appeared to be wearing a loose, man's black suit, complete with white shirt and tie. He was horrified that she felt it necessary to mask her assets to advance in the FBI. He hoped he could change that.

Jack laughed out loud when his personal security exited the Tahoe after Janet. He thought he left them in D.C., but they obviously had caught up. Dir. Setliff said, "Hello Special Agent Welch. I see you made it here. Sorry for the quick last minute change. Where did you pick up my security agents?"

Agent Welch laughed and said, "I don't mind driving fast. I got to use the lights and siren. Your security flew into Luke AFB on a military plane, and they were waiting on you there. So, I brought them along."

Jack said, "I guess my Executive Assistant arranged this?"

Both Agents laughed and Agent Brown said, "Yeah, you know how she is. She worries about you and your mandatory protocol. We kind of thought you actually wanted to leave us behind. I mean we weren't worried, since we knew you would be surrounded by other Agents, but here we are as she instructed."

76

As they left the AFB they were taking their time. Special Agent Welch must have sensed Dir. Setliff's relaxed attitude and said, "We received Dir. Jones' information, and request for verification on the vehicle. We found the Yukon almost immediately and have located where they are staying. It's a safe location and guarded. We also located Dr. Wisscroff's office and called to set up an appointment. That is where we are going. We checked him out. He's well respected and even has a Top Secret clearance from us."

Jack was reading over the dossier Agent Welch had passed to him on Dr. Wisscroff and said, "Thank you, Janet. Good work. You say he is expecting us?" She nodded.

Dir. Setliff and Special Agent Welch entered Dr. Wisscroff's office and introduced themselves and shook hands. Dir. Setliff didn't think it was him at first and asked, "Dr. Wisscroff?" He nodded. "Sorry, your dossier picture led me to believe you were older."

Dr. Wisscroff laughed and said, "Well, I am eighty, but that is probably my Dorian Grey picture you saw. I stay young and my picture grows older." They all laughed and said no more about it."

"I knew you would show up sooner or later. We have been expecting you, and you are right on time. I assume you are here about the Star Children?"

"Yes. Are they safe?"

"They are very safe, safer than you can imagine. They are more than able to defend themselves. Obviously you have the clearance level, but before I brief you I need to ask about the clearance level for Special Agent Welch, or at least give you the opportunity to exclude her from this discussion, as it will be above Top Secret. And, yes, I know everything and expect to be included in any future developments with these kids. They want me to be their guardian, mentor and protector, even from our government. They have a trust issue with our government since they were almost eliminated under your watch."

Dir. Setliff thought for a moment and said, "She will be tuned in. I want her in the discussion and her insight."

"Very well. You did the right thing by coming to me and not acting like storm troopers. As I said, they are well able to defend themselves, but they don't want to hurt anyone. In fact, they are listening to us and watching right now. Tom you and Sue come on over. These kids have powers they are just now learning. I'm helping them. Some of these powers are controlling gravity, temperature, and time, to name a few, plus they can read minds, hear and see through obstacles. Let me warn you up front. Do not try to deceive or lie to them. They will know it instantly."

From the hallway, they heard, "We are expected."

Dir. Setliff said, "It's ok. Let them in." He recognized Tom and Sue from surveillance videos and personnel files when they entered the office. He stood and greeted Tom and Sue and introduced

Special Agent Welch. After the introduction, they all settled into a tight circle of chairs due to the limited space.

Dr. Wisscroff continued as if he had never been interrupted, "Dir, Setliff, we have made some discoveries, some provable, some not. The Star Children are genetically enhanced, but not by the Greys. I believe another alien race did the genetic splicing for reasons unknown at this time but apparently to help the human race. We know the Greys are hostel to the children, fearful, also. That is why the Greys are trying to destroy them."

Tom interrupted, "Why did you allow the Greys to kill almost all of the Star Children at Area 51, and why are you chasing us? What is your goal? We will not go back to Area 51 or anywhere the Greys can have access to us, and you can't force us to."

Dir. Setliff said, "I'm not sure how to answer you. You have to understand that very few even know about the existence of the Greys or the Star Children. These subjects are classified far above Top Secret." He looked at Agent Welch to impress on her the secrecy. She nodded. "I didn't know either existed until after the explosion and the death of so many children. That whole project was done by previous administrations and kept hidden. President Thompson was appalled at the children's death and subsequently put me in charge of the operation to save you. Only then was I given access to the hidden files. My orders were to find you children and protect you from further harm, which

79

was no easy task. You covered your tracks quite well. We are gathering as many Star Children as we can find and protecting them at the CIA Headquarters at Langley."

Sue interrupted, "You found other Star Children?"

"Yes, I started an investigation and found that there were adopted children that weren't included in the original project. We have identified a plot to assassinate those also, but we managed to save twelve and take them to Langley."

Sue said, "But you don't trust the CIA. I see it in your thoughts.

Doc said, "Don't lie! They will know."

Dir. Setliff said, "Let's just say I have some potential doubts."

Tom said, "The Greys killed almost 200 of us. I see that also in your mind. We will not go to Langley. Bring the others here instead. We will look after our own safety. We may have a place of safety. We will know soon."

Dir. Setliff said, "My orders are to take you to Langley. Besides, this isn't a defensible location."

Tom said, "Mr. Setliff, following your government's orders has killed almost 200 of us. We will do what *we* think is right, and you can't stop us. At least I wouldn't suggest you try. You and Agent Welch, however, are welcome to go with us to Antarctica. I think you might find it interesting and productive."

"Antarctica? Why would you want to go there?"

Dr. Wisscroff said, "I believe they will find answers there as to who they are and why they were genetically engineered. Some of them were given instruction in dreams on how to find the location, and that location is in Antarctica. I suspect the dreams were only given to the younger ones, most of which were killed, except for one here."

Tom said, "I believe there might be more than information there. I feel that the aliens lived there, and they want us to go there for some other reason. Besides, we are not sure we can trust you completely."

"Mr. Setliff, we might have more confidence in the government if you destroy the Greys for killing 200 children. Have you done that yet? If not, why not?"

Dir. Setliff said, "I think the president is waiting to see more evidence, but according to the file I read there are only about a hundred of the Greys. They shouldn't pose much of a problem to us."

Tom said, "No, that is incorrect. I've seen images in their minds of other massive underground bases here on Earth. There are many of them hiding and waiting. For what I never saw in their minds. They didn't know I learned to understand their language somewhat. That's how I learned of their intent to kill us, and I escaped and saved the other five here."

"Mr. Setliff, I think we can help each other, but I need you to get my other kin out here with us so we can teach them. I have a feeling that before this is over we will need all of the Star Children active and ready."

Dir. Setliff said, "I believe you, Tom. I will, however, need to talk to the president about our discussion. Agent Welch and I will go back to the base and have an encrypted video conference with the president. In the meantime, I will assign additional security and establish some air cover if necessary."

When the FBI had gone, Tom and Sue embraced to celebrate the addition of twelve more Star Children … hopefully. During the embrace the simmering emotions could not be held back. His lust for her had burst forth. The reward was in the returned feeling of her desire for him that flooded his mind. They wanted each other. The only more embarrassing was his erection, which no doubt she felt when they embraced. The emotions couldn't be held back, but doc had said they could and must be held and controlled. This might be the hardest power to learn to control.

***

As they were driving to the air base, Dir. Setliff said, "Well, Agent Welch you were quiet in the meeting. How do you think that went?"

She said, "That is exactly what I knew you wanted me to do, remain quiet, listen and analyze. That's what I did. My first observation is that everyone in that room had a high IQ. That's for sure, even the doctor, far beyond just knowledge. It is also plainly obvious that those kids have powers we can't understand. Our minds were clearly open to their inspection. I agree with the doc, they would have instantly known if you tried any deceit, and I'm pleased that you didn't. We would have been totally rejected, and we might have seen some of those powers in use. As it is, I think they trust us to a point, and that's good. They should, since you are obviously trying to work with them and help."

"I cringed when the question came up about the CIA. I happen to agree with all of you. The CIA does necessary work, but anyone would be insane to trust them completely. I'm not sure even Dir. Martinez knows all that's going on in the CIA, too many secret deals going on. We probably should get the kids out of there, and here is as good as anywhere on a temporary basis. It will help the Star Children learn to trust us."

"I guess the most important fact to be gained out of this entire interview, is that this situation might turn out big, very big, especially if there is an alien base under the ice. And, we were invited to go with them. I think we should go. I think we have only scratched the surface. By the way, thanks, I think, for getting me so deeply involved. I am like the doctor, I know too much now, and I realize I can't get out. So, I guess I'm your new assistant."

Jack laughed and said, "I'm afraid you're right. You're my new Deputy Director of Alien Interface, and NO you can't put that on your business cards." Janet laughed.

"When we get back to the base, I need you to get hold of Bob Woodall and find out if anyone else is tracking the progress of Tom and the other kids.

If so, we need to know and find out who they are, and who they work for. I'm worried about the assassins that have been killing off the kids. We are also investigating a D.C. law firm that may be funding them. Oh, and pick your own replacement for the Phoenix Bureau."

"Oh, get some Agents for guards, maybe some military with heavier equipment and air support." Janet simply nodded.

Dir. Setliff leaned back and started writing his report to the president. He heard Agent Welch talking and turned to respond, but realized she was talking into a phone and returned to his report. He made sure to list all the key facts without the voluminous details, but he covered it all. Since the information was Top Secret for the president's eyes only, he would send the report to the president's personal secure data address and mark it "Urgent" from the base's secure line with the highest level encryption. He believed the president would read his urgent message immediately and call him soon after, and that is exactly what happened.

President Thompson called on a secure phone but not with a video conference as he thought. The president said, "I want to keep this exchange as low profile as possible. It's too sensitive."

Dir. Setliff said, "I understand, Mr. President."

"This is a very interesting report, and at the same time, it's very disturbing. The disturbing parts are the powers these Star Children seem to have and the potential threat the Greys could present. Both are disturbing, but the Greys' threat more so. It's a potential disaster. As I've said, I never trusted the skinny bastards, and it looks like I was right. We have to identify if in fact there is a hidden Grey base and where it is. It looks like we need the Star Children to help us, since they seem to know more about them, well, this Tom Bradley anyway. Do they trust you?"

Dir. Setliff said, "I've given them no reason not to trust me or the government. This is another reason to make the recommendations I have made."

"And I agree with your recommendations. Give them anything they want. I want their friendship. We just might need their help if things go wrong with the Greys. I want you to stick close to them, help them and protect them. That goal hasn't changed, and by all means, go to Antarctica with them. If there is any chance at all there might be an alien base with advanced technology there, we must control it or at least have access to it and keep it away from anyone else, especially the Russians and the Greys. Jack, you have full authority over everyone involving the Star Children Program and the children. Keep up the good work, Jack."

Dir. Setliff's next secure call was to National Security Advisor Tom Canton. When he answered Jack said, "Hey Tom, I need you to set up air transportation for at least twenty-five people and take personal charge of the twelve Star Children at Langley and bring them to the Air Force Base here in Tucson. Keep in mind that on the next leg of our journey we must be able to land on ice. Bring a couple of security guards for the children, your people, only those you can explicitly trust and with Top Secret clearances."

Mr. Canton said, "Christ, Jack. Where are we going?"

"Antarctica, somewhere close to the South Pole. We have facilities there don't we?"

Tom said, "Well, yeah, but they are Top Secret."

Jack quickly came back with, "What do you think this is? That's perfect, actually."

Tom continued, "I'll have to run it past the president and get his approval."

"I know. I would expect that. You're his man, but I'm following his instructions. Trust me. He will want you on this mission. It's important. So, hurry up, Tom."

***

Tom, Sue and Dr. Wisscroff left the doc's office and walked back toward the gym, both trying to ignore the images flooding at the other. In some ways, these images took any secret feelings away. She knew exactly what he was thinking, and he knew exactly what she was thinking. The images of them naked and having rough sex excited him, only to suddenly realize that Tom was viewing her enjoying it being radiated out from her. If they were lovers the intimacy would be acceptable, even desirable; but the others of their kind would be able to view them as well. She blushed brightly at the thought. As it stood right now each one of them was connected to each and every other one. This equated to total confusion as their telepathy powers grew, which in itself was the problem. As Dr. Wisscroff had said, this must be controlled, and she began trying different methods toward that goal, quite unsuccessfully.

Finally, she compared their unorganized communication to the closest thing she could think of and created a matrix in her mind with each member having their own separate line of communications, not unlike a telephone exchange. She then disconnected all the lines. That was successful in shutting off all mental telepathy and communications, from her end anyway. Sue then began planning and imagined how an individual phone rang when another called. The ring in her mind became a ping. Once she would receive a ping she could answer it by making a mental connection. If she assigned each one of the children a separate leg or line of the matrix, equivalent to a phone number, she could create her own set of rules for manipulating the matrix. In this way, she would learn to identify the caller and accept the mental ping and connection for one on one telepathy. She knew the mental matrix system would work, but it would require all the others to create their own mental matrix of their own.

To test her theory she opened a connection to Tom and sent a mental ping. Of course, he didn't know what it was, but responded, which went out to them all. She flooded his mind with the details she had worked out.

Tom stumbled and almost fell with the sudden flood of information. It took him a few seconds to see the wisdom of the plan and duplicate it. His next transmission was single-line telepathy communication, *"This is great, Sue. You solved the problem, and I like it very much. But, I didn't mind getting those other images you were sending before."*

She blushed and sent, *"Shut up!"* Tom laughed out loud, which drew Dr. Wisscroff's attention.

Tom shrugged and said, "Sue solved the problem with telepathy that you requested we work on. She and I now have control over our communications. Sue is pretty smart. We can get the others oriented and in control quickly, since we have also learned to mentally transmit data now."

"Fantastic!"

As soon as they got back to the gym they explained the matrix system Sue had come up with to the other four, and Sue downloaded the data she had worked out. Within minutes they were all communicating individually one on one and group talking. It went just that fast.

Tom made an observation and said to all, "You know it is almost as if one of us learns something the others can pick it up immediately from the originator's mind directly. Like I learned gravity control and passed it on to you, and you picked it up immediately. Sue came up with a way to perfect telepathy communication. Jerry learned time control, and we quickly learned it from him. Mary taught us temperature control. The reinforced sight and hearing we all learned together. Even Tina, our youngest, showed us new mental capabilities. I guess Fred is next to surprise us."

Fred absentmindedly stroked his now missing hair spikes, laughed and said, "I hope so. I want to contribute, too."

# Chapter 4
## (Gathering)

Dir. Setliff had just finished his secure phone conversations with the president when Agent Welch burst into the office he was using. He realized she must have been monitoring the phone lights and saw immediately when he hung up.

Janet said, "Director, I got a call from Bob Woodall. They caught the agents tracking Tom Bradley and the others. They caught them at the car dealer. Bob didn't know what to expect from the agents, so he played overkill. There were five of them, so Bob called in their Enhanced FBI SWAT team of fifteen and took them down at gunpoint outside the dealer. They were overwhelmed by sheer force and surrendered. They were handcuffed and swept off to the Las Vegas bureau's detention center. All of them carried federal IDs, which were traced back to the CIA. They are remaining silent at this point and demanding to be released. Bob provided us with copies of their IDs."

Dir. Setliff smiled hugely and said, "Tell Bob he did great work, and he was absolutely correct to bring in a SWAT team. If I'm right this was a kill team and highly proficient at it, and there might be more. Be alert. Tell Bob to hold them without contact by anyone and no phone calls, no matter who demands their release. I want their capture to remain a complete secret. Investigate anyone calling for their release, because we need to know who is running them."

"Oh. Please forward the ID information directly to CIA Dir. Martinez."

Janet nodded and said, "I will do so immediately."

Jack picked up the secure phone and called Dir. Martinez on his direct line, which was answered on the second ring. Jack spoke in a steady, firm stream, not allowing the director to respond. "Dir. Martinez. This is Dir. Setliff. We just arrested five of your men in Las Vegas. We believe they are a hit team sent to kill the Star Children. I'm sending their ID information now as we speak. I want to know who they are, and who controls and sent them. I want to know their chain of command. I strongly suggest you give this your highest priority, because you will not have much time before I send a report to the president. Am I understood?"

"Yes, Sir. I understand the implications completely. Thanks for giving me some lead time to clean this up."

Dir. Setliff did not respond. He simply hung up the phone, knowing Dir. Martinez had no choice but to quickly investigate and weed out the alien mole or moles in his office. Jack also knew that the director knew he was giving him a chance to clean it up and contain it. Jack would not stick his neck out very far, but Dir. Martinez could clean it up and contain the situation much quicker than the FBI, and that was the ultimate goal.

Agent Welch said, "You know you are taking a big chance by letting Dir. Martinez clean up his own mess. What if he is part of it? He could be using the time to cover it up."

"I don't think he is part of it. I think it was you that said the CIA has too many secrets, and even the director can't know everything that's going on. No, I don't think he is part of it. Hell, even if he is, he will shut it down to cover his own ass, and that is our goal here: to protect the Star Children."

When they returned to the gym at the University of Arizona the first thing they saw was a barricade surrounding the gym, and a full company of Marines, probably out of Yuma, stationed around the gym. They had to go through security to be granted access, but they were listed on the Marines security approved list.

They went directly to the conference room when they entered the gym, where they were quickly surrounded by the children, Mrs. Wilks and Dr. Wisscroff, obviously curious about the director's conversation with the president.

Dr. Wisscroff started, "Well, Dir. Setliff, we are anxious to know what the president had to say."

Dir. Setliff chuckled and said, "In short, the president said to give you whatever you want. The other Star Children received new and additional guards, and transportation is being arranged to bring them here. The National Security Advisor to the president, whom I totally trust, is taking charge of their protection personally and will deliver them here as soon as possible. Also, arrangements are being made to transport us all to a South Pole facility close to where you indicated you wanted to go. Yes, the president agrees that we should accept your invitation and go with you."

Tom said, "Of course he agrees. He and you are as curious about us as we are. We don't believe we have anything to hide, and we will find out together. So, I guess we feel like we can trust you … with limitations."

"Thank you, Tom. The president is on your side. Look into my mind to verify what I'm saying."

Sue laughed and said, "We already have." At that, everyone laughed, including the director and Janet.

Jack said, "There is something you should know. We arrested a five-man team in Las Vegas tracking you kids. They worked for the CIA. The director is closing down this rogue operation, but this stresses the need for security. Hopefully, the threat has been eliminated, but I would feel far more comfortable about your safety if we moved you to one of our underground facilities."

Tom interrupted, "*No!* Sorry director, but we won't go anywhere near one of those underground bases. They are populated or accessed by the Greys. I have seen it in their minds. They are working with humans and in vast numbers. I can't tell you exactly where, but in many of them, and I have seen miles and miles of deep tunnels that they use that interconnect the bases. We will not go inside one of those bases."

Dir. Setliff was speechless and shocked by what Tom had just said. His lips moved, but nothing came out.

Agent Welch took over, "Tell us more of what you have seen in their minds. What about weapons?"

Tom thought for a moment and said, "Weapons? I've seen caves full of flying saucers all lined up, hundreds, maybe more. I think I saw several different caves … all the same."

Janet asked, "What emotions did you feel coming from the Greys concerning the flying saucer."

Again Tom closed his eyes, then said. "Hostility! War! They want war. But, but, it seems they feel they are already at war, a secret war … and winning. They already control some of our military, especially the deep underground bases and tunnel networks."

Dir. Setliff found his voice and said, "Holly, shit! War? Flying saucers? Hundreds? This is extremely serious." He was silent for long moments processing the information. When his eyes refocused, he said, "I think I see it. The existence of the Greys and the recovered alien spaceship, hell, everything to do with aliens, has been covered up for decades. Even the knowledge of their existence has been locked up and buried in archives. The government labeled it Top Secret and hid it away, and who did we put in charge of the secrecy? I'll bet some autonomous Top Secret agency under the CIA with no government oversight. Still, the Greys wouldn't be able to secretly control much without substantial support from our own government. Hell, we may have already lost the war and don't even know it. The president must know about this immediately, but we must know just who we are at war with. Is it just the Greys, compromised humans or both?"

"Tom, how close to a person must you be to see his thoughts?"

Tom didn't yet see where this was leading, but answered, "I would say within talking distance to be able to focus on an individual. Why?"

"Will you travel with me to D.C.? We need to identify how far up the chain of command the Greys have managed to compromise or corrupt. Will you help us? I mean they are also after you, too. Just maybe because you can identify them."

The firm resolve shown in Tom's face. "Yes, of course, I will go with you."

Jack said, "Janet, please call Advisor Jim Canton and have him get those kids away from Langley immediately and get them on the plane for here. Tell him we have uncovered a major threat. He needn't know what at this point. Tell him to put fighter escorts on the plane. If this is what I think it is, the Greys will stop at nothing to keep their secret. These Star Children are in serious danger."

"Also, call and get my plane ready for a fast trip to D.C. After that, take charge of this operation and get those kids here as soon as possible when they land. Oh, have that corrupted FBI Deputy Dir. waiting for me in an interrogation room when I get there. My secretary will know who. Thanks, Janet."

A fleeting thought flashed across his face. "Oh, Janet, we don't know who to trust at this point, so don't trust anyone. Be suspicious of everyone." Janet nodded again.

Tom said, "Sue, take charge of the children and the others when they get here. I'll be back as soon as possible. If this is as big as Jack seems to think, we are not safe anywhere. Watch and expect an attack. If humans can't get to us, the aliens may come out of their hole to do the job. If they come I'm pretty sure their saucers operate using gravity drive, so disrupting gravity is probably our best defense."

"Teach the other Star Children how to fly as soon as they get here and be ready to escape to Mexico. I'll find you there."

Sue leaned forward and up and kissed Tom on the lips and said, "You will be in danger yourself. Be careful and come back to me. We have some images to fulfill." They both smiled. Dir. Setliff, his two bodyguards and Tom raced back to the base. Janet must have called ahead to clear security, because they waved him right through. Jack made a quick stop at communication to type up another "Urgent" message to the president he had been writing in his head during the drive. After only a short delay, they were in the air violating all kinds of governing flight regulations, but he didn't care. The president would get him out of trouble … this time. The flight would be long, but considerably shorter than it could have been. He hoped to get to know Tom a lot better by the time they arrived, and know better how Tom could help him identify the bad guys.

***

Agent Welch was sitting in the conference room visiting with the others when her cell phone rang. It was Marine Major Burns in charge of their outside Marine security. Major Burns said, "There is a detachment of Air Force Security Forces specialist here with orders to relieve us from this detail. I thought I better check with you."

"Where are they from?"

"Their orders say Nellis AFB."

Janet thought, this doesn't make any sense. Something is not right. Nellie AFB is in Las Vegas, where the kill team was arrested. She didn't like the smell of this. It stunk! She trusted the Marines, because they had been ordered to come by Tom Canton, but an AF team? How would they even know where the Star Children were?

Agent Welch said, "You did right calling me. Listen to me very carefully, Major Burns. Consider them hostile, I repeat, *hostile*. Under no circumstances are they allowed to replace you. I believe them to be an assassination team for my wards. Here is what I want you to do. Very carefully and suddenly surprise them and hold them at gunpoint. Use deadly force if necessary. I want them disarmed and held until you hear from me. Once you do that, bring me the officer in charge. Do you understand?"

"Yes, Ma'am."

Janet said more gently, "Be careful, major. They're professional assassins."

"Will do, Ma'am."

Janet said, "Kids, be prepared to escape if I tell you. We have a situation outside." The Star Children ran to their rooms and picked up a prepared bag, which Mrs. Wilks had made them pack. Each emergency bag had water, food, miscellaneous items and money for survival if they got separated.

Sue said, "What about you, Mrs. Wilks and Dr. Wisscroff? We can take you with us." The other kids were nodding their agreement.

It was Mrs. Wilks that answered, "Don't worry about us. It's you kids they want. They won't bother us if you kids are gone. They will be more interested in finding you."

Two shots sounded from outside but only two. Janet assumed a full armed conflict would generate far more shots than two. Janet asked Sue, "Did the Marines capture the Air Force Security Forces? Take a look." When Sue started to walk toward the door, Janet said, "No not that way. Look through the wall."

Sue said, "Oh. I forgot." She concentrated for a second and said, "Yes. They are dropping their weapons. A couple of them got shot, but they are still alive. The Marines are making them lay down, and the major is bringing an Air Force officer here."

Agent Welch said, "Good. When we talk to the Air Force officer search for whatever you can detect, especially images. We want to know who sent him."

Sue said, "I'm sure I can help."

When the Marine Major brought the Air Force Lieutenant into the gym at gunpoint and handcuffed, Agent Welch said, "I am FBI Special Agent Janet Welch, Bureau Chief in Phoenix. Who are you, and who do you work for?"

The Lieutenant didn't answer. Instead, he bellowed, "Are you fucking stupid, bitch? You just fired upon federal agents. I'm going to see to it you are prosecuted." He then spat on the floor to accent his rage.

Janet bellowed back, "Shut up unless you want to be shot for treason? Hell, I might even do it myself. I suggest you calm down and answer all my questions fully and truthfully."

Sue saw the rage in the Air Force officer, but she also sensed an underlying high level of deceit. She sensed this officer would never be truthful and thought, *"I want this man to be open and truthful."* The reaction was immediate. The Air Force officer's body became rigid, his face turned visibly pale and blank, his eyes stared forward and unfocused.

In a monotone voice, he answered Janet's questions, "I am Air Force Lt. James Barker, Special Intelligence Operative for … (the list continued up the hierarchy detailing squadron, sub-branch, branch, several layers of departments, ending with the NSA in D.C.).

Janet actually stepped back in shock and disbelief at the voluminous and detailed answer. She was happy she had turned on her recorder. The officer looked like a zombie, and she didn't understand until she saw Sue smiling. Janet asked, "Sue, is that you?"

Sue continued to smile and said, "Yes, I didn't know I could help, but, guess what? I can. Ask your questions, he will answer them."

Janet said, "What were your orders and who gave them to you."

Lt. Barker said, again in his monotone voice, "My orders were to convince the Marine detachment to allow us to relieve them. Failing that, we were to eliminate them and kill the Star Children and all housed here. The order was verbally given to me directly by Col. Martin, Commanding Officer of the Security Police at a secret underground base near Nellis AFB with no name."

"Why were the Star Children to be eliminated?"

"I don't know, Ma'am. I just follow orders."

"What is the function of this secret base?"

"We provide security at several stations for the underground tunnel system in Arizona."

"Where does the tunnel system go, and who uses it?

"I don't know where it goes, Ma'am. We are only allowed to know about the stations we maintain. We don't know who uses the tunnel system. We remain topside when it is being used."

"Who do you think uses the tunnel system?"

Lt. Barker's face broke out in sweat and the muscles strained tense, but he finally said, "I am sworn to secrecy. They will kill me."

"Who will kill you?"

"The Greys!" At that his face contorted, and he collapsed to the floor.

Dr. Wisscroff ran to his side and checked him out. When he again stood he said, "He is dead, bleeding from the ears, eyes and nose. It looks like his brain burst from the strain of trying to resist interrogations. Either that or he had a brain implant explode triggered by the stress of revealing secret information, possibly the mention of Greys. That's when he died. I can't imagine conditioning so strong as to cause death resisting. I don't know what you intend to do with the other Air Force men outside, but I might suggest brain scan MRIs be run on them. Let's see if any others are hard-wired to explode. My guess is the lower ranks aren't implanted.

Mary said, "Can't us Star Children take a look with our enhanced vision? Just tell us what to look for."

Dr. Wisscroff said, "Well I be dammed. Why didn't I think of that? Of course, you can. Just scan a normal brain then look for something different. Let me think. If an implant exists it would almost have to be inserted through the nose canal." Doc went back to the dead lieutenant and inspected the base of his neck and behind the ears and came back and said, "I don't see any marks. I guess it could be some nanotechnology, but I still suspect the nose canal would be the best guess."

Agent Welch asked, "Major Burns, please bring the others inside by small groups so we can inspect them. Also, everything you saw and heard in here is above Top Secret, even above your Commanding Officer clearance. There will be no debriefing about inside here. Do you understand?"

Major Burns said, "Yes, Ma'am. I understand completely, and Ma'am, I want to thank you for the warning outside. It saved all our lives."

"You're very welcome Major. You did great, and thank your men."

Major Burns was back within minutes with a few Marines and a body bag for the dead Air Force Lt.. They bagged the dead man up and carried him back outside.

Agent Welch said, "Hold him outside. I'll call the FBI to come to get him. We'll want an autopsy done right away."

Dr. Wisscroff said, "We can do that here, probably better than anywhere and much quicker. The University of Arizona in Tucson trains doctors and is considered one of the leading medical training and research facilities in the country. I think they would love the opportunity, and as I said, I have a lot of pull here. They can take care of the wounded airmen, also." Janet just nodded.

While doc was on the phone making arrangements, Major Burns brought in the first five Air Force soldiers. The soldiers had not seen Lt.

Barker since he had been brought in, and now they just witnessed an occupied body bag carried out. All this made for an anxious group, and Agent Welch increased the stress by not addressing them at all. She just motioned the kids over and pointed at the soldiers.

Jerry was the first one to step forward and begin an intense focus on the soldier standing in front of him. Initially, he sensed extreme fear but forced his mind to ignore the sensation and refocus and enhance his vision to view his target's brain. It took several tries to learn how to adjust his enhanced focus to only see a slice of the brain and another few seconds to learn how to move that narrow focus through the man's brain like an MRI would do. Soon, however, Jerry had mastered the ability and telepathically sent the instructions to the others.

Jerry began slowly slicing through the brain looking for anything that didn't look right. He almost missed it and had to back up. There it was, a very small metal cylinder embedded in an open bone pocket at the far back of the nose canal under the center of the brain. From its location, a small explosion would definitely instantly kill the host's brain and person. He pinged the others and relayed the exact location. Soon the others verified their targets also had the same implant. Jerry nodded to Agent Welch that they were finished.

Janet said, "Thank you, Major Burns. You can return these men outside. Please hold them all until we can come up with a plan to deal with them."

103

After the five were gone, she said, "Can I assume that they all had implants?" When they nodded, she continued, "Since these soldiers were low ranks we must assume that all members of this security force have implants. "I guess that is one way to ensure total compliance and loyalty. Dr. Wisscroff, do you think these devices can be safely removed?"

Dr. Wisscroff said, "If they are where I suspected, right under the center of the brain in the bone structure at the back of the nose, I believe they can. Am I correct about the location?"

Sue said, "That's exactly where I found it. It is small and metal. It appeared to be lodged in an open hole in the bone."

Dr. Wisscroff said, "Yes. An explosion, even a small one, at that location would cause maximum damage and instant death. The device probably would be triggered by a chemical reaction from stress or possibly an electronic signal. It would be a fairly simple surgical procedure to remove them, but in the event of a potential electronic signal detonation, we should undertake the removal immediately. The Greys are probably not aware of the failed assassination attempt. I will get a surgical team mobilized immediately and begin the removal."

Janet said, "Thanks Doc. If you haven't already thought of the potential stress, you might want to sedate them before you take them to the hospital."

"It's already in the plan."

It had already been an eventful day, and they were more than ready for their evening meal when it arrived. Mrs. Wilks was already dishing out the food.

Mrs. Wilks said, "Someone has been trying really hard to kill us. Sooner or later they may try poisoning our food. I think after this meal I will go shopping for food and start cooking our own meals here."

Janet said, "That's probably a very good idea, and it's also a good idea to send a status report to Dir. Setliff and let him and Tom know what has been going on here."

\*\*\*

Jack and Tom had spent some productive flying hours getting to know each other, and they were nearing the D.C. airspace when he received Agent Welch's encrypted message. The message was a detailed and concise report of the activities at the gym and included the video of the interview and death of Lt. Barker. They both read the report and watched the video together in disbelief.

Tom said, "That was close. I should have been there to help."

Dir. Setliff said, "I should have been there, also, but Agent Welch did a great job. They are safe because of her quick action. You know that Dr. Wisscroff is one smart SOB. How did you ever find him?"

"I didn't. Mrs. Wilks found him. She steered us toward Tucson and found him. He kind of took charge of us from then on. I think he got you and us together, too."

Jack said, "Yeah, I like them both, too." After a smile and a moment of serious thought he continued, "You know, Tom, this is a lot bigger than we thought. It will take a major effort to clean this up, assuming it's not already too late. When we get to D.C. we will have to clear a basic core of insiders to fight back. I think you will be a big help, especially with those new powers."

Tom said, "We will have to work fast, though. We have our own problems that we must solve. I have to get back soon, and we must get to Antarctica. The answers are there. I feel it."

When they landed at Andrews AFB their plane was directed toward a remote area of the field, where the parking lot was filled with flashing lights. When they came down the plane's ramp they were met by Marines in full-dress uniforms that guided them toward a large, stretch limousine. The FBI called this type limousine a "Tank" because they were bulletproof like the one the president travels in. A Marine opened a backdoor for Dir. Setliff and Tom. The director stiffened when he was halfway in at the sight of President Thompson setting in the back.

FBI Dir. Setliff entered, pulling Tom Bradley inside and said, "Mr. President, I didn't expect to see you meet me. Oh, Mr. President, this is our Star Child, Tom Bradley." They shook hands.

President Thompson said, "I'm glad you were surprised. Hopefully, no one else would expect to

106

find me here. I wanted no one to know about this meeting. Mr. Bradley, I am happy to finally meet you. I've heard much about you. I understand you may be able to help us … each other, actually."

Tom said, "I will do what I can, and yes, I hope we can work together for each other's benefit." He searched the president's emotions and felt nothing but open, honest and cooperative feelings as they related to him and the other children.

The president said, "I was most disturbed by your last report, most disturbed. The situation appears to be far worse than we originally believed. In fact, it could be disastrous to the country."

Dir. Setliff took the opportunity to jump into the conversation and said, "Mr. President, it has gotten worse. May I suggest you read this last report I received from Agent Welch and watch the video attached. It will answer many questions you might have." He handed his tablet to the president, and he and Tom set back and watched the president's reaction, which was varied. There was initially surprise, then anger flushed over his face, followed by worry. After a few moments, determination and resolve settled on his face.

President Thompson said, "Unbelievable! I can't believe the propensity of our government to think the citizens of our country aren't smart enough to handle the truth. So aliens are here. It's the truth, so deal with it. This Top Secret crap allowed this problem to develop in this secret environment without any oversight, and it looks like they could have taken over while we weren't watching. Enough of my ranting. Let's try to solve the problem. I need to find a core of dependable patriots. I'll start with the military, and the first place to start is with the Joint Chiefs." He was thinking out loud and they knew it, but they were gaining insight. "The way I see it, we have at least two directions we can approach this. We need to identify the enemy within our government. We can start with this Col. Martin that gave the order to kill the Star Children. We can work backward up the chain of command."

"The other direction is the implants your agent discovered. It's possible that the aliens are in full control without human conspiracy involved in this corruption. I would like to believe that, anyway. The use of implants was an ingenious plan. By placing the implants in humans it made them totally compliant and would ensure complete control. The implants are encased in metal?"

Dir. Setliff said, "That's what I understand."

"I like this Dr. Wisscroff. I think we will need his help and analysis of the implants. If we don't already, we must modify or add to our security screening to identify those with an implant. We will set up a surgical operational team to extract the implants. I'll have my team work closely with this Dr. Wisscroff. Once the human is clear of the implant we'll have to determine if he is capable of coming back to the human side. And director, get those five you have in custody down to Tucson. They are obviously high operatives and can give us great intelligence on the alien operations."

108

"I will call a meeting for early in the morning with the Joint Chief; Secretaries of the Defense, Army, Navy and Air force; Directors of NSA, CIA, you will be there Jack and Tom, of course. Tom, I understand that you can sense emotions in a person. Will you be able to clear the group I bring in, or do you need individual one on one monitoring? I guess I should have asked if you are willing to help, first."

Tom said, "Of course I will help. They are trying to kill us. I want to end their reign. I believe I will be able to isolate emotions to an individual among a group. If necessary, assuming they don't have an implant, I can interrogate an individual more forcefully, like was done at the university gym. I can do many things, Mr. President, even search for any implants. I'm happy to report that none of your group here that I have seen, including yourself, have any implants."

The president chuckled and said, "That's nice to know. Where are you two going now? I will drop you off."

Jack said, "We are going to FBI Headquarters to interrogate my corrupted Deputy Director and CIA Dir. Martinez."

The president remained calm, even cheerful, for the trip to the FBI office. In parting, he said, "Be at the White House early. We'll see what we can get started."

When they walked into the interrogation room they found a very intimidated and nervous Dir. Martinez, which was uncharacteristic of him and a dejected Deputy Dir.

It was Dir. Martinez that began, saying, "Dir. Setliff, you're not going to be happy with my report."

Before he continued Tom stopped him and said, "Dir. Setliff, before this goes on, let me notify you that the Deputy Dir. is compromised. Do you understand?"

Jack said, "I understand." He called in an agent guard and said, "Take the Deputy Dir. back to his detention cell. No phone calls allowed." After he was gone Jack said, "Sorry Dir. Martinez. You can continue."

"Well, what I was going to report is I couldn't find anything ... nothing at all on those five men you captured. They simply don't work or even exist in our files. They don't exist anywhere. The IDs were printed in our office according to the embedded serial numbers, but our records don't even list them. Somehow, someway our system has been compromised, but I am at a dead end."

Dir. Setliff looked at Tom for a reaction, receiving a nod and a shrug, as if to say, "No deceit and no implant." Jack decided to commit to Dir. Martinez and trust him. He needed an ally he could trust. Jack said, "You know what director, yesterday I would not have believed you, but after what I have seen lately, I do believe you."

With this belief in mind, Jack spent some time totally briefing Dir. Martinez on the happenings of the last few days. He even let him read his last report from Agent Welch and watch the video.

They could see the facial expression change, much like those of the president.

Director Martinez looked extremely serious, then said, "This is far, far bigger than any of us thought possible. Are we too late?"

"Well, I'm certainly not giving up, and neither is the president. We're meeting at the White House in the morning. You're invited and come early. There are things we *can* do. I would say we can try to eliminate any of the forced enemies, those with the implants, so everyone in our departments are on the right side. We can also try to keep it secret as long as we can and ignore any cross-agency competition and work together."

Dir. Martinez said, "Yes, I agree. Our security X-Ray will identify the implants now that we know what to look for, and I will have a team standing by to take immediate charge of them. I'm thinking I will just sedate them and get them to a surgical team. We apparently won't be able to interrogate them until the implant is gone. We will probably kill them if we do, because we do know how to get results from our enhanced interrogations. Once we get started, we will be able to gather a lot of intelligence." He fell silent for a moment in deep thought then said, "Jack, this can't be just the U.S. This conspiracy almost has to be worldwide, also. Maybe we should let something slip to our counterparts around the world, even the Russians, about some worldwide conspiracy involving brain implants. We could give them just enough information to make them curious, and they would quickly find the cause. Actually, they need to know, and it will keep them busy and keep them from banging around our doors for a while. We can't deal with their games right now. We have too much to do."

Jack said, "That's actually a great idea, and the CIA is the expert of dissemination of misinformation. I'd say do it, but keep the lines open for feedback. I'd bet the Russians have the same problem."

"Tom and the Star Children is another direction we can go. They seem to think they might be the key to the whole problem, or at least a major source of intelligence, possibly even a solution. We're leaving tomorrow after the meeting with the president to go to Antarctica, where they believe answers can be found.

***

Sue was amazed and shocked at the activity around her. There were so many really smart people looking after the Star Children. They were very lucky to have met them. Each one had jumped into the fray to protect them in some form or another. Now, Agent Welch, well, Janet, surprised her again.

Janet came in the gym door and said, "Sue, I've got them, all twelve of your kin."

Sue was all smiles, but of course, it wasn't that big of a surprise. She knew Janet had gone after the children, and she had already seen them through the wall as they arrived. The poor kids huddled together and looked frightened and lost, like they had no idea what was going on; which of course they didn't. They had been ripped out of a loving home and thrown into a completely hostile world. Apparently, no one had bothered to tell them who they were and where they were going. But then no one at that end had even known what was going on, and hopefully, they still didn't know.

The kids seemed to be of equal numbers of male and female ranging in age from about twelve to maybe her age. They all had light blonde hair, green eyes and were similar in appearance, definitely from the same genetic line.

Sue stood before them and said, "You must all be frightened and wondering what has happened to your world. Well, let me try to explain." Waving her hands to include the other children, "We are called Star Children. The rest of us are still trying to figure out what that means, but nevertheless, that's what we are told. Somehow we and all of you are kin from the same genetic line. You can tell that by the similarity of our looks and hair color, although some of us have dyed our hair color to help us hide. What you need to know is that you are in danger, and we are all under attack. About 200 of us have already been killed." At that statement the new group huddled even closer. They all at that point were starting to realize the seriousness of what they were being told. "You have been taken from your homes and families to protect you. All here are friends trying to save us."

"What we are, we have no idea, but we have some amazing abilities, which at this point you are

113

probably totally unaware. We will teach you some of these abilities quickly so you can defend yourselves." Sue turned to Fred, Jerry, Mary and Tina and said, "Demonstrate to the others what I am saying."

The four immediately floated up in the air, and Tina began an elaborate exhibition of twists, rolls, spins, etc. Tina loved to fly and obviously liked to show off, too. The others stared wide eyed in obvious disbelief, but a couple of them after watching began to float upwards. Maybe they had already discovered this ability previously or completely accepted the possibility by seeing it done. Some may have been pinged by the original kids. Their expressions turned from fear to astonishment and cheerfulness. With this look of acceptance, the original kids floated back down to the floor and began greeting and meeting the others. As with Tom before, they knew the truth and could sense the friendship and their acceptance. Talk was easy flowing between the kids.

Sue introduced Mrs. Wilks, Dr. Wisscroff and Agent Welch, which the new kids had already met. The National Security Advisor, Tom Canton was also introduced. It took him a minute to recover from the shock of the demonstration to shake hands all around.

Mrs. Wilks announced, "I've been cooking today and have dinner ready. So, gather around and get some food and continue getting acquainted."

Most of the new kids gathered around Sue to quiz her. Hope was now filling their minds, finally beginning to understand who they were and wanting to know more about their dormant powers. Due to the limited space around the conference table, some were already taking instructions from the older kids, many already flying around the gym. Chatter and laughter filled the gym.

That's when Dr. Wisscroff's phone rang, changing the mood completely. Doc listened for a while, then raised his hand for silence. Doc said, "The secret is out, and the enemy now knows their attempt to take over here has failed. Many of the Air Force Security Forces soldiers have died at the hospital. Apparently, their implants were detonated. We were, however, able to remove about ten of the implants. The rest are all dead. The five just received from the FBI in Las Vegas are still alive. Evidently, the Greys don't know they have failed also. They came in sedated, and they will be kept that way. Hopefully, their implants will be removed immediately before the Greys know we have them. By tomorrow you should be able to interrogate them.

Tina tugged on Sue's shirt and said, "They are coming."

"Who's coming?"

"The Greys are coming. They're coming soon." She hadn't spoken very loudly, but there was total silence in the gym and all were listening.

Sue asked, "What do you see, Tina. Tell us everything you see."

"I see saucers diving down on us in the gym and shooting beams of light at us."

"How long do we have before they come?"

Tina hugged her and said, "Not long. They are coming now."

Sue began screaming orders. "Jerry, Fred and Mary, look for them and be prepared to use gravity to disrupt their flight. Mrs. Wilks, get the other children in the back room, underground if possible. Mr. Colton, get us some air cover to shoot them down. Janet, tell Major Burns to get ready to repel an air attack." Everyone seemed frozen until Sue screamed, "Move it, people. They are coming *now*! If Tina says they are coming, you better believe it." At that, they all burst into action."

Dr. Wisscroff said, "They know their attempt to kill you kids has failed, so they are coming themselves with their best weapons. It sounds like they will attack with lasers. Okay, kids think about light. How can you control it? Remember, what she saw in the future is only one version of the future. It can be changed, so change it."

Mary was looking up through the ceiling and said, "I see them coming. I only see two. They are fast. They're firing rockets at them from outside, but the saucers are so fast they are just skipping out of the way."

Sue, Jerry and Mary shot their arms upward sending gravity pulses. Fred was bent over concentrating hard on something. The gravity pulses began disrupting their flight and making them wobble in flight, but they kept coming, skipping from side to side to avoid the gravity energy. When the first laser beam shot out toward

116

them it got about halfway and mysteriously bounced back and curved its trajectory back into the saucer. The saucer exploded immediately. When the second fired the beam immediately reversed back into the saucer. Both saucers disintegrated into smoke and small debris. It was over as soon as it began, and all stood in total disbelief.

Dr. Wisscroff was the first to say, "Okay, who did what?"

No one spoke for a full minute, then Fred began laughing and said, "I learned how to control light. Doc, I just did what you said, I thought about light and how to control it. My projected energy became a mirror, and it worked. It *was* my time to introduce a new power."

Cheering broke out throughout the gym. The new Star Children were jumping and hopping around, proud of their new kin and mentors.

It was Doc that ended the cheering by saying, "We've got to get the hell out of here. They won't make that mistake again. Next time they will come with more saucers and possibly different weapons."

Sue remained in charge. She said, "Mr. Canton, please get our plane ready and when the jets get here, keep them in the air to protect us. Agent Welch, tell Major Burns to maintain security here after we go to maintain the illusion we are still here. Now, all of the rest of you hurry and load on the bus. Let's get out of here before the Greys come back. Mrs. Wilks, bring the money. We won't be coming back here." This time everyone jumped to comply without further prodding.

# Chapter 5
## (Preparing for War)

Dir. Setliff's cell phone chimed, indicating he had a text message. He froze as he read it. Janet simply said, *"We were attacked again. See full report in e-mail. We are leaving here. When you finish there head south. We will contact you and tell you where to meet us."* Jack then opened the report. The news was mostly all good, but it had almost been disastrous. For security purposes Jack and Tom were sharing a room near the White House. When he finished reading it he handed his tablet to Tom.

Tom's face flushed with anger and said, "I need to be with the children. We need to leave immediately after the morning meeting with the president."

Jack said, "I will call and have the plane ready, and we will leave as soon as the president lets us go. I promise."

Dir. Setliff and Tom were up early, had an early breakfast and were the first ones in the security conference room. CIA Dir. Martinez was the next one to enter, followed by NSA Dir. Jones. After a short wait the seven Joint Chiefs of Staff came in with their boss, The Secretary of Defense. The Secretaries of the Army, Navy and Air Force came in next. The president came in last.

Tom had been watching them all and wasn't too surprised to see an implant in NSA Director

Jones. Someone high up had been leaking information, and it made sense that it was the NSA. The officer that died from an implant had admitted to be working for the NSA and at a high level. Dir. Jones knew where the children were hiding and many other details from their joint investigation.

Tom barely controlled his seething anger and wanted to kill him personally … now, but he came up with a better idea and leaned close to Dir. Setliff and whispered, "Dir. Jones has an implant, but the others are clear."

Dir. Setliff was initially shocked, then after a moment of thought began to realize what Tom had pieced together: Dir. Jones was the enemy, mole and leak inside the security screen who had been informing the assassins so they could be killed. Jack went to the president and quietly informed him. President Thompson nodded and continued as if nothing was out of the ordinary.

After the security shield came up the president started the meeting saying, "I want to ask some questions before we get started. Be honest when you reply. How many know we have deep underground tunnels crisscrossing America and how many know about the Greys?" He looked around the room then at Tom and waited for a reaction.

Tom sensed panic from Dir. Jones, which he ignored. From the others he sensed varying degrees of confusion some acknowledgment but no panic or deception.

The Chief of Staff of the Air Force said, "I know we have deep tunnels here in D.C. and the

119

east coast, but I'm not aware of tunnels all over the country. I'm also aware of the existence of Greys in Area 51, but that is a deeply guarded Top Secret subject. Isn't It?"

Dir. Jones blurted out, "It *is* Top Secret, and we can't talk about it."

President Thompson's deep baritone voice bellowed, "Dir. Jones, shut the fuck up! I'll tell you what's Top Secret and what we can and can't talk about, not you." The conference room fell into total silence.

The president looked directly at Tom and received a shrug and nod toward the Air Force general, then said, "General Freeman, I am very pleased to know you aren't part of the problem, since the Air Force is deep into this problem. I needed to know your level of participation, because I need you to help correct it. The Secretary of Defense has already been briefed. Now I will brief the rest of you, since you all have been cleared by Tom." Pointing directly at Tom. Continuing, "Tom is a Star Child. That project is also Top Secret, and most have probably not heard of them. Around 200 of them, children, were killed, assassinated. That's what got this current investigation started that brings you here today. We are still trying to figure out what Star Children means, but suffice to know that if any of you here were part of the conspiracy Dir. Setliff uncovered, Tom would have known. As it turns out, only one of this group is compromised, and that is Dir. Jones."

At the president's statement, Dir Jones broke into a dash for the door, but with the security shield up the door was locked.

Tom said, "Mr. President, may I take it from here?"

The president waved his hand toward Dir. Jones. Tom took control of his mind, like Sue had instructed him. Dir. Jones froze with the blank look. Tom knew what he wanted to do and where to look. He concentrated on the implant, held it tight with his manipulation of focused gravity and yanked it out. It would have been painful to Dir. Jones had he been fully awake, but Tom wouldn't have minded inflicting pain to the man that had been part of killing the Star Children and tried to kill him and the other children. Blood gushed from his nose along with the tiny implant, which floated to the center of the conference table where everyone could see. Tom wanted the director to talk, so he burned the ruptured area with generated heat to seal it and took pleasure in the smoke coming out of Dir. Jones' nose and the smell of burning flesh.

Tom watched those around the table stare at the implant on the table and said, "We can interrogate him now without the Greys killing him. Dir. Jones, answer the president's questions fully and completely."

In a monotone voice Dir. Jones said, "Yes, fully and completely."

The president said, "How much of our government and military have been compromised and are controlled by the Greys?

121

"Mostly only the NSA, since the NSA oversees the Top Secret alien liaison. Also, some of the Air Force, mostly security, those forces that provide security to the deep underground secret facilities."

The president asked next, "How extensive are the underground tunnel systems and where do they go?

"There are thousands of miles of massive deep tunnels. The Grey's saucers and the high-speed trains travel from coast to coast in them. I'm not aware exactly where they go, but I know several bases in California are connected together. The tunnel system started out from Area 51 and extends into California and through Arizona into Mexico. There are also terminals in New Mexico, Colorado and Oklahoma that I am aware of."

The president began thinking out loud and asked, "Where the hell do they get their money to do all this shit?"

"Mining from all the tunnels and the government."

The president asked, "How many Greys are there and where do they live?"

Dir Jones continued to stare unfocused and said, "I'm not sure. They don't let us in their areas, but there must be thousands of Greys. I do know there are three main bases, but I don't know where. One is in Arizona I think. Another is far away and they have to fly there … no tunnels.

"What are their intentions?"

"They are hostile to humans, even those they control with implants. It is obvious to us that are

122

around them that they intend to rule Earth, and they are close."

"What weapons do they have?"

"Flying Saucers. They have many stored underground."

The president stopped his questions, because the room appeared to be in total shock. So, Tom released Dir. Jones' mind. He immediately fell to the floor and burst out with sobs from pain and shame.

The president stared at Dir. Jones pathetic, wintering form on the floor. His face wrinkled up in disgust and said, "Your implant has been removed, so the Greys can't kill you, but those in this room might do it for them, and I'm one of them. You are a treasonous bastard, and you and your fellow conspirators have done major damage to this country."

The president looked at the others and said, "I could simply have briefed you, and I will now; but I think you are getting an idea of what we are up against. We now must plan. Tom, thank you for your assistance. I can handle it from here if you and Dir. Setliff want to leave. I know you are anxious to rejoin your group."

Dir. Setliff said, "Thank you, Mr. President. Yes, the other Star Children are under attack, and we must rejoin them as soon as possible. May I suggest that CIA Dir. Martinez be given custody of Jones, so he can subject Jones to some of his enhanced interrogation techniques. I will pick one of my Deputy Directors, Robert Hawkins, to

123

temporarily fill my post while I'm gone, but only after Tom gets a chance to meet him for obvious reasons."

President Thompson said, "That's a good idea, Jack. Dir. Martinez, he's yours, but call some of your agents to get him the hell out of my sight." The president lifted the security shield. "Hurry back, because I need you here to help me brief the others." Dir. Martinez nodded and hauled Jones up and pushed him through the door in front of him.

Dir. Setliff and Tom immediately left the White House and met a waiting Lemo. One of his Deputy Directors, Robert Hawkins, was waiting in the back for them. His secretary had organized it all while he was in the secure room. One of Jack's personal security guards was driving. They quickly got in and sped toward Andrews AFB and his waiting FBI plane.

Before Dir. Setliff spoke he looked at Tom. He had known Robert for years. Robert was intelligent and very competent. Jack was sure Robert was clear, but looked for assurance and got it. "Robert, check in with my Personal Assistant and she will get you all set up. You are now in charge of the FBI until I return, assuming I do. You need to get back to the White House as soon as possible for war council with President Thompson, The Joint Chiefs, and Secretary of Defense and many others. They will need you and the FBI." Dir. Hawkins' body stiffened at the news. His eyes bulged and face turned chalky, but he said nothing, much to his credit. Much was happening involving him and much too fast.

After a pause Dir. Hawkins said, "May I ask what this is all about?"

"I'm about to tell you. I'll give you as much details and facts as I can during the trip to Andrews. That's all the Top Secret time I have to give you, but CIA Dir. Martinez and President Thompson can complete your briefing. You will understand the severe nature of the problem immediately, but you are needed to help plan our future actions, and I must devote my time to an equally important aspect of the problem. In short, we are at war with aliens." That set the shock and mood of the briefing, which lasted the full thirty minute trip to Andrews AFB.

They said their "Good-Byes" at the ramp of the FBI Gulfstream V and left immediately, leaving a bewildered and stressed Dir. Hawking waving. Jack thought that if what just happened Dir. Hawkins had happened to him he might be waving a finger.

The pilot asked after takeoff, "Where are we headed? I need to file a flight plan."

Dir. Setliff said, "Forget about a flight plan and just fly south. We'll tell you where we are going when we know."

They had been in the air for some time, and the pilot said he had begun a swing west around Cuba's air space. Jack was beginning to wonder if Janet had forgotten. That's when he received a message. The message was not terribly informative, and he assumed she was just being careful. It said, "We will meet you at the International Airport in Buenos Aires."

Dir. Setliff told the pilot, "Our destination is Buenos Aires."

He flashed an annoyed roll of his eyes and said, "Wow. That's a long ways. We will have to stop for fuel somewhere. Where would you like to stop?"

Jack ignored the eye roll and thought for a moment and said, "Well, Buenos Aires is a public airport. I think Janet is telling us to use public facilities. I think she doesn't trust military facilities. So, let's see, stop in Bogota, Colombia. That's a large airport, and we have to fly over it to Buenos Aires anyway."

"Very well, I'll call in a flight plan and order the fuel for our stop."

Tom listened to the conversation and said, "With all that has gone on I think Sue and Janet are afraid of letting our destination out in military communications. I wouldn't want to take a chance either."

"Yeah, I agree. Well, Tom it's going to be a long trip. We should spend it sleeping. It might get busy once we get there."

***

After Tom and Dir. Setliff left, President Thompson said, "The FBI and its resources will be important to our overall strategy and investigations. So, let's take a break until Special Agent Hawkins goes through the Star Child security check and briefing by Dir. Setliff. This will give you all a

126

chance to grasp the implications of what you have heard and seen this morning. We'll meet again in about an hour. I don't think I have to tell you that secrecy is vital." Animated nods passed among the group.

When the group gathered again, including now Dir. Hawkins, the look was completely different. Where shock and disbelief highlighted the looks of the group before, now could be seen concern and firm resolve.

The president closed the security shield and said, "I see the hour wasn't wasted. I no longer see disbelief. I see acceptance of certain facts. Trust me, it gets worse." The president began at the beginning, which was only a few days ago. He gave as much detail as he could, and often called on Dir. Martinez or Dir. Hawkins to elaborate. Over time they built a very good picture of the problem.

At one point the president said, "As I have said, the Greys, with the help of conspiring humans, have killed over 200 of these Star Children. We know little about the Star Children, but apparently they are a major threat to the Greys, and they want to eliminate them. You have seen some of their powers demonstrated here today, but they have many other powers. I've been told that if you ever see them fly you would easily believe. At any rate, the Star Children are enemies of the Greys. That makes us, the human race, friends. Dir. Setliff is working directly for me. You will consider his directions as my direction. Right now he is working with the Star Children to help them, first, to stay alive, secondly, to help them identify themselves and how we can work together against this Grey alien threat. The Star Children claim to know where they will learn their history, and they are headed there now. They say Antarctica is their destination."

"Now, before I open this forum up, let me just say, much damage has been done under the mask of Top Secret. That ends here and now. All department secrecy and jealously ends now. We have a common problem and enemy, and it is a major one. Let's work together and prepare jointly for this coming war."

"I'll leave now and let you experts begin your planning, just keep me informed. Dir. Hawkins, for right now I want you to take over supervision of the NSA. We need to clean it out secretly."

*** 

Sue believed they were safe once they got in the air, but she had Mr. Canton maintain fighter protection. But, after they crossed the Mexican border she ask him to call them off, believing it could draw too much attention to them from other governments and even the U.S. military. Sue didn't want the military to know where they were or where they were going. She didn't know how far up the chain of command had been corrupted, and it was better to remain invisible to everyone. Sue called the group together and expressed her concerns.

It was Dr. Wisscroff that got everyone's attention by saying, "There is a whole lot more to think about and plan. For one, where are we going?

Antarctica? Where are we going to stay when we get there? We will need cold weather gear once there. I, for one, don't plan to stay in a military base underground, for reasons Tom explained. So, first things first."

Janet said, "I agree with Sue's concerns. So, let's stick to public airports for fuel. We just tell them we are a high school science class. I also agree that we should stay clear of McMurdo. It is the main location of air flights in and out of Antarctica. We would not be able to land there without everyone knowing."

National Security Advisor Canton said, "Well, the military does exercises in Antarctica all the time to train troops in cold weather survival. We could schedule an exercise there. I mean, this is a Boeing C-40-A Navy plane and is equipped with hydraulic skids that can be engaged to allow us to land on ice. We can plot a military exercise location on the Ross Ice Shelf in West Antarctica. It is close to the coordinates you want, and the Ross Ice Shelf is somewhat protected by a mountain range. We certainly don't want to get on the ice dome. The weather is really nasty there. If I get them moving now they can be set up quickly, and we can land there. At least we would have a secluded place to land, stay and eat.

As far as foul weather gear is concerned, I did have foul weather gear, equipment and supplies loaded on the plane, but survival there takes skills the military must provide."

Janet said, "That sounds like an excellent idea, and I know who to send. Marine Major Burns did an excellent job of protecting us at the gym. I'm sure he won't like going from the Yuma desert to Antarctica, but at least he knows who the enemy is and won't need to be briefed."

NSA Canton said, "Good. I'll get it started. In the meantime we need to find a place to hold up and stock up on more equipment and supplies."

Janet said, "The FBI has a large presence at the American Embassy in Buenos Aires. I'm positive they could put us up. That location is far south, and Buenos Aires is a large city. We should be able to find anything we need there. I'll send a message to Dir. Setliff to meet us at the airport in Buenos Aires."

Within an hour Agent Welch and NSA Canton met again. Both were amazed at how fast their plans had been initiated.

NSA Canton said, "I was notified directly by the Sec. of the Navy. The message was encrypted and said, *'I have been briefed. The orders have been issued, top priority. Let me know anything else you may need.'* Things must be happening at that end, also."

Agent Welch said, "I agree. Things must be happening there. I also received a message notifying all FBI offices to give top priority to any requests coming from Deputy Dir. Welch (me) or Dir. Setliff. I guess I have been promoted to Deputy Director level. Strangely, the order came from Acting FBI Dir. Robert Hawkins. I know Mr.

Hawkins, and he is a great agent, but I wasn't expecting him to be the director. That's new, too. I'm not sure now what Dir. Setliff is the director of. The same thing I am I guess. At any rate, the Buenos Aires FBI office notified me that they will meet us at the airport with a bus and escorts to the American Embassy. Now that we know where we are going for sure, I will notify Jack where to meet us."

Sue had been following all the communications and activities up to this point and felt comfortable. Still, she didn't like being out of touch with Tom. Suddenly, she realized that they hadn't even tried to communicate with each other via their Ping Network since they split up. She sent a Ping to Tom, which was answered immediately.

*"Sue, is that you?"*

*"Well, of course it's me. Duh! No one else can use my number."*

*"I know that. I was just surprised to hear from you. I didn't think we would be able to communicate from a distance. I was wrong with that assumption, obviously. Where are you?*

*"We are still flying en route to the FBI at the American Embassy in Buenos Aires."* Sue went on to give Tom a complete report on what they were planning to do and where they were going.

Tom pinged, *"That sounds like a good plan. We are stopping in Bogota, Colombia for fuel, then straight to Buenos Aires. I'll let you know when we are close."* Tom then gave her a rundown on the happenings with the president.

Sue called the group in the plane together and told them about her communications with Tom via their Ping Network and passed on the information Tom had given her.

Janet said, I'm glad they caught Dir. Jones. He was definitely the main source of the leaks concerning the Star Children. The problem is that the Greys now know their secret is out, but with him sequestered, they won't get any new information."

Dr. Wisscroff said, "It's important to note that the communication network you kids developed is much stronger than you, or we for that matter, believed possible. Apparently there is no reasonable distance limit. We must all stop trying to put limits on your powers. You new kids need to develop your communication matrix links, if you haven't already. The older kids can help you greatly by transferring Sue's data."

The remaining part of the trip was uneventful. Sue worked with Tina, trying to learn how to trigger the ability to look into the future, unsuccessfully. They finally gave up and joined the others in sleep.

Sue felt the change in pressure in her ears and was awake when they landed. As promised, there was a bus and several black Suburbans at the end of the runway they were steered to. Janet steered the pilot and small crew of the Navy C-40 A toward one of the Suburbans. Sue assumed they would be taken to a nearby hotel. NSA Canton and Deputy Dir. Welch got in the other one. They would be giving instruction to the Agent in Charge during the ride to the embassy. All the others were directed toward the bus.

As the bus pulled out, Mrs. Wilks said to the driver, "Take us to a large mall with a large sporting goods store. We need to buy some supplies."

The driver didn't argue, but he stopped to report the request. NSA Canton came waddling back to the bus and asked, "What kind of supplies do you need?"

Mrs. Wilks said, "Mostly winter gear for the children."

"Buenos Aires is not a great place to find winter gear. It hardly ever snows here. Besides, I stocked up on the winter gear back in D.C. for adults and all sizes for children. I brought lots of extra and all the accessories like boots, gloves, arctic coats and pants, thermal socks and underwear. I think we have all that covered, but if there are other things you need we can go to the mall. It will make the FBI agents nervous, but we can go. I think we are safe enough, since only now are some aware we are here … not enough notice to plan anything."

"I wasn't aware that you had taken care of foul weather clothing. Thanks. That was one of my biggest worries, but, these kids have been under a lot of stress for days. Having just gotten here, I too think we are safe. I just want these kids to have a little fun before we get locked back up. I want to let them shop for personal items to make them feel comfortable and just cruise the mall just for the fun of it."

"You are probably right about the kids having been under severe stress. Let's do it."

Cheers rang out from the kids, and the excitement level increased dramatically. The FBI Agents went crazy once they reached the mall. Mrs. Wilks was handing out money like it was Monopoly money, and the kids took off running and laughing. After a few futile attempts to keep the kids herded together, the agents finally shrugged and gave up. They watched closely, however.

The kids had a ball playing video games in an arcade, buying games, tablets, clothing, food and everything imaginable. It was a pleasure to see the enjoyment on the faces of the kids after so much seriousness over the last few days. A couple of the kids came back to Mrs. Wilks to ask for money to buy musical instruments. One girl wanted a violin, and another boy wanted a guitar. They got the extra money from a smiling Mrs. Wilks. After a three-hour spending spree, the happy kids reloaded in the bus and they completed the trip to the American Embassy.

It was a disappointment when they got there, because the embassy didn't have the facilities for so many extra bodies. They were taken to another gym, where foldout beds were stacked in rows.

Once everyone was situated, Sue began a training session with all the Star Children. She started with levitation just to show off to the astonished spectators. She knew they would love showing off. All the Star Children now had the gravity power mastered and began flitting all over the gym, led by a jubilant Tina. Sue evolved the exercise in gravity manipulation by having them move other items, as in telekinesis. She had them stacking barbell weights, then playing mental catch back and forth with one hundred pound weights. They began to become comfortable and quite proficient. One of the kids brought out a football he bought at the mall, and the kids soon had a game going. That game soon evolved into a mental game of Dodge Ball, that tested all the kids' abilities. It only took a few hard smacks by the ball to make them perfect their skills in time control and telekinesis. Another of the inventive kids, probably Fred, created an arrow of light and sent it floating into the group. The kids began altering its direction, shooting it back and forth across the gym. The speed kept increasing to the point that the human observers couldn't follow it. As an observer, Sue suddenly realized that not only were they controlling the light, but they were sharing the minds of the other players to anticipate their moves. That was the only way it could have been done, even with controlling time. She opened her mind and sensed the players and their moves. She joined in this challenging game. It was stimulating to the point of excitement. Not only were the Star Children (Kids) mastering various powers, but they also had obviously mastered their communication Ping Network.

Agent Welch got Sue's attention when she said, "The kids probably shouldn't be displaying their powers so flagrantly. There might be some compromised witnesses."

Startled, Sue realized Janet was right and wondered why she had been so negligent. Sue looked around to see the kids all gathered around in chairs, totally immobile. This would be good for their concentration but would also focus the observers toward the kids, and they had drawn quite a large crowd that she hadn't noticed before. Sue Pinged the kids *"Stop the exercise and mingle with the crowd to see if any have an implant or if you detect deceit or hostility. Immobilize them if you do."*

Sue said to Janet, "You're right. I'm sorry, I wasn't thinking. I've sent the kids searching for any implants among the crowd."

Janet quickly waved the FBI Agents over and informed them, and they quickly dispersed following the children. The kids quickly spread out through the large crowd and went directly toward the exits, so no one would be missed. Janet directed her agents toward three men seemingly frozen in a trance. One of the zombies was the FBI Bureau Chief standing in front of one of the Star Children, Jerry. Janet motioned for the agents to vacate the other witnesses out of the gym.

Once they were gone Agent Welch said to the agents, "Tranquilize him and keep him sedated until I tell you what to do with him. No, wait. Jerry, can you pull the implant out, like Tom did in D.C.?"

Jerry said, "I believe so. Right here?" Janet nodded.

Jerry had read the shared report from Dir. Setliff and knew what Tom had done. He did likewise. He viewed the implant, grabbed it and yanked it out, then he cauterized it. Jerry never touched it, simply dropped it on the floor of the gym, just in case it exploded.

Janet motioned for Jerry to lead the zombie to a tabled area, then motioned Mary and Tina to bring their zombies to the area, also. The seized men remained at stiff attention. The Bureau Chief had been a surprise to her, but he should be a valuable source of information. The other two were Marine Embassy guards.

Sue said, "Tina, your man does not have an implant."

Tina said, "Yes, I know, but his emotions were hostile, and if allowed to remain free, he will do harm to us in the future. We must keep him imprisoned to prevent that."

Agent Welch said, "Someone get the Assistant Bureau Chief here. Let's start with Tina's man while we wait. What is your name?"

"I am Lance Corporal Jeremy Abdul"

"Jeremy, are you working with the Greys?"

"No Ma'am. I don't know anyone named Grey."

Janet looked confused, then asked, "Why are you hostile toward the Star Children?

"They are not of this world and are an abomination to Allah. They must be destroyed."

Janet shook her head and said, "Sadly, I understand. He is a religious zealot. His hostility would have surfaced sooner or later. It's good that it showed up now. I guess the best place for him now is with the other terrorist at Cuba. One problem solved. Tina, you can release him."

Once Lance Corporal Abdul was released he was grabbed by two other Marines guards and hauled off rather roughly.

As this was happening the Assistant Bureau Chief came bustling in. Janet looked at Sue for confirmation that he was clear. Sue nodded her approval. Janet asked, "What is your name?"

"I'm Special Agent Gary Brawley."

Janet said, "Well, Special Agent Brawley you are now Bureau Chief Brawley, because this Bureau Chief is a traitor, as you will soon see." She noticed an agent at his side whispering in his ear and pointing to the implant on the floor. Janet looked directly at the zombie FBI agent and asked, "How long have you had that implant, and how long have you been working with the Greys?

Again the monotone voice said, "Ma'am, I was forced to take the implant over twenty years ago when I worked security at Area 51, and I have been forced to do their bidding ever since. If I don't they will kill me."

"Your implant has been removed. They can no longer kill you."

"The Greys are very powerful. They will still kill me when they take over the world. They can't be stopped. It's too late."

"Have you told them the Star Children are here?"

138

"No, we didn't know they were coming. I just now figured out who they are. The Greys sent word to all to watch for them and report."

"Are there others at this station with implants other than you and this other lance corporal?"

"Yes, there is another in the Ambassador's staff. His name is John Meeker."

Janet looked at Agent Brawley and said, "Please take that man into custody with no calls or outside contacts. Actually, bring him to me, now." Agent Brawley nodded and spoke to his agents.

Janet continued, "Now you will tell us every FBI agent that has an implant."

I can only tell you my single upper contact. The others above ground here you already know. We are not allowed to know more. My contact is ...." He named the Deputy Director in D. C, the one they already knew about.

Why is there a presence of so many Grey agents here at this facility?"

"This is a stopover location for the Greys. They have a tunnel network underneath us."

That answer shocked Janet, but she continued, "Stopover to and from where?"

"We don't know. They give us little information, but we believe they must be going between main bases, since there is a lot of traffic."

Janet told the others, "This is frustrating. You have to ask the right questions to get meaningful information. Sue, are you getting any emotions from these zombies?"

Sue said, "No emotions at all in this state."

Janet continued probing for information, but very little additional information was obtained, even less from the other lance corporal. He had been a low-level worker, and not a very good one.

Tom had been listening in to the interrogation via their Ping Network and passing on the intelligence to Dir. Setliff. Tom said, *"Sue, when you interrogate this John Meeker, try doing it after you remove the implant and without seizing his mind. See if logic might work with him. If it doesn't you can always seize his mind."* Sue told Janet about Tom's suggestion.

Janet said, "Good suggestion. We might as well try it. What do we have to lose?"

When the Marines brought John Meeker into the gym everyone forgot about the suggestion. All they could do was stare with open mouths. John Meeker looked to be an identical twin to Tom, only older at about 25 years old. Even being older and with a beard and mustache, John Meeker was a doppelgänger to Tom in size and looks, complete with the darker complexion accenting platinum blond hair and green eyes. Sue just stared … speechless.

It was John that broke the spell when he said, "I'm John Meeker. What is this all about, and why have you arrested me?"

Sue actually jumped when he spoke, because he even sounded like Tom. She opened her mind immediately and searched for his emotions. All she saw was confusion … no hostility or deceit, but when she searched his brain she found the implant. Sue whispered her findings to Janet.

With John's identical look and Sue's report, Janet was unsure how to proceed and said, "Are you aware that you have an implant on your brain?"

John said, "I have a what? There must be a mistake. I have no implant."

"I can assure you that you do. It looks exactly like those." She pointed to the shiny implants on the floor. "It is currently being observed in your head. And, you say you are not aware of it?"

"No, it's news to me. What's it for?"

"Well, honestly, the intent of these implants is to kill its host."

Sue detected shock and dismay, even fear with that statement, which she relayed to Janet.

John Meeker looked at Sue and said, "Are you probing my mind? I feel you inside my thoughts."

Surprised, Sue said, "Yes I am. Would you like the implant removed? I can remove it, but, I warn you, it will hurt."

"Hell yes! Get it out. Get it out, now."

Sue tried to seize his brain to prevent the coming pain, but nothing happened. Regardless, she mentally latched on to it and jerked it out. Mr. Meeker squealed in pain but didn't resist. Sue immediately cauterized the small wound and continued to pull the implant out. It dangled in the air in front of him for a few seconds, then fell to the floor to join the other two.

As soon as John overcame the pain and bleeding he blurted, "Someone want to explain to me what the fuck is going on?"

Dr. Wisscroff stepped forward and said, "I think I might be able to explain. Mr. Meeker, were you adopted?"

"No, I was raised in an orphanage."

"That makes sense. Mr. Meeker, I think you better sit down. What you are about to hear will come as a great shock to you. It certainly comes as a shock to me, but the evidence is undeniable. I believe we will find that your DNA comes from the same lineage as these other kids, which in all likelihood was genetically engineered. This lineage hasn't yet been determined. That's what we are currently doing. I believe you, possibly, came from an earlier DNA release. I believe you and probably others of your type have been monitored by the Greys and were scheduled to be eliminated at some point in the future. This is probably why you were assigned to this location. The Bureau Chief was your monitor."

John Meeker said, "What the hell is a Grey?"

Dr. Wisscroff said, "Don't worry about that. Everything will be explained to you."

Doc turned to the others and continued. "To the rest of us, this means we have more work to be done to find the remaining Star Children before they too are eliminated. To you, Mr. Meeker, meet your kin and let them teach you what you have been missing all of your life. It will most likely take you longer to learn about your powers, because you must unlearn much of your understanding of the laws of physics."

A very dazed Mr. Meeker looked around the room and, as if for the first time, seemed to recognize some of himself in the other children: the bronze skin, white hair, green eyes and generally the same features.

Sue said, "Tina, see if Mr. Meeker can fly."

Tina took Mr. Meeker's hand and led him off into the gym. In a few moments she began levitating in front of an extremely jolted Mr. Meeker. He began listening to her intently. Tina returned to the floor and lay Mr. Meeker down on the floor and pulled his eyes shut. Sue could hear Tina telling him to relax and just believe. It took a few moments, but she saw Mr. Meeker slowly rise up. He got up to about six foot above the floor before he realized he had done it, at which point he panicked and fell back to the floor with a loud bang. The excitement didn't allow him to feel it, or at that point, he didn't care. It meant more to Sue, because it proved Dr. Wisscroff was right about John. He was one of them.

Tom continued to follow all of the activities through Sue's Ping Network, relaying the information to Dir. Setliff. A few times he had to rebuke Jack, because he kept pumping him with questions. Finally the interrogation was over and Sue closed the link. Tom said, "This is amazing. There are more of us."

Dir. Setliff didn't hear him. He was already on the phone with Robert Hawkins instructing him to initiate the research on John Meeker's background and DNA file. He was telling Robert to find a link through Meeker's records to find others.

They had refueled in Bogota, Colombia and were well underway toward Buenos Aires, Argentina. The pilot had given them a time of arrival of 05:45 am. Based upon that time, Dir. Setliff scheduled, through Agent Welch, a departure time of 10:00 am for the Boeing C-40-A.

He had traveled on one before. As he remembered, it would transport about 120 people plus cargo, more than large enough for their growing numbers and needs. He told Janet to meet them at the airport for breakfast. There was nothing left to do but sleep. He and Tom reclined back in their plush seats for the rest of the trip.

# Chapter 6
## (Antarctica)

Dir. Setliff woke as the plane began its approach to Buenos Aires, freshened up and changed clothes. He then checked his messages. There was one from both Dir. Hawkins and Dir. Martinez. He quickly read through them, but basically they were the same. They provided a copy of the Plan of Action from the president's joint committee. Jack perused the plan, but it was a list of the obvious standard things: find out how many Greys there are, where they are, what weapons they had, locate the tunnel network, etc, etc. The committee was working on developing hand-held implant detectors, which Jack thought was a great idea. One item got his attention. They planned to capture some Greys undetected and wanted a Star Child to monitor them and eavesdrop on their conversation, maybe even learn their language.

Jack asked, "Tom, can you understand the Greys' language?"

"I can follow some of their conversation by detecting their emotions and images they generate, but understanding their spoken language? No."

"The president's joint Committee wants to capture several Greys and asked for one of the Star Children to eavesdrop in on their conversation to get intelligence, maybe even seize their mind for interrogation. What do you think?"

Tom thought for a moment and said, "It's possible. I think we have learned that our internal communication will work over great distances, and that was my main concern in being separated. I'll ask the others."

At ten till seven an FBI Suburban pulled up beside the Gulfstream V. Dir. Setliff, Tom and the two personal security agents got in and were taken away from the airport to a large restaurant. Evidently, Janet wanted more security and privacy for their morning meeting and meal. Jack liked that about her, she took charge.

When they went in the waitress led them to a back room. There were two sections, and everyone gravitated to their respective areas. Dir. Setliff was greeted with a big hug from Janet and firm handshakes from the new Bureau Chief, NSA Canton and various other FBI members. Tom was greeted with a big hug from Sue, followed by a very wet kiss that he liked a lot. All the kids greeted him like they had known him forever, even though he had never met most of them. His attention was drawn toward a large man that looked very much like the man he saw in the mirror every morning. Sue introduced him as John Meeker.

Sue said, "Now you can see why we were surprised. You look like identical twins, only John is older. Dr. Wisscroff says it's genetics, maybe you both had the same mother or egg. He said he will figure it out."

Tom normally remained serious, but he felt the need to lighten the mood, if only for himself. He

146

said, "You said we are identical? I think I'm more handsome."

John's face flushed and he broke out in laughter. He said, "I was thinking the same thing." They both laughed as they shook hands.

Before he sat down, Tom went around his table meeting the new Star Children. He was proud to see so many finally gathered together. Tom then circled the other table greeting the others and the new ones, especially NSA Canton.

When he rejoined Sue and John he said, "John, I like your beard and mustache. I always wondered what I would look like with a beard and mustache. Sue we need to take a picture. Actually, I like it, but seriously, you probably should shave it off. We need to fit in and become invisible, since they are trying to kill us off, and assuming you are now one of us, you are now a target, also. My hair is even dyed."

John said, "Well, I'm definitely one of you. I've never had a family before, and I always wanted too. I just didn't expect to find seventeen brothers and sisters all at once."

Sue said, "Sadly, there were two hundred more of us not long ago."

Tina said, "I've been teaching John how to fly."

John looked at her and winked and said, "Well, she has been trying, but it's coming much slower for me. I honestly had no idea these powers were in me. Now they are deeply dormant, but I'm slowly breaking down the wall. I've seen enough to know I have most of them."

Tom asked, "What is Dir. Setliff thinking right now?"

John laughed and said, "He's thinking about sex with Agent Welch."

Tom already knew that, since he had just screened the other table. He turned and said, "Janet, have you shown Jack your tattoo yet?" Laughter broke out throughout the group of kids, because they all had seen the tattoo with their enhanced vision, certainly the boys.

Janet said, "What tattoo. I don't have a tattoo."

"Sure you do. You know the butterfly tat below your belly button."

Janet flushed bright red and said, "Tom, that's not fair."

Tom softly said just to those close, "I'm just stirring the pot. They like each other."

Just as Tom took another bite, John said, "Just like you and Sue like each other."

Tom almost choked and his face grew hot. "Well, that's true. If she likes me as much as I like her … well … you know." He then leaned over and kissed Sue on the lips, and she kissed him back.

Mary said, "Tom, did you meet the president?"

"Yeah, he is a nice man, but under stress right now with all this crap going on. He has to deal with all this political crap. That can be a real pain in the butt."

John said, "I would have loved to see that. I majored in Political Science in college. That's what I was doing here, advising the Ambassador, at least I thought that is why I was here."

148

Tom asked, "Truthfully, John, have you mastered your powers yet? There may be a place for you back in D. C. They need a Star Child's powers, and we need one of us there to look after our interest, but you would have to be proficient in our powers. So, what do you think?"

John pinged Tom, *"I have initiated my Ping Network, and I am progressing in the training. We haven't had a lot of time together, but all the kids have pinged me with downloads, worked with me, and I have the concepts down. I have talked extensively with Dr. Wisscroff, and I understand the powers. I just need time to work through my disbelief, but I am confident I can master them. I would love to have the chance to do this for the Star Children and my country."*

Sue pinged, *"John included me, and I think this is a good idea."*

Tom turned to Dir. Setliff and said, "Hey, Jack, I have your candidate for the presidents joint committee. Meet John Meeker, Political Science major and Star Child."

Dir. Setliff said, "Very pleased to meet you, John Meeker. You are needed indeed. Mr. Canton, you can take my plane and take charge of Mr. Meeker's security and guide him in Washington. I will be able to communicate through Mr. Meeker of our findings in the south. This is a nice plan."

By 10:00 am they were all back in their appropriate planes, fueled and ready. The next stop for the C-40-A would be near the South Pole, where

149

Major Burns, hopefully, would have a base camp set up.

Tom had never flown in a military C-40-A before, hell he had never flown at all before he met Dir. Setliff and his Gulfstream V. Still, looking at this plane and the way it was set up looked plush with many extras he suspected were not standard in normal air passenger planes. In the front was an area that looked much like a lounge conference area. It looked like the lounge area could accommodate ten, maybe twelve adults. The next section was equipped with recliners for about seventy-five people. There was a kitchen and bathroom area, and behind that he could see an open storage area full of crates. He took a seat in the lounge area next to Sue, and of course, Tina was beside her. Dir. Setliff and Agent Welch set together facing him. Tom smiled when he saw Dr. Wisscroff and Mrs. Wilks sitting together and laughing. He noticed that Mary, Jerry and Fred also claimed seats in the lounge area. Some of the older kids from the new group claimed the remainder of the seats in the lounge area. Tom noticed that Janet had commandeered several Marines to go with us, plus Dir. Setliff's two agents.

Tom asked, "Janet, do we have to refuel anywhere before we get there?

"This is a military plane, and as such, this one is equipped for mid-air refueling. Unfortunately, there aren't any bases near enough to send tankers up from. We will have enough fuel to get there, and we should be able to get a fuel truck out of

McMurdo on the coast. If not, we can schedule a long distance air tanker after we take off to come back."

The mother hen, Mrs. Wilks, busied herself during the trip in the back unpacking the winter clothing, gloves, boots, etc. and outfitting all the kids, then she started on the adults. The Marines knew what was needed and helped. It was a long trip, and it took most of that time to be ready.

Janet got a message and read it then said, "Major Burns says, 'Thanks a lot for dragging him out to Antartica'. They have a ground base set up and ready for us. Good timing, We are heading there now, following their homing signal. So, get dressed. It's -10 degrees outside.'"

They had all been outfitted in foul-weather gear long before they got there, and the cabin attendants were picking up gear from our hot meal when Tom felt it. At first it was just a tingling sensation, but it got stronger the closer they got. He looked at Tina to see if she was feeling anything. She obviously was, because she began to hold her stomach. He said, "Tina, I guess you feel the beacon? Does anyone else feel it?" Tom knew Tina would feel if anyone else did. Several of the younger kids nodded. Others looked like they didn't know what I was talking about.

Tina felt the beacon, but at first she didn't understand what it was. At first she thought she was getting seasick until she noticed the rhythm. Her head felt the rhythm of pressure throbbing, that continued to gain in strength. It began to hurt and

151

spread toward her stomach. Queasiness and nausea spread and threatened to make her retch. She held her stomach tight, and was finally able to make it subside through pure willpower. It was easier to control, once she knew what it was.

Tina said, "It's a message for us Star Children. It is calling, drawing us toward their beacon. I don't think we will have a problem finding it."

Tom said, "Dr. Wisscroff, we are feeling the beacon. How in the world did you get us so close? Well, I assume we must be close."

"Logic my friend ... logic and intelligence. I took the hints Tina gave me like going south, flying over flat ice, deep ice tunnel, low midday sun at noon, cave, etc. I then studied the terrain on maps and concluded the location would have to be on the Ross Ice Shelf near the Transantarctic Mountain Range. Elementary deductions."

Sue said, "Don't get cocky. We could still be a long way off. We'll let you know soon." They all laughed, including Dr. Wisscroff.

After a few more minutes the pilot came on the intercom and announced that we would soon be flying over the base camp, circling and landing near the structure. As they passed over, Tom could see the structure. It was still daylight, but of course it would be, since it was mostly daylight here 24 hours every day during the summer. The structure looked like a cloverleaf of attached blowup tents. The landing seemed smooth over flat, relatively smooth ice, and the plane came to rest near the structure.

Major Burns came up the lowered ramp and entered the plane after all inside were blasted with painful gusts of frigid cold air rushing in. It was Major Burns, because he said he was. All Tom could see of him were his two eyes peering out between layers of fur. Janet could, however, recognize his voice when he said, "Bundle up good. It's eleven below outside. Follow me. We have a short walk to the entrance."

Thankfully, there was little wind outside, and it was relatively clear. Even so, Tom felt the bitter cold burning his lips, but he was determined not to generate a heat bubble for himself. He wanted to experience what all the non-enhanced people were feeling. As he exited the plane he saw bundled workers rigging cables to the airplane, which he assumed were electricity. He then quickly entered the flap entrance of the structure into a second entrance and marveled at the engineering. He wanted to call the structure a huge tent, but it was far more than that. The long arch shape consisted of double walls, apparently filled with air between them. There were few actual solid struts, most of the supporting struts looked like they were tied into the air pressure system filling the walls. Even the floor felt like a tight cushion of air, obviously heavily insulated. The engineering was amazing and obviously highly efficient, judging by the increase of temperature inside. The structure was not built for comfort. This was an arctic weather survival structure, but there were three wings of them.

Janet said, "Damn, Major, this is impressive. How long did it take to set up?"

Major Burns said, "I can't take credit for the base camp. I brought an extra crew for that, experts in arctic survival. I was amazed, also. We landed, they pulled these tents out, rolled them out, tied them together and aired it up like a basketball."

"We appreciate your support and quick action."

"Let's just say, my commanding officer had never received an order directly from the Sec. of the Navy before. That speeded up things greatly. I think I know why. Same enemy?"

Dir. Setliff answered, "The same potential enemy. Are you deployed? Hopefully, they won't know we are here … yet, but we can't take any chances."

Instinctively Major Burns recognized authority and said, "Yes, Sir. We are deployed as best we can under these conditions. We brought a lot more surface-to-air missiles this time. I figured it would be harder for a saucer to dodge multiple missiles coming after them."

Tom said, "Sue, Tina and I are going to search for the beacon. Jerry, Mary and Fred, you guys stay with this group … just in case." They nodded understanding.

Major Burns asked, "Don't you want some Marines to go with you?"

Sue chuckled and said, "Maybe later. This time we are flying. Just tell your Marines not to shoot us." His blank and confused expression said he didn't understand but said nothing.

They received many stares as the three of them went outside and jumped into the air and kept going. Definitely, they protected themselves with bubbles of warmth this time. They continued to rise above the Ross Ice Shelf and saw a vast sea of flat ice. Tina said, "This looks just like my dream, even better. I really love flying. I have never felt so totally free of restraints."

Tina came back from her comforting daydream by the pull of the beacon in her gut. She activated her enhanced vision and began searching through the ice as they flew north along the mountain range. After about fifteen minutes she had seen nothing and the beacon's throbbing seemed weaker. She said, "Let's turn around. We are going the wrong direction."

They raced back toward the base camp and proceeded south. They hadn't gone but about two miles when she saw it. At first the red glow was faint but got brighter as they approached it. It was deep, maybe as much as a thousand feet deep in the ice shelf. She pointed and Tom and Sue nodded. They dropped in elevation to the ice shelf directly above the beacon.

Tom was the first to probe the ice with heat. At first there was no visible beam, but as he learned to adjust the power a visible orange beam began to show on the ice. When Sue's radiation and Tina's joined his, the beam turned bright red and began melting a large hole in the ice. Steam bellowed out of the growing hole and floated a rising column of white clouds of steam into the air. Already the hole was deep, but the rising column of steam was becoming very visible. He motioned for Sue and Tina to reduce the heat. Their progress slowed, but the cloud reduced. Eventually, the emptying hole approached the beacon and they ceased radiating heat and sank down in the hole toward it.

Tom pinged Sue and sent, *"Please remain above to give us warning if something approaches." She nodded and floated back up out of the hole to hover above."*

Tom and Tina were able to more precisely clear the ice away from the beacon, but once there, it was only a beacon, nothing more. The first thing Tina did was flip a switch to stop the offending nausea and throbbing. There was visible writing on the beacon, but nothing he could read or understand. Surely there must be more to discover. He began searching outward from the beacon and looked toward the mountain through the ice and saw it. There was a massive metal door in the rock. He pointed it out to Tina and they began melting a horizontal path in the ice toward it. The door was about a hundred feet away, but it took both of them a good thirty minutes to clear the way and clear the door, but he saw no way to open it. He pulled and pushed but could find nothing. Frustrated, he bellowed, "Damn, there has to be a way in. What are we failing to see?"

Tina said, "It must have to be opened from the inside."

Tom thought about it. Yeah, that made sense. Only a Star Child should be able to open it, but how? He had already tried to burn a hole in the door, but this metal wouldn't melt. It didn't even get hot.

Tina said, "There is a latch on the inside."

Duh. Of course there would be. Then he realized he was directing the "Duh" at himself. Tina was telling him how to open the door. He allowed his enhanced vision to begin to probe the metal layer by layer. He saw the latch mechanism on the inside and followed it to the lever Tina told him was there. He focused gravity to push the lever as if he were standing inside pushing it toward the door. They heard a heavy snap, then a creak and a gush of warm air exhaled on them. As the massive doors began to swing open outward they were flooded by bright light.

\*\*\*

John Meeker's life had changed drastically. One moment he was a floundering politician just arriving on the scene, without sponsors or family. The next moment he belonged to a large family and he was now off to assist the president in a critical situation. What more could he hope for? He had been alone his entire life, relying solely on himself. Now he could rely on others, and it was a satisfying feeling. He liked Tom and the others and felt completely accepted, more than that, he felt like he was one of them. He felt the bond in ways he never thought possible. The Star Children were his priority, and he would not let them down.

Now that he was alone with NSA Canton on the Gulfstream V, Mr. Canton began to share information he had missed over the last few days, namely the execution of all but Tom at the Star Children school, Tom's escape from Area 51, the rescue of the other five, the involvement of President Thompson, Dir. Setliff and the other's involvement, the attacks, implants, threat, in essence a full briefing on everything Mr. Canton knew, and since he had been involved from the start, he knew a lot.

During the briefing John felt the anger and rage boil up inside him. His family was in danger, and he would do anything necessary to save them. John was determined to do his task to the best of his ability, so at Johns insistence, Mr. Canton then began briefing him on the backgrounds of the Joint Chiefs, CIA Dir. Martinez, and the others on the presidents joint committee.

They were taking an evening dinner break en route when he received a ping from Fred, *"Tom wanted me to keep track of our communications as distance increased. This is one of those checks, but Janet wanted to let Mr. Canton know that he will be receiving a message from President Thompson soon. He called here for Dir. Setliff, but he is unavailable right now, so he asked for him."*

*"I will let him know, Oh, the communication is great. Thanks, Fred."*

There was no need to tell Mr. Canton, since he was already on the phone with President Thompson. John heard Mr. Canton say Mr. President, but he could also tell from his stance. He was sitting up straight in his seat and absentmindedly adjusting his

158

tie. They talked for a while and ended the conversation.

NSA Canton said, "Something has come up back in D.C, and the president wants us there as quick as we can get there. It seems that CIA Dir. Martinez let slip some keywords about internal conspiracy problems, implants and aliens. Of course it slipped accidentally on purpose, and it wouldn't take the Russians long to tie those three things together and realize we weren't talking about Mexican aliens. We were trying to get the rest of the world looking for implants. Apparently, the Russians did a little checking around there and discovered something. The Russian president is flying in for a secret early meeting with our president, and he wants us at Camp David. He wants your analysis of the Russian President to find out if they are here for a serious discussion of the problem or just fishing for information. Since the Russians are flying here, my guess is that they discovered the same problem exists there. We should easily make it. Hell, we are probably only an hour out. The president will know when we get in and have a car pick us up."

John said, "I'm glad I brought a bag. I guess I better clean up a bit, and I think I will follow Tom's suggestion and shave this beard and mustache off."

True to Mr. Canton's promise, there was a car waiting for them, but it was a short trip. It only lasted long enough to take them to a waiting helicopter, that took them directly to Camp David. When they landed on the grass and disembarked,

President Thompson himself was waiting by the pool outside his retreat residence at Camp David, Aspen Lodge.

As they turned toward the house the President said, "Hello Tom Canton. It's good to have you back. I need your always welcome advice." Turning to John he continued, "I assume you are John Meeker, our Star Child. Damn, you look like Tom."

"I wanted to meet you both outside so we could have a brief unheard discussion before we get inside. The Russian President with about five of his people are already inside. Please check them out when we go inside. I've kept the conversation casual so far, because I wanted you here. I desperately need to know his level of deceit or honesty in our upcoming discussion. I don't think he knows about the Star Children, so I won't mention that fact unless he brings it up. So, Mr. Meeker, you will be an NSA Agent in there, and I'm glad you are dressed like one."

"Very well, Sir."

John was actually surprised when he went inside. From outside it looked like a normal suburban house, but surprisingly, it looked like a normal house on the inside as well. They entered into a large living room with chairs and couches positioned for a conversation. There were about twelve people, some in a center circle, while the others were spread out, obviously security for both sides. With his freshly awakened powers he was immediately bombarded with strong emotional

160

signals of stress, panic, fear, hostility and others he didn't take time to identify. His eyes quickly searched the people in the room and focused upon only one, one of the men standing. He was about to do something hostile, and he had an implant. John instantly pointed directly at the man and seized the man's mind and yelled, "Who is this man? He has an implant and is intent on killing someone."

The reaction was immediate. Secret Service (SS) and Russian Federal Security Service (FSS), the old KGB, drew their weapons, but didn't really know who to point them at. John remained completely still, still pointing at the man. They did, however, take the man's weapons.

President Thompson said, "Are you sure?"

"Yes. I'm positive."

Anger flashed across the president's face and he bellowed, "President Pramin, you called a meeting to discuss this very problem and you bring one of the SOBs with you? You brought one into MY house."

John thought that politically, it was a smart move to put the Russian President on the defensive, but it was dangerous. Then again, it could have just been anger. Either way it was up to John to prove it. He said, "I can prove it. I froze his mind. He can't act now. I can show you the implant. Want me to remove it?"

The Russian President looked hard at John and said in Russian, which was translated into English by his interpreter, "If you can prove this allegation, do so."

161

John was fluent in Russian but decided not to reveal that fact just yet. He had figured if politics was to be his future he should know Russian. John looked at President Thompson for confirmation and received a nod. So much for keeping his powers secret. John said, "Watch the man." He then enhanced his vision again and latched on the implant and pulled it out like he had been instructed. It floated out of his nose, and he let it drop at President Pramin's feet. John wanted them to see the blood to know for sure it had been implanted inside him. Now he cauterized the wound.

John said, "I wanted you to see it so you would know what I said was true, but I suggest you not touch it. It is a small explosive." President Pramin's feet jerked back from it even before he heard the interpretation, which told John the Russian President also spoke English.

John said, "Now ask the man whatever you want and he will answer, but I believe we all would like to hear what his orders were." After a slight delay for interpretation each way President Pramin asked that question.

The monotoned zombie said in English, probably in response to John's original question. "Once we were all gathered here in Camp David I was ordered to assassinate President Thompson and President Pramin."

Shock filled the room with disbelief, not disbelief of the order but disbelief of the audacity of the order. What could possibly be gained by

162

causing conflict or war between the U.S. and Russia? John already knew that only the Greys would benefit from the chaos, and the rest of them would soon figure that out.

President Pramin asked in English, "Why?"

The zombie said, "The Greys don't tell us. They just give us orders, and we must obey or they kill us."

President Pramin looked at President Thompson and asked, "Is this the conspiracy you worry about, a conspiracy of the Greys?"

President Thompson said, "It is indeed. We have discovered the conspiracy goes deep, and you obviously have the same problem. Now can we dispense with subtleties and work on the problem?"

"Yeah, let's have some coffee and let me settle down from the shock of almost being assassinated."

They asked no further questions of the FSS agent, most likely waiting for later when they had no witnesses. John released the man's mind, and he fell to the floor, to be rushed out under heavy guard. Further scanning of the parties on either side revealed no other worries or implants, and President Pramin seemed completely open to honest discussion. John looked to the watching President Thompson and nodded.

While the coffee was making its way around, the Russian President leaned toward his interpreter and said in Russian, "Did they teach you any of these mental abilities at that special mind control school of yours? If not, find out about this man and how he learned them."

Now John was pleased he hadn't let it be known he spoke Russian, and he detected no hostility, only amazement. Additionally, he had learned that the lady was more than simply an interpreter. She had been trained in mind control, whatever that was. He would have to watch her emotions to make sure she didn't pull any mind tricks.

While things were calming down John pinged Fred and give him a telepathic report of what just happened and thanked Dir. Setliff and Tom for their decision to send him. It had prevented an all-out war between the U.S. and Russia.

Fred pinged, *"Yes, we have been lucky. Good work, John. I will pass it on to Dir. Setliff. Tom, Sue and Tina have found the beacon and are actually in the cave now. I will let them know when they check in."*

Due to the pending crisis and John's interference, he had not been introduced to her, nor anyone else for that matter. She was young, about his age, with brown hair and green eyes. She was quite striking, but there was something familiar about her he couldn't quite place. He went to her and said, "Hello, we never got a chance to introduce ourselves before. I'm John Meeker. I'm with the NSA." His introduction startled her because he spoke in Russian.

She recovered fast and said in English, "Hello, John. I'm pleased to meet you. Thank you for what you did. I just wished I knew what that was. My name is Jane Turret, and you already know I'm the President's interpreter."

John felt her tickling his mind with a probe and actually laughed. Her probe was extremely weak. John said, "I know you are far more than an interpreter, and you're wasting your time trying to get inside my mind. Please don't try that with anyone else here, especially President Thompson. I will be forced to intervene." He had said it in English so President Thompson could understand the conversation. Jane interpreted what he said to President Pramin.

It was President Pramin that responded in excellent English, "Who the hell are you?"

President Thompson said, "That is the second part of the conspiracy. They are called Star Children, and John is one of them. We don't know where the name came from, and we had no idea they were among us. We believe they have been genetically engineered, possibly from other aliens, since the Greys somehow worked their influence in our government to identify them. I'm assuming you know who the Greys are. Right?" President Pramin nodded. "We did their work for them and gathered them together, and they destroyed most of them. That's what alerted us to the problem, which has been getting deeper by the day. We have been trying to save them, and we did save some of them. Our friend here is a Star Child, and as you can see, they have certain powers. The Greys are afraid of them, and that makes them humanities friends."

"Now, before you ask, we don't know if you have any Star Children in your empire, but I can't see them being introduced only in the U.S. So, my assumption is yes, but you have to figure out how to find them. We can give you a sample of their DNA to help in the search, but my guess is the Greys have already begun working through your own secret departments of your government and other governments around the world to find and eliminate them."

"Shall I go on? Are you as worried about the Greys as we are?"

President Pramin stared in silent thought and finally said, "Yes, we are worried. Please continue."

"Here's what we know and what you will discover. There are many Greys, but they remain hidden and are protected by compromised departments of our government. By compromised I mean over time the Greys have installed implants in many humans to guarantee allegiance to them, implants like the one you just saw removed. They have a vast network of massive, deep tunnels and deep bases where they have been dispersing and storing up flying saucers for a war on humans to take control of Earth. We believe they started infiltrating our government as far back as the late 1940s, so they have done much damage. Scary? You bet your ass."

"Obviously, I am keeping nothing back, because if we lose this war we lose our countries and Earth. We need to work together. Now, do you have anything to add?"

John noticed that the president was keeping back some information, and did not mentioned the current excursion to the Antarctic to find an alien base. That was probably a good omission, since the U.S. would want to have the first rights to the technology, if any were found.

President Pramin and several of his top advisors stared wide-eyed as Jane Turret completed the translation. Slowly, he said, "This is indeed scary. I'm afraid we have little to add. We are only now beginning to find bits and pieces of information, but when we would hear anything to catch our attention, someone else would tell us otherwise. I guess we now know why. I suspect our government is also infected with this treason virus. We have a lot of work to do, and you are way ahead of us, but as you say, we have to work together. Who do we coordinate with here, since we have to worry about channels of communication?"

"My CIA Dir. Martinez will be your contact at Langley. He and my former FBI Dir. Setliff are key to our planning and secrecy. I hope you can find some Star Children in Russia that haven't already been killed. They have been a great help to us and might possibly help with a solution to the problem. We wouldn't even know about the problem if it hadn't been for them, but you should also know that they are an independent group outside of any government control. They answer only to themselves, but their goals are our goals. Check, also, with Dir. Martinez about plans for a hand-held implant detector. Identifying those with implants and getting them out of the loop is key to our survival."

They continued to converse, but little new came from it. There was determination to work together, and John sensed it was genuine. All those in the conversation continued in English. It seemed for the Russians that secrecy among themselves wasn't something they needed anymore. But, that left Jane free from her interpretation duties, so John and she moved to a separate sitting area and struck up a conversation. With everyone being so open now they were comfortable and let their guard down.

John said, "How did you wind up in a mind control school?"

Jane was started at first until she realized her president had let that slip and said, "I was kind of drafted into it from college. My IQ is super high, according to the school, plus I had demonstrated some paranormal abilities such as minor telekinesis and clairvoyance in some of my classes. The government sort of told me to go to the advanced school. No one, however, at that school can do what you did here tonight. Have you always been able to do those things?"

"Oh, no. I never knew I had those abilities until just a few days ago. I guess I had the abilities always, but they were dormant in me until I met the others. They knew I was a Star Child and finally convinced me. Actually, Jane, I had an implant and never knew it. What I did, removing it, was done to me. It saved me from a Greys assassination"

Jane said, "Really? You had an implant? Why?"

"I didn't know I was a Star Child, but the Greys did. They apparently were monitoring me, studying me for some reason. I'm sure at some point they intended to kill me if I became a threat to them. I dare say I am a threat to them now, so I'm glad it's out."

"How many of you are there?"

"At this point there are only seventeen of us, but there were far more. The Greys have killed over two hundred of us that we know of, but like me, there may be more if we can find them before they are killed."

Jane said, "I was impressed at what I saw you do. You say you just learned of these powers? How can you have them inside and not know. Why the sudden change?"

John sensed her curiosity and said, "Mostly, it is a mental process. I just had to believe in myself. They convinced me that I was a Star Child and demonstrated some of their powers. Trust me, once you see them fly, you begin to believe, and once I learned to fly, the rest came much easier with that confidence."

Jane asked, "You can fly, really?" John nodded. "I have got to see this!" She looked around and saw that no one was paying us any attention and continued, "Let's slip outside so you can show me." She didn't wait for a response she just grabbed his hand and pulled him along with her. They continued to hold hands all the way out past the swimming pool and out on the grass. "Show me, please. I have to see this."

John smiled and allowed himself to float up off the ground. It was worth it to see her beautiful green eyes sparkle in amazement and hear her squeal of excitement. He shot off, circling her in widening loops. He then settled down to the ground in front of her and suddenly wrapped his arms around her waist and lifted her into the air with him. He was having fun and could feel her warm breasts and body press into his. Her arms wrapped around his neck and her legs looped around his, as she held on to him. He soared high and looped around the golf course, listening to her high pitched squeal of pleasure and feeling her hot breath on his neck. John ended the flying lesson before either of them was ready, but her closeness was arousing him greatly. He knew she would know soon if they remain aloft and tightly together much longer.

As their feet again felt the grass, Jane jumped back into his arms and kissed him solidly on the lips and then said, "That was wonderful, John. Thank you so very much for taking me flying." Her arms lingered around his neck but finally slipped to her side. She did grab his hand in her's again, as they walked back toward the house. Jane stopped and turned to look at John and said, "That was amazing. I would love to be able to do that. What other powers do you have?"

John laughed and said, "Well, you are a show me type girl I see. Let me think." He clicked in his enhanced vision and took a look at her up and down and said, "Enhanced vision is another power, and I can tell that you that you are not a natural brunet. You are a blond."

Jane thought about that, then flushed in embarrassment and said, "I knew I should have shaved before coming on this trip." They both laughed out loud, and she kissed him again. This time he kissed her back… hard.

Something was going on between them, a connection, and John couldn't explain it. It was like they were so comfortable with each other, like they had known each other all their lives. He wanted her, and he could sense that she felt the same. The images filtering out of her mind were very erotic. He wondered if she could see what he was thinking. She kissed him again, and he knew she could.

Their passion exploded and they were pressing and rubbing against each other. Somehow they stumbled into a pool lounger and fell into it. Thankfully it was dark and secluded as they shed some of their clothing and fell into each other. They made love like neither had ever experienced before, like they belonged together.

Afterwards, they tried to recover as best as they could. They both knew this was something real. They connected in every way possible, mentally and physically, and they knew it was real.

# Chapter 7
## (Star Child Archive)

Fred went to Dr. Wisscroff and said, "Doc, John pinged me with a question for you. He suspects that he may have found another Star Child and wants to know how he can be sure?" Fred went on to relay what John had reported in detail about what happened at Camp David and what he knew or suspected about the Russian interpreter, minus the sex part.

Dr. Wisscroff thought intently and finally said, "Tell John he can't know for sure until she demonstrates the Star Child powers. But, from what he reports, he may be correct. Having very high IQ, a blond bush," He laughed, "High Russian government placement in mind control, etc. Just to reach that level in Russia, she would have had to be rare among the population, like a Star Child would be. You said this woman also had the ability to visualize mental images. John could very well be right. Tell John to simply ask her … mentally. Speak to her with his mind like the rest of you do."

"I have been thinking about Dir. Martinez's last report that he couldn't find a link to any other Star Children through John's history. The only thing I could come up with was what I just recommended you tell John. Since there is no apparent limit to your telepathic abilities, send out an open message and tell them how to find you. I was going to tell everyone at our next discussion, maybe when Tom and Sue come back."

Jack and Janet had been listening to the conversation and Janet said, "That sounds like a great idea. You kids can send a message to call my cell number. You know like, 'If you hear this message call #######'. Who knows, maybe a Star Child will hear it, wonder about it and call. Even better, they might answer directly and talk to you."

Many of the kids had listened intently and began nodding and chattering among themselves. They seemed to think it was a great idea and must have begun mental transmission, because one of the kids said, "Hey Timmy, you don't have to send that message to me. Use your matrix exclusions." Many of the kids were chiming in with their annoyance also, and a few said "Sorry."

Fred immediately pinged using the matrix to notify those not there to ignore the messages to call, that nothing was wrong. It was a misunderstanding.

Thousands of miles away John had gotten both messages and laughed, but it faded quickly when he noticed the shock on Jane's face. He had the answer to his question even before Fred told him seconds later.

Jane said, "Did you hear that? Is that a phone number? What does that mean?"

John cupped her face in his hands, kissed her and said, "What it means is, is that you are a Star Child. Only a Star Child would have been able to hear that message."

Jane just stared at him in disbelief for a long while. She then began to understand, and a huge smile split her beautiful face just before she leaped into his arms and kissed him. She said, "Yes! Yes, I so want that to be true. Can it really be so?"

John said, "Well, let's find out. We need to tell the two presidents what we believe and find a place we can be alone together to test the theory."

John and Jane went back into the living room and noticed the conversations had continued, and just stood waiting to be noticed.

President Thompson noticed them and said, "Mr. Meeker, was there something you wished to add?"

"Well, Sir, Miss Turret and I have made a rather startling discovery. I believe Miss Turret is in fact a Star Child. I was hoping there might be a private place we might go to test out this theory?"

President Pramin said, "You think Miss Turret is a Star Child? How can that be? We were under the understanding Star Children were all blond."

John said, "This is true, but then Miss Turret *is* a natural blond." Jane nodded in confirmation.

"I've known her for three years and she has always been a brunet. How do you know this?

"Please don't ask, Sir."

President Thompson came to the rescue and said, "One of Mr. Meeker's special powers is X-Ray vision, like Superman."

President Pramin thought, suddenly smiled and said, "Oh. I understand. How nice that would be." Both presidents and several others laughed.

174

President Thompson said, "With your permission, Sir," He waited for President Pramin's nod and continued, "We have lots of cabins here at Camp David. I'll have one of them assigned to you both. Please let us know when you are positive."

As they left, one of the many bustling attendants came rushing up and handed them a key and small map. The key had Dogwood printed on it, and the map showed it only a short distance away. They took off on the connecting path holding hands. They were both more excited by what they were going to do once they got to a bed than being a Star Child. They finally made it through the front door of the Dogwood cabin and stumbled into the first bed they could find, stripping as they went. By the time they reached the bed both of them were naked. They fell, locked together. He saw the images in her mind of what she was hoping he would do and did them. Likewise she did what he imagined. This being a Star Child really had its advantages. They made love so completely and satisfying it was magical. They went hard and fast, then slow and sensual. Hours went by, but it seemed like only minutes. Finally completely exhausted and totally relaxed, they lay beside each other reveling in the desires they had so realized.

John said, "Do me a favor, Jane. Don't ever shave that beautiful blond bush off. I love playing with it." They both laughed.

"Now, let's talk about those dormant powers you have. It's all about believing. Once you do, it's like flipping a switch in your mind. I've been told that our own mind prevents us from exercising our powers. It tells us that it's impossible, and if you believe it's impossible, it is. I've also been told that our powers are without limits, and it's a fact that we have discovered new powers by simply needing them ... again the mind. You also need to understand that flying is not levitation. That's just a word to describe one of the results. What flying is, is manipulation of gravity. Flying is only one use of gravity. Telekinesis is another word, but it's altering gravity on an object. Now, close your eyes and think to yourself, *'My body is weightless, gravity is not pulling me down,'* then reverse gravity to lift your body upward. Once you can do that you can use gravity to propel yourself in any direction you wish."

Jane closed her eyes and lay there. Sweat broke out on her brow, but nothing happened. Frustrated, Jane said, "I can't make it happen."

You're trying too hard. It's not hard and shouldn't be something that you have to do. Just let it happen and believe. Ok, wait, let's try something different. Imagine you are floating four feet in the air above me. When you see it in your mind, close your eyes." When she closed her eyes he floated in the air four feet above her and said, "Open your eyes and when you see me below you let go of gravity and fall." When she opened her eyes her body shot up and slammed into his. It hurt, because she hit him with the same force of a four-foot fall, but she had done it. He floated them back to the bed and said, "See you can do it. We just had to trick your mind into believing it was a fall. You bypassed the restriction of your mind. Your mind told you, you can't float, that you had to fall. Now do it again."

Jane said, "I did do that didn't I?" He nodded. Jane smiled and lifted her body off the bed and floated up above him. "Now I understand how it works. Let's go flying. I've got it."

John said, "Shouldn't we get dressed first?"

"Hell no! Who would believe two people were flying, especially if they say they were naked."

They both laughed and ran outside. Jane immediately jumped into the air and shot up. She stumbled around some in the air until she tuned her mental controls, then it looked graceful. He joined her as she darted back and forth, up and down.

Jane said, "I love this, and I love you, too. I am so excited and aroused. Let's make love in the air."

It shocked him to hear what she said, but she came directly to him and kissed him in mid-air. He had never thought about making love in the air, but the idea seemed like a great one. Making love in zero gravity has its pluses and minuses, but the pluses definitely won out, and they enjoyed it immensely. Afterward they floated back down to the cabin, and were thankful that no one had seen them humping in mid-air. That thankfulness lasted only a few moments.

Fred pinged and said, *"Did you have fun having sex in the air? We all certainly enjoyed it."*

John pinged, *"Oh crap! I didn't think you would get my emotions once the matrix was established."*

*"Your right, but Jane hasn't created a matrix yet. Her mind just recently activated, and we got her images and emotions. She sure does love you, you know."*

John said, "Jane, sweetie, I'm sending you a download from Sue, one of the key Star Children. She came up with a method of isolating and controlling the telepathic communications between all the Star Children. I strongly suggest you establish this matrix as soon as you can, since most of the other Star Children just shared your emotions and imagery of what you experienced in the air. I just found out."

"OMG! Really? All of them? How can I ever face them now?

"Oh, don't worry about it. Star Children share much, and we all have had similar embarrassing moments in our history, but the matrix does help."

They spent the rest of the night working and learning about the powers. By daylight Jane knew everything that John did about Star Children powers, and she had established her own matrix network. She could probably learn more from the others, but that would have to wait.

Jane got a call from one of the Russian staff members letting her know that breakfast was being served in the Laurel Lodge if we wanted to come. We were more than ready to eat something, so she said we would be there.

178

John said, "There is a golf cart assigned to this cabin that we can drive over."

Jane smiled and said, "Why ride when we can fly."

They laughed, but she was serious. They showered, got dressed in their yesterday's clothing and flew over to the Laurel Lodge and surprised the Marine guards when they landed. They entered the lodge and received stares from all present. The group continued to stare, so John and Jane stopped and waited, as if to say "what?"

John realized what they were waiting for and said, "Yes, Miss Turret is a full-fledged Star Child and totally operational. Cheers of congratulations rang out, especially from the Russian delegation.

President Pramin said, "This is great. We can get a lot more done when we get back to Moscow."

Jane said, "Mr. President, I won't be going back with you, not yet anyway. I have further indoctrination with my new Star Children family."

President Pramin's face flushed bright red and bellowed, "You are Russian, and you will do as I say!"

Jane said, "I'm sorry. I no longer belong to Russia. I am a Star Child now and will do what is best for us. We will help you because it is in our own interest, but we will do it in our own way and on our terms. That's the deal, and you can do nothing about it. I am now a Star Child first and foremost."

President Pramin bellowed again, this time to his security, "Take this bitch into custody until we leave."

Russian security moved toward Jane, but they were immediately thrown to the floor. Jane did it before John could. The security men were trying to get up but found themselves far too heavy.

President Thompson said, "Mr. President, I suggest you let it drop. If Jane is like the other Star Children, she is being lenient, because she could have done much worst. I warned you that the Star Children have become an independent group, and we need them for the battle to come. So far they are on our side. I hope you don't do anything to change that.

President Pramin thought, calmed and said, "Yes, of course. I'm sorry Miss Turret. I truly apologize for my outburst. We want to work with your group."

Jane released the Russian security and said, "Of course we can work together as long as we have common goals, but I must go with Mr. Meeker to meet with the others of my kind. We have been summoned to our Star Child Sanctuary."

NSA Canton asked, "Do you need me to fly you back in the FBI plane?"

John said, "That won't be necessary. Tom Bradley and Sue Chambers are en route to get us now, and they are landing on the golf course as we speak. We must go, but you can come out and meet them if you like."

John and Jane didn't wait for a response and turned and walked out. By the time they got to the pool most of the room occupants were rushing to catch up, but everyone froze in place when they saw a bright shimmering on the grass. The shimmering brightened then flickered out, leaving a shiny, slightly pink saucer sitting on the grass. John and Jane walked toward it, as a slice of bright light emerged from underneath, highlighting a ramp lowering. By the time they reached the ramp Tom, Sue and Tina were waiting.

Tom smiled hugely and said, "The situation has changed dramatically. We need you back, so we came to get you in one of our chariots. Plus we wanted to meet Miss Turret, our new recruit and flying acrobat."

Jane blushed at that comment, but kept staring back and forth between Tom and John. Jane then turned her attention to Sue and said, "Hello Miss Chambers. I'm Jane Turret. I am very pleased to meet other Star Children, since I guess I'm one too."

Sue just smiled and hugged her. Introductions were made all around, then they all turned to meet the others still staring in awe at the flying saucer. Introductions were then made with the delegation.

Tom said, "Hello Mr. President. I think you will be getting a very interesting report from Dir. Setliff tomorrow. I think you should look forward to it."

President Thompson said, "This may sound trivial with all that's going on, but we were all about to have breakfast when you came. I know you're busy, but do you have time to eat before you leave? Maybe we can discuss a few things while we eat."

Tom looked around at the others and received energetic nods. Tom nodded and said, "I think we will join your group for breakfast. I hadn't realized how hungry we are."

All of the Star Children had multiple helpings and steered the conversation away from the elephant parked on the grass. President Thompson had commented only once about it being a nice flying saucer.

Tom said, "Both of you presidents have a saucer, except ours works." Area 51 hosts the one that crashed in Roswell in 1947. Who knows where the KGB put the one in Russia back in 1969. Neither president acknowledged their possession and let the comment drop.

Finally, the star group finished eating, said their "Good-Byes" and entered the saucer. Tom slipped a flexible device on his head. It looked like a clear belt with sensing devices all around the inside of it. John saw no other controls in the saucer, only the head crown. There were six chairs in a circle facing outward with very thick forming cushions. When he sat, he sank into the cushion and it formed to his back and wrapped around him partially. There were other head belts hooked around a central, cushioned post for up to four additional people. A clear dome surrounded the central area of what he guessed was the cockpit of the saucer. Visual images and indicators were superimposed on the inside of the dome. John felt a slight vibration, then the circular wing of the saucer became invisible. The saucer lifted off and suddenly shot up and away at an extremely fast pace, but he felt no acceleration inertia. It was amazing.

Tom said, "I guess you noticed that there are no controls. This ship was designed solely for use by a Star Child. Only we can operate it through our minds and powers. John, you and Jane can slip on one of the headgear units and the ship will teach you how to operate it. It also connects you to an Arcadian database, which is full of information about them and us and archives of advanced technology you wouldn't believe. We are Star Children, but we were genetically engineered by Arcadians. I do, however, suggest you wait until we get back to our Sanctuary. It won't be a long trip. Dir. Setliff, Agent Welch, Dr. Wisscroff, Mrs. Wilks, Major Burns and the other Star Children are currently en route there now. The Arcadians have a full presentation for us ready."

Tina said, "You guys are not going to believe what we found when we opened the door to the Sanctuary. You have to see it to believe it."

True to Tom's prediction, they were over solid ice within an hour and slowing. The saucer circled back and plunged into the sea and went deep under the ice shelf. Elaborate and detailed three dimensional images displayed on the inside of the dome, which guided them toward a deep underground cave opening. They followed the cave entrance far into a mountain then upward out of the

183

water to a huge circular iris door, that was opening as they approached. Inside the iris door the scene changed abruptly. They rose into a smooth circular shaft hundreds of feet straight up until they entered a massive open cavern. Tom guided their saucer to an open top slot in a docking structure designed to stack saucers like plates in a cabinet. There were fifteen saucers already stacked, with ten vacant slots. All the stacked saucers were pulsing slightly with energy. Once docked, Tom, Sue and Tina led John and Jane out the lowered ramp to a stairway joining stairways from the other saucers. The final single stairway led upward to another iris door. It opened as they approached.

John and Jane froze and stared in amazement. In front of them was a pristine white city complete with building lined streets. Tall pine trees jutted up from numerous locations throughout the city before them. The entire, high ceiling radiated light that looked like natural sunlight. As they neared one of the streets they noticed that the streets moved, like an airport walkway. They let the street take them through the small city to the far end, where a huge door was swung open. They could see solid ice outside through an orange light barrier and didn't feel the cold from outside. Inside was a comfortable 75 degrees. Two hundred feet inside the door was a circular gathering area. In the center was a raised platform. In the center of the platform stood a small, cream-colored man. He was no taller than four feet. The arms and legs were skinny, but he was humanoid in appearance. No, the head was larger, no hair, small nose and lips, but the eyes were overly large and dark green. The man just stood there clothed in a snug silver garb. It looked very much like a wet suit, except silver.

Sue said, "That is an Arcadian, but it isn't real. It's some sort of holograph. He scared the crap out of us when we first came in. He has been standing there for years waiting for us to come. They must all be dead now, but they wanted to leave us a message and explain our heritage. We've heard the message. That's when we called everyone here."

Tom said, "We wanted all involved to hear this, their last words, thoughts, blessings and warning."

Fred pinged Tom and said, *"We have all arrived. We came with the others in track vehicles, so we are a little late. We are beginning our descent now."*

Tom motioned for the rest to follow him, as he walked to the open-door entrance. Fred was the first to be seen, and he was lowering Dir. Setliff in a gravity and warmth bubble. As they reached the bottom, Jack was released from his bubble and stumbled in awe into the entrance. His eyes were wider than Tom had ever seen before, and he said nothing and did nothing but stare with a wide open mouth. Tom pulled Jack farther into the entrance out of the way, and Jack followed like a child in a toy store. Tom could tell Fred was also in awe, but Fred was laughing, like he usually did.

Mary and Janet were the next to reach the bottom. Their reaction was much the same as Dir. Setliff. Jerry and Dr. Wisscroff came next, and

Tom was surprised at Dr. Wisscroff's reaction. He was not in awe, quite the opposite. He was sporting a smug smile, as if he was expecting this. Mrs. Wilks and Major Burns followed in succession with two of the newer, recruits. Gary and Don looked to be around sixteen, maybe seventeen. The remaining Star Children then came down, each with a security guard or a Marine. Even the young ones seem to be proficient in their powers. Tom was proud of them.

John was making the introductions of Jane to the other kids or their supporters, but he could tell everyone's attention was on the sparkling city. He certainly could understand that, since its existence was so totally unexpected.

When all were inside Tom raised his hands for silence and said, "Thank you all for coming. Sue, Tina and I came in first and discovered these facilities and listened to the welcome you are about to hear from Mr. Mum on the podium there." Tom pointed toward the holograph image. "As you will hear, he is not a living person, he is a visual image programmed to present a message, mostly to the Star Children but includes a message to humans as well. Please follow me to the small arena designed for this introduction."

The small crowd mechanically followed Tom to the arena and took seats on the circular benches. Tom said, "We are gathered Mr. Mum and ready."

The standing Mr. Mum looked very lifelike and began to move and looked around, as if seeing everyone and said, "I am Mum, one of the few remaining Arcadians left alive. I am making this recording in the event of my death. Obviously, if you are watching this I have since passed in this life."

"We have waited so long for you to find us. This facility was built for you. It is your Sanctuary, and it will protect you. As you have undoubtedly discovered, you have powers or you wouldn't have survived, and you wouldn't be here now. You have enemies, as you have surely also discovered. They include both alien and human. I will talk more about them later."

"The Arcadians came to this planet nine hundred years ago. Our world was dying, and we were and are a dying race. When we first arrived we numbered in the thousands. We are a benevolent race, and we originally wanted to assimilate with humans and help them develop, but we quickly discovered we had no natural immunity or resistance to human diseases. Each time we made contact with humans hundreds of us died of various human diseases we would be infected with. We were forced to withdraw from humans and built a Sanctuary here, isolated from humans, but we continued to want to assimilate."

"This brings us to who you are. Since our race was dying, we attempted to merge our DNA with human DNA. It took us many years of genetic engineering to create a new Arcadian race in a human body that could resist the human diseases and finally be able to help them evolve. We created what we called a Star Child ... You. You are both Human and Arcadian, the best

187

of both races. You have our powers and the keen intelligence of the Arcadians, and you have an enhanced Human body. You are capable of surviving in both worlds. You have the ability to assimilate with humans, but many humans will resent your powers. They will be an enemy you must avoid, but we believe you will also find many humans worthy, value them."

We strongly suggest, however, that you live here in this Sanctuary, but saucers are available to quickly travel wherever you wish to go. Through the town and down the steps you will find these saucers parked. Simply slip the headset on and the saucer will teach you how to fly it. There are weapons on the saucer, but your main defense is your own mental powers."

This Sanctuary will keep you safe from your enemies and provide all that you need to survive. We suggest that you continue to live together here in order to propagate our race. A Star Child can mate with humans, but each subsequent generation will find the Arcadian powers weaker until they are no more. We hope you keep our race alive.

"Your other enemies you need to know about are the Resis, the humans call them Greys. We were never positive if they migrated from outside this solar system or evolved here on this planet, but they existed here on this land body as an advanced civilization long before humans civilization emerged and spread. The Resis are now typically an underground race and exist in vast numbers, many here on this land mass. We believe they once had a thriving culture and advanced technology before a polar shift of this planet occurred, turning this land mass into a frozen wilderness. This sudden polar shift destroyed many Resis and drove the survivors deep underground and caused their culture and technology to collapse. They reverted to a primitive and isolated existence. After we Arcadians arrived here we attempted to make contact with them on several occasions, but they were fearful and hostile toward us, so we left them alone"

"We have reason to believe that something happened before and during what human's called World War II. A group of human warriors and scientists discovered the Resis and their abandoned ancient technology. These human NAZIs conquered the primitive Resis and began to reverse engineer the Resis' forgotten technology. We know they produced flying saucers and laser weapons during that war, but were unable to produce them in sufficient quantity and lost their war. At the end of that war the NAZIs came here in mass, and they have remained hidden here on this barren land mass ever since. The Resis have become their slaves and warriors. These groups are your enemies. They know about us and fear us, but our defenses are too powerful, so they leave us alone. You will be in danger if you live outside of this facility and are identified."

"Again, we welcome you here. You are what remains of our Arcadian race, and we wish you well. I am interfaced with our database and programmed to answer specific question, just ask."

No one spoke up, so Dr. Wisscroff asked, "How many Star Children did you create?"

Mum said, "We created five batches using harvested human female eggs. The first two batches mostly died in infancy. Very few survived in the human environment. All total in the later batches we created 550 Star Children dispersed in several developed countries."

"When were the batches dispersed?"

"The first batch was dispersed thirty years ago, with the next four at five-year intervals."

Tina asked, "Where do you get your food? What do you eat?

"Our race primarily eats a cultured algae, but knowing your body eats differently, we stocked up food humans would normally eat. You will find a completely stocked and usable cafeteria on the main avenue. There are also underground caverns with artificial lighting that can grow crops for consumption and house Earth native animals."

Mrs. Wilks said, "This Sanctuary is so pristine and white. How is it maintained like this?"

"Arcadians, as mentioned earlier, are susceptible to Earth germs. Germs can't survive in this frigid climate, which is the main reason we chose this location. We also added a comprehensive air filtering and processing network to maintain sterile, dust-free air. As a result, nothing much ages in our Sanctuary."

John Meeker said, "Mr. Mum, I noticed coming in via the iris door to the docking area that even the saucers are constantly alive, along with the Sanctuary's equipment and lights. How do you maintain almost perpetual energy?"

"That is a difficult question to answer, since humans do not yet have the technology to understand, but I will try. The planet itself has an abundant supply of energy. We simply capture that energy through crystals calibrated to absorb this radiated energy and store it. Beyond that I can't explain it where you would understand. If you would like to learn this technology our data archives can provide additional information and engineering calculations and drawing."

Mrs. Wilks said, "Where do we reside here, some of the children are tired and need to sleep?"

Mum said, "There are many residential complexes here and thousands of sleeping units, many are next to the cafeteria."

Tom said, "Thank you, Mr. Mum. I'm sure we have many more questions for you, but as Mrs. Wilks said, we need to check out the cafeteria, find something to eat and find sleeping quarters. Group, let's head toward the cafeteria and do a little exploring while we are at it." Most everyone nodded.

Dr. Wisscroff said, "you all go on. I'll meet you in the cafeteria later. I just have a few thousand more questions to ask Mr. Mum."

Knowing Dr. Wisscroff and his thirst of knowledge the way he did, Tom knew they would be lucky to see him again at all. They left him behind, but extracted a promise that he would meet them at the cafeteria soon.

As they were about to leave, Major Burns said, "Is it alright if I bring my Marines down here? If so, I will order the crew to move base camp over here, set it over the entrance of the hole and built an elevator of sorts.

No one spoke, but they all looked at Tom for an answer. Tom said, "I guess I am the de facto leader of the Star Children and thus the Sanctuary. Major Burns, I think that is an excellent idea. Do you need us to help?

"No Sir, the crew I brought is expert. Honestly, the rest of us would just get in their way and slow them down. Plus, they now have a major incentive of getting in out of the cold."

Before they left Dr. Wisscroff said, "Director Setliff, please wait for a minute. I need something from you. Hearing what Mr. Mum told us reminded me of something that happened here at Antartica just after WWII. My memory is vague, but America had just fought a brutal war with Germany and we were war-weary. The war was over, but a year later America and many of our allies launched a fleet and soldiers to Antartica. They called it a training exercise, but at the time there were many rumors about a secret NAZI base here and that they remained operational. Without doubt that force was sent here to clean it out. The only problem is that the fleet returned with many casualties. Some reports claimed the fleet limped back defeated. It was quickly labeled with the accursed 'Top Secret' tag and hushed up, but I think we need to know what really happened with Operation High Jump, since we may be dealing with that same NAZI group."

Dir. Setliff nodded and said, "I agree. I'm sure that's one of the files deep in the vault. I'll get NSA Canton to review it and give us a report. Operation High Jump, right?" Doc nodded and turned back to Mr. Mum.

Tom, Sue, John and Jane followed a focused Mrs. Wilks as she led the younger children in search of the cafeteria. It wasn't too hard to find, since it had a large sign on the front that said, "Cafeteria." Tom wondered if the Arcadians actually used English or were simply preparing for the Star Children, since all the writing on signs seemed to be in English and even the introduction by Mr. Mum was in English. Oh well, it worked out well for the current occupants, now.

Mrs. Wilks hit the cafeteria like a dynamo, checking water facets, stoves for heat, shelves for food, etc. All was in order and worked, and she soon had powdered egg omelets cooking. At least they would be nourishing until she worked a few things out. She had found stored powdered milk and made up pitchers. The younger kids were helping, fetching and stirring. They found dishes and glasses, and I'm sure they would be doing the dishes afterward. Tom couldn't believe it. He smelled coffee brewing.

Tom was first in line for coffee. Sue was second. Once they had their coffee they found a table and set across from each other. Tom and Sue finally began to relax as others of their group began to enter. Each of them seemed to have an exciting discovery to share and came directly to him to report.

Mary had found a library and school together in one building, Jerry found a forest on a lower level complete with animals, Fred found shops along the main street of all kinds fully stocked, Tina found a park and equipped playground, Gary had found a fully equipped gym and Don excitedly reported finding a building with a Bank sign on it but no vault or bars. He said it was full of gold bars just stacked on the floor. To emphasize that statement, he plopped a gold bar on the table. Bridget, one of the older of the new group, reported finding a sophisticated hospital. Karen, another new one, came in wearing a form-fitting silver suit and silver lightweight boots that looked very much like Mr. Mum's. She reported that a building was full of them, and they were extremely comfortable. In addition, a foundry, advanced machine shop and laundry facility were reported. Tom was sure they would find everything they might ever need here in the Sanctuary.

John and Jane finally came in and reported that the building next door was like a large two-story motel with about 200 large rooms, two bedrooms, large shower, the towels and linen were in vacuum packs, operational swimming pool, etc.

John said, "I took the liberty of claiming part of the bottom wing. Jack and Janet in the first one, Jane and I in the next, You and Sue in the next. I simply put occupied on the next few for Mrs. Wilks, Dr. Wisscroff, Major Burns and the rest of the kids. I figured Major Burns would also billet his crew there, but then there are many other living units in other buildings to choose from. This one was the closest to the cafeteria, though."

Tom knew he showed surprise at John's comment about him and Sue staying together and said, "I'm sure Jack and Janet will be surprised, like Sue is probably surprised.

John, realizing his error, said, "Oh, that's awkward. From the emotions I sensed from them I just assumed they were together, like you two. You are, aren't you?"

Sue flushed but said, "Yeah, I'm surprised, but I'm OK with it if you are, Tom. You needed a push anyway. Thanks John. You too, Jane." The girls exchanged winks.

Dir. Setliff and Agent Welch came in and sit alone at a corner table. Jack said, "Janet, I need your help putting together a detailed report for the president. He will be surprised at what we found."

Sue noticed several Marines come into the cafeteria and take over from Mrs. Wilks. Major

195

Burns must have sent his Combat Cooks down first, since this is where they would be needed. Sue was pleased to see Mrs. Wilks relieved. She had been working hard and had fed most of the children.

Mrs. Wilks joined them and said, "That is a fantastic kitchen, and you wouldn't believe all the stores back there. There are huge freezers and storerooms brimming with food, enough to feed an army. In fact, they stored thousands of the MREs, like the military uses. Many of the younger kids have eaten something. Now I need to find them a place to sleep."

Sue said, "Next door. John has already assigned rooms."

Tina said, "Tom and Sue are sleeping together tonight. Can I stay with you tonight Mrs. Wilks?" Sue blushed profusely.

Mrs. Wilks eyes bulged, but she covered it well and said, "Of course you can. Let's go check out the rooms."

Tina gave Sue a mischievous grin and a hug and said, "See you tomorrow. I'm moving back in with you."

# Chapter 8
## (Doom & Gloom)

President Thompson received Dir. Setliff's report with much interest and immediately called a meeting of his secret committee. They were there in the masked conference room within an hour and ready to provide their own reports.

President Thompson had Dir. Setliff's written report posted on a large screen TV for them to read. Afterward, he played the video of base camp, snow, descent into the hole, entrance of the Sanctuary, Mr. Mum's welcoming presentation and then the video inside the Sanctuary. Between the written report and the videos they all had an excellent understanding of the situation in Antarctica, and it was both disturbing and exciting.

President Thompson said, "I can't believe how devastating this 'Top Secret' hiding seems to be. I haven't the slightest idea what Operation High Jump was. Mr. Canton, please do as Dir. Setliff has suggested and go to the 'Top Secret' archives and find out what you can about it. Send Dir. Setliff an encrypted report, a summary anyway. And, we all need to know here, too. Jack seems to think the NAZIs from WWII may be behind the whole thing and control the Greys. He also seems to believe the NAZI main base is somewhere there in Antarctica. At least we now know where the main base is. Now we have to find the others."

"Mr. Canton, learning about the Star Children is enlightening, but learning about the potential of incredible technology is even more intriguing. Ask Dir. Setliff if we can send some top-level scientist down there to investigate this technology."

Mr. Canton said, "Well, we already have one of our best scientist already there, Dr. Wisscroff. He is probably the one we would have chosen to send."

"Very well, but more scientist would be better. Ask anyway. OK, what can you tell me from your end, Dir. Martinez?"

CIA Dir. Martinez started and said, "We found a contractor for the hand-held implant detectors. Thankfully, most of the individual parts already exist. It was just a matter of putting them together for our purpose, which has been done. I might add, rather quickly. In fact many have already been distributed, and many more are becoming available. We started at the top of the chain of command. So the screening has begun working down the commands. The FBI headquarters has been cleared and so has Langley. The Secret Service was among the very first department cleared. The military is also working expeditiously. We have established an isolated compound at Langley for housing all those we have found with implants. Sadly, we have found too many already through the security screening modification. We snatch them up immediately, take their cell phones and transport them to our compound, where the implants are removed before being locked up. Enhanced interrogations will be employed, and we hope to begin gathering intel soon."

"Surprisingly, we have identified four Senators, fifteen Congressmen, five Generals and one Admiral so far. Most of these are involved in appropriations, so now we know where the Greys got their funds."

"Dir. Hawkins has just started at NSA, but he has already sent us twenty-five. No one is very surprise, since we knew the NSA was heavily compromised. We are keeping all these in a separate compound for priority investigation. I'm not sure how we are going to keep it a secret for very long. The news media are already asking questions."

President Thompson interrupted, "Hell, probably most of the media have those damn implants already. It sure seems like they are trying to destroy the country already. Be sure they are checked. Too bad we can't detonate those implants." The room filled with laughter, but the president wasn't smiling.

Dir. Martinez continued, "Actually, Mr. President, we have scientist researching that possibility now."

The president said, "That is a great idea. They are committing treason, and traitors can be shot. Detonating the implants in compromised soldiers should be an option, especially if they start shooting at our forces."

Dir. Hawkins said, "The FBI's main priority right now is identifying the implanted personnel and

199

quietly removing them. This is taking most of our time, but we are making great progress. The hardest part is quietly whisking them away before our progress can be reported. So far I believe we have been successful. At the FBI we now have many SWAT teams being deployed, many at the various military branches and targets of their choosing. Each service branch has developed its own assault teams. Overall we are making much progress.

Each Joint Chief sequentially gave a report, but little new information was gained, other than identifying the deep underground bases and connecting them with dots to estimate the potential tunnel routes. The Secretaries of Defense, Navy, Air Force, Army, etc. offered no report at all. President Thompson thought, *"These appointments are nothing but political positions and useless now when action is required. He decided to replace them with action-oriented retired generals and admirals."*

They were getting nowhere, so the president said, "OK, let's resume tomorrow. By then I want some intel coming in, and Mr. Canton, get that report out on Operation High Jump to Dir. Setliff and myself. We will talk about it tomorrow. Let's get moving guys."

***

Activities increased in the cafeteria once the Combat Cooks got rolling, and hot meals were available for all in short order. They were most likely MRE, but they were hot and actually tasty. Sue had no idea what it was she ate, but it was good and filling. There was powdered milk and water to drink, and the water was as pure as she had ever tasted. Everyone had their fill, and Mrs. Wilks ushered most of the younger kids off to assigned quarters. Most of the Marines had finished their move of the base camp and moved down into the Sanctuary, and the cafeteria was filling up fast with hungry Marines. Sue hadn't realized just how many Marines there were, enough to fight a small war for sure. Major Burns joined them at their table to tell them the good news.

Dr. Wisscroff, who had just joined them, asked, "Major Burns, do you have a medical doctor with your detachment?"

"Yes we do, two actually. Do you have a need for medical attention?"

"Yes and no. We don't have immediate needs, but we don't have a medical doctor among our group. Mr. Mum mentioned that the Sanctuary has a medical facility. I would appreciate you sending them to find it and report the status of equipment and capabilities. My guess is that they will find much new medical science and technology and potential cures at the facility. They, however, may come back feeling like witch doctors in comparison to the Arcadians' advanced medical technology."

Major Burns nodded and said, "That sounds like an excellent idea. I'll send the whole medical team there to set up. I'll have my guys explore the Sanctuary and identify the areas of potential interest."

Sue said, "Bridget found the hospital. Tell them to find her and get directions." He nodded.

Fred came up to the table and said, "Have any of you been getting a weak and garbled telepathic transmission? I've heard some transmissions, but they didn't make sense to me. I thought it might be a response to the telepathic messages we have been sending out."

Jane shocked us all when she said, "The signal seems garbled because the person sending is thinking in German and not English. I heard it too, but I'm so new here I thought it might be coming from one of you guys."

John asked, "Do you speak German?"

"Yes, I am an interpreter, remember? I'm fluent in Russian, German, English, French and a little Spanish."

John said, "What are they saying or thinking in German?"

"She is complaining about the voices in her head, wondering if she is crazy."

John said, "Well, it looks like you are elected to be her mentor. Put her in your telepathic matrix and talk to her. Find out all you can about her and where she is."

Dr. Wisscroff said, "German? That is extremely unlikely, since the Arcadians didn't trust the Germans during the dispersement of the infant Star Children. I would have thought they would try to keep all the kids in English speaking countries, since everything here in the Sanctuary is geared to

English. Jane, I am even surprised that you came out of Russia."

"I'm originally from England. I was adopted from an English orphanage by a Russian family. English was my original language."

Dr. Wisscroff said, "That explains it, then. Maybe something like that happened to this girl. Wait … Oh, I think I see. Maybe she was adopted by a German family when she was very young and never learned English. Oh my, be very careful in dealing with her, Jane. If this NAZI theory turns out to be real, this girl may be a NAZI or possibly living with them in isolation. There may be more of them. The Greys gathered the Star Children together before at Area 51. Maybe they did it again in one of their strongholds, maybe even here."

Tom said, "Damn, Doc, you sure are cynical, but you could be correct."

Dr. Wisscroff said, "If this lady or potentially a group of them have lived among a NAZI group for that long, long enough to have forgotten their native English language, they may feel an attachment to them. They may know no other life. It's called Stockholm Syndrome, where the captured develops a bond with their controller. I'm just saying, be careful. We may not want to educate them about their powers until we know what side they are on."

Jane said, "I'll talk to her in German, but I understand the risks, and I'll be careful."

Jane had another cup of coffee, relaxed then pinged the lady and thought in German, *"You are not going crazy. This is called telepathy. Others like you have that ability. You don't have to speak the words, simply think them. Do you hear me?"*

After a moment the lady transmitted, *"Yes ... I hear you in my mind. You said this is telepathy? Thank you for explaining it. I thought I was going nuts. Who are you? Are you close? I don't see you."*

*"My name is Jane. No you can't see me, and I can't see you. For now we can only communicate through telepathy. Please tell me all about yourself: name, age, location, are you alone or with others, etc."*

*"My name is Berta. I'm seventeen years old. I'm here. I don't know what you are asking. I'm just here at the camp. I am not alone. There are twenty of us in the camp. We work on projects given to us by the watchers."*

*"What kind of camp is it? Can you take a look at the camp and think about the image? I think I will be able to see it through telepathy."*

Berta said, *"It's just a camp like any camp I believe. It's where the watchers keep us when we aren't working. We have always lived here."*

An image flooded Jane's mind of a fenced complex filled with small barracks-like buildings. There were far more buildings than needed to house twenty people, suggesting the numbers may have been a lot more at one time. The fence was high on three sides and abutted against a straight rock wall on the fourth side. Looking past the fence Jane could see they were inside a huge, lighted cave, really huge. She could also see Greys, at least she thought they must be the Greys she had heard the others talking about. They were walking around outside the fence, maybe guards.

Jane pinged, *"Berta, do you like it there?"*

*"We work hard, and the watchers are mean, but it is what it is. Where else would we go?"*

Jane said to the others watching her, "It's horrible. There are twenty of them confined to a prison-like complex in a huge cavern. They are working slaves to the Greys. Berta is seventeen, and I'm assuming the others are about the same age. They apparently know no other language but German. I think they have been imprisoned since they were very young. When I asked where they were she had no concept of there being any other place. I'm positive they are not educated at all. She talks childlike, illiterate. We have to get them the hell out of there."

Jane pinged, *"Berta, I have to go right now, but we will talk more. I have much to tell you about, and I will. I think for now, I would keep our communication our secret. I will tell you, however, that there are many other places to go to. We have a place you would love. Bye for now."*

Dr. Wisscroff said, "They almost have to be here in Antartica, since they speak only German and live underground. Let's go ask Mr. Mum where the cave is located, since the Arcadians have been there." All their group stood up as one and followed Dr. Wisscroff out.

After Mr. Mum heard the explanation and question from Dr. Wisscroff, he replied, "It's not hard to find. Go exactly to the coordinates of the

South Pole. You will find a large opening that leads down into a hidden world. Yes, there is a large cavern, but it is far more than that, it is large enough to be an underground continent. You can fly one of the saucers. It is invisible in flight and cannot be detected. Search that world until you find the Star Children. Please save our kin. If you have to leave the saucer use your light bending stealth power to remain invisible outside the ship if necessary."

Dr. Wisscroff said, "We haven't gotten that far yet. Jane is the only one that speaks German, and she is having to go slow, because those Star Children are illiterate and don't understand common knowledge."

Mum said, "A Star Child can simply slip the control head ring on in the saucer or library and the Arcadian data archive will teach you what you want to know or need to know. It will also educate the illiterate ones to catch up."

Tom said, "Thank you, Mr. Mum. It's late, and tomorrow is likely to be a busy day. I think we should all go get some sleep. But, I'm out of clean clothing. Does anyone know where Karen found the warehouse with all the silver suits? I think I want to pick up some for myself."

Mr. Mum pointed and said, "There, and they are more than simply clothing. The suit has protection built into it to prevent injury to us. Your human body doesn't require as much protection as an Arcadian body, but they would be beneficial."

Dr. Wisscroff said, "Well, in that case, I want one too."

They all followed Mr. Mum's pointed direction and entered the warehouse to find thousands of the

206

uniforms. Tom even found one in his size, although the way they stretched, they could have gotten by with one size fits all. The suit was soft to the touch like silk, yet there was a firmness about it. Tom wondered if it was some advanced form of Kevlar ... probably. They all managed to find a place to change, and soon everyone was admiring themselves, even Dr. Wisscroff. The boots weren't heavy at all, but they did support the ankles. It almost felt as if he was naked, because there was no binding or rubbing, and it was almost weightless.

They didn't stop back by the cafeteria, but went straight to their quarters. Tom noticed a quick look between Jack and Janet, but they went into their quarters without being pushed... too hard. Tom took Sue's hand and led her into their quarters. Tom had been thinking a lot about being alone with Sue ever since John mentioned the sleeping assignments. He pinged Sue and released his emotional images. Sue did likewise. They were certainly imagining the same thing. Sue fell into his arms and their kisses became a storm, complete with lighting. They floated up together as the uniforms slipped off just as easily as they slipped on. Since Jane's inadvertent transmission of zero gravity sex, the desire had been on her mind. They slowly drifted toward the bed locked together in a heaving undulation of bodies. They climaxed simultaneously in a whirlwind of zero gravity. That first time was almost animal. They calmed and settled upon the bed wrapped in each other arms and legs. The second time was slow and passionate, and they seemed to continue till morning, but at some point they managed to finally put the sheets on the bed.

There were no locks on the doors and Tina came busting into the room early and jumped in bed with them, between them actually and said, "Breakfast is being served in the cafeteria by the Army guys. I was sent to let you and the others know." Tina looked back and forth between them and asked, "Did you guys have your 'Honeymoon'? Mrs. Wilks said you were. I guess Dir. Setliff and Agent Welch did too. They were in the same bed when I woke them up."

Sue and Tom looked at each other and started laughing, laughing at their own situation and laughing at Jack and Janet's.

Sue hugged Tina and said, "Well, yes, Tina. We sure did have our Honeymoon. We'll just get a shower and join you at the cafeteria." Tina giggled and took off, slamming the door as she went.

At the cafeteria table Dir. Setliff was reflecting on his night, although night never comes to the Sanctuary. Nevertheless, it had been wonderful. It all started when Tom opened his door and pushed Janet and him inside. At first Jack panicked, worrying about sexual harassment allegations, but he needn't have worried. As soon as the door closed Janet turned to him and kissed him. She kissed him and waited for his reaction. He liked and was attracted to her since the first time he saw her, but like all government executives, especially at the director level, you just don't make unwanted sexual

208

advances. It could cost you your job and reputation. In this case, however, it must have been a mutual attraction, it certainly wasn't an unwanted sexual advancement. His reaction was almost immediate. Jack took her in his arms and kissed her back. He was unattached and so was she, and they were likely to be together isolated for quite some time with the Star Children, maybe longer. He certainly wouldn't mind that. She was beautiful and smart, a great combination.

When she kissed him it was like releasing him from his forced self-control. He let his desire for her explode, and Janet did likewise. They maintained a passionate kiss, while trying to maneuver toward the first bed they could find. This became hard to do while they were stripping each other of their now cumbersome clothing. Her desire matched his own, maybe more. Janet pushed him back on the bed and straddled him. He was deep inside her wonderful, hot sheath before he realized what was happening but offered no resistance, not one iota.

Janet was riding him like a cowgirl on a horse and panted out, "I've been wanting to do this since we met in Phoenix. I thought we would never be alone together."

He didn't want to talk, and pulled her face to his and continued their kisses. She never missed a stroke. They moaned and groaned at the same time in climax, and she collapsed on top of him. They both knew it was going to be a long and satisfying night, and it was. It was until Tina came bursting into the room to tell them breakfast was ready. It didn't seem to bother Tina that they were still naked, as they scrambled to cover themselves.

Her job done, Tina left and they showered together, dressed and meandered to the cafeteria. They were both still smiling as they entered. With food and coffee inside them, his mind remembered the night. Jack knew there would be many more.

Jack's mind jumped back into focus when his secure satellite phone chimed. He looked and said, "It's from Mr. Canton. It has to be the report Dr. Wisscroff requested." Jack opened it and read.

\*\*\*

NSA Tom Canton (Operation High Jump)

Operation High Jump was launched in 1947, authorized by President Truman. It consisted of three Battle Groups and thirteen ships including a Flag Ship, Aircraft Carrier, Ice Breaker, two Destroyers, Submarine and miscellaneous support ships. There were almost 5,000 elite and seasoned combat soldiers from the U.S, United Kingdom, Russia, Norway, Australia and Canada. It was advertised as a training mission, but the real mission was to find and destroy a secret German base believed to be in full operation long after the end of WWII. The world was war-weary, so the mission goals were kept secret, and no one wanted to admit that the war wasn't over.

Investigations gathered after Germany's final surrender by underlings uncovered disturbing data. There were 250,000 unaccounted for scientists and soldiers consisting of many of Hitler's elite SS and radical elements of his inner circle. The investigators uncovered information that Hitler himself may have been with the missing group.

Investigators uncovered records that indicated Hitler was keenly interested in Antarctica long before the war started. Some records referenced discoveries of an ancient civilization and advanced technology there. Hitler had sent many scientific and military expeditions to Antarctica long before the war and continued sending ships and supplies throughout the war. When the inevitable defeat of NAZI Germany loomed near at least forty German submarines disappeared, believed to be carrying escaping NAZIs and the plundered wealth of Europe, headed for their secret base in Antarctica. One of the crippled, missing submarines surrendered in Argentina after the war ended, which, ironically, is in a direct route to Antarctica.

So, believing the NAZIs intended to continue their war for domination of the world from Antarctica, Operation High Jump was conceived by Adm. Nimitz and launched to finally end that bloody war and defeat the NAZI Reich once and for all. Unfortunately, the operation failed miserably. Admiral Byrd's strike force was reportedly attacked by flying saucers with swastika insignias coming out of the water and firing what we now believe were laser weapons. Many men were lost and much damage inflicted to the fleet, with at least one Destroyer cut in half by these lasers and sank.

The flying saucers were totally unexpected and impossible to defend against their speed and weapons. Adm. Byrd retreated and reported some of these facts in a public interview on board his Flag Ship. The whole episode was quickly declared "Top Secret" and hushed up. Adm. Byrd was silenced and incarcerated in a mental hospital for the rest of his life. He was more fortunate than the then Sec. of the Navy. He too was silenced and put into a mental hospital, but supposedly committed suicide by throwing himself out of an upper story window.

I found additional research describing Hitler's obsession with Antarctica. Something of significance was discovered there by the original German scientific research team, something so significant that Hitler became totally obsessed with it. Many believe they found a wealth of new technology there, which explains their planned advanced technology of guided missiles, space orbital lasers, jet planes, helicopters, stealth technology, even anti-gravity. The NAZIs had abundant plans for altering the course of the war, but fortunately, allied forces destroyed most manufacturing plants before they could produce a final product. One of the more "Science Fiction" rumors was that they were developing flying saucers, but no evidence was ever found. Now, based upon what Mr. Mum reported, maybe they did find technology in Antarctica. The advanced technology Germany was developing must have come from somewhere, unless we are to believe their scientist were far smarter than the rest of the world's.

Also, add to this what we learned from Operation High Jump. I must conclude that the NAZIs did in fact develop flying saucers technology during WWII and moved the whole operation to Antartica. I must also remind you that they had flying saucers and its technology as far back as probably 1945. If they continued to develop this technology over the last 70+ years, the world has little chance of standing against them if they intend to attack us. I have no reason to doubt the NAZIs intend to do just that, based upon what we have already discovered. I'm beginning to believe that this was their ultimate long-term goal even before WWII began. I don't think they cared if they won or lost the war, even though, with their developing advanced technology, they came within a breath of winning WW II. Now, they have had many decades to implement their ultimate plan and build many flying saucers to disperse throughout the world, readying for the final attack.

I find we face a grave and potentially hopeless situation. We may have lost this war already.

***

Reading Mr. Canton's report tended to wipe the smile off his face. Jack passed it around the table, starting with Dr. Wisscroff, who's frown matched Jack's.

Dr. Wisscroff said, "That's what I was afraid of. Actually, it is worse than I was afraid of. I seemed to recall Operation High Jump and wondered at the time why it wasn't reported more. No wonder they kept it a secret. They didn't want the world to know we got our asses kicked by the very NAZIs we supposedly won the war from. Still, keeping it a secret was wrong. The rest of the world would never had allowed the NAZIs to have decades to continue their preparations for world domination. The world would have insisted we continue the war and end the threat. As it is, the secret kept anyone from knowing or even remembering the threat, except for very old farts like myself. We are in serious trouble now."

It was Jane that brought everyone back to the here and now and said, "Well, I don't know what happened back then. Maybe we are in trouble, but for right now we know for sure we have twenty Star Children that need help. Let's go find them, and just maybe we can find out about the existing threat in the process."

Tom said, "That sounds like a good plan. Let's go to the saucer cavern."

Tom and Sue took off. When they looked around the entire group was flowing behind them. Tom said, "We can't all go. There isn't enough room, especially if we find the Star Children."

Jerry said, "We can if we take several saucers. Mary and I learned to fly yesterday. It was easy. All you have to do is think about what you want to do. The saucer just does it. It's kind of like flying ourselves the way we originally learned."

John said, "If it's that easy, I will learn to fly on the job."

Tom nodded and said, "OK, we will take three saucers. Jack, you and Janet will go with Sue and me. Dr. Wisscroff, you go with John and Jane. Jerry, you and Mary go alone to carry more Star Children if we can find them. The rest of you will have to wait here to give us room to load more."

John, Jane and Dr. Wisscroff went down the stairs to the third saucer and stood there waiting for something to happen and nothing happened, then john remembered hearing that you had to think about what you wanted to do. He thought, *"Open the hatch."* Down it came. He led the other two up into the craft and sat. When he slipped the headset on the ship talked telepathically to him. *"We are one. I can only be accessed and flown by an Arcadian mind. I will know what you want to do when you think it. Try thinking of me as an extension of your mind. When you fly me I will be your surrogate body. Your powers will work through me amplified. Some powers will operate automatically and generated by me like gravity drive for the ship, but you control the speed and direction. Invisibility will be automatic, anti-detection also. I will also emit protection in the form of a shielding forcefield. Time control is also deployed for exceptional speed. Still you can use your own powers at will. Telemetry is displayed on the dome. Flying is just that easy. If you have any questions simply ask and your mind will be connected to the Arcadian archive."*

*"How long does it take to learn to speak and understand German?"*

*"A language is fairly simple to learn from the archive. Information from the archive is sent*

*directly to the sub-conscience mind. Information feeding there does not get challenged or need to be understood by your rational mind. The sub-conscience mind absorbs the information as absolute. As a result, a language can in essence be downloaded directly. It takes only a few moments. Would you like this information downloaded? It can be done while you fly. In fact it is more easily done while your conscious mind is occupied with other tasks."*

*"Yes, I would like that. Please proceed."*

John continued to fly, and after a few moments he was unaware of the download activity. It was like it was being fed directly into some sub-file and bypassing his thoughts process.

John couldn't see the other saucers visually, but he could follow them through a digital and graphic display on the dome, even as they disappeared under the water. He followed them through the tunnel down into open sea under an ice shelf and eventually they burst out of the water into the air. He felt not the slightest difference between water and air. John could feel Jane sharing his controls, like they were flying jointly. They soared high and flew over their base camp, realizing as they did that the Marines had also moved the planes as well. The saucers went toward and over a high mountain range and out over a vast ice dome. Tom's lead saucer circled over a wide hole in the ice dome and reduced speed and sank deeper and deeper into the black hole, possibly miles. They continued to sink lower until light could be seen getting closer.

216

Suddenly, the opening expanded out into what must be a huge cavern filled with light. The light wasn't bright like the sun, but it was certainly bright enough to see well.

Dr. Wisscroff said, "Would you look at that. I can't even see the sides or ends of this cavern, and it's all lit up. It has to be some form of organic plant or algae that generates lite. There are fields of crops on the surface, so the light must be sufficient for growing. This cavern is far too big to be man-made. This has to be a bubble inside the Earth's crust when it cooled. Unbelievable! I've heard of this before. It's called the 'Hollow Earth' theory. The entire theory gets a little crazy wild and unbelievable, but apparently it isn't all so crazy."

Tom pinged Jerry and John saying, *"This is too damn huge. Let's split up and explore. John, you take the right side. Jerry, you take the left. I'll take the center. Let me know if either of you find the Star Children. If we don't find them in this direction we will try the other."*

John realized Doc was right. This cavern was unbelievably huge. They traveled to the right side, following the downslope of the bubble, which must be a mile high at the center. Even though they could not see the ends or the sides, they could judge where the end was by the declining slope. The floor was relatively flat, filled from ancient sediment to the approximate center, maybe lower, of the bubble and covered by woods and forests, some roads, an occasional city or industrial complex. It looked like any rural surface on the top, except the light was of

217

lesser intensity and of a slightly different shade than our sun. It almost looked fluorescent, and there were no shadows, since the light came from the entire top of the bubble. It took a moment to adjust to the change.

Doc said, "Oh, look up ahead. There is a massive lake. No, it's not a lake, it must be connected to the sea. See all those submarines? Damn, there must be ten of them at the docks, and they look like our modern nuclear subs. This is not good."

A sprawling military base surrounded the internal water inlet, and humans and Greys could be seen working together everywhere. Up on the shore another submarine was in the process of being constructed, which meant this was also a shipyard. John noticed Jane taking pictures. This was good to be able to show and not have so much to tell.

Doc said, "Oh my God, look at the other side of the bay."

John looked and saw a series of open vertical "I" beam platforms with stacked rings each holding a saucer. They were stacked like plates in a rack, each platform held ten saucers and there were at least thirty platforms. Thankfully, two of the platforms were empty, suggesting they were not yet at their target goal. John hoped that meant they still had a little time. Behind the platforms was a large warehouse, where it appeared they built the saucers. Jane captured the scene with pictures before they moved on.

They continued their survey following the curvature of the bubble. No more bases were discovered, but they did find ancient structures closer to the outside wall, which appeared to be housing for the Greys.

As they continued, Tom pinged and said, *"John, we found the Star Children."*

John glanced at the dome display and located Tom's saucer. It was toward the back of the bubble. He shot forward toward Tom's location. They reached the area almost immediately and hovered. The fenced area was quite large, and they noticed some Greys patrolling the outside fence. Inside the fence there was an open area blocked from view by the small barracks. John brought his saucer to the open area and lowered it to the ground and waited.

\*\*\*

Berta was the only name she had ever known. When she was young she and the other children required attention for their basic needs. She remembered mean women taking care of her and teaching her how to speak, but once they were able to understand instructions and take care of their own needs, the women stopped coming. Then, when they got old enough to work, all the children were moved to their camp, where they were now. The only contact they had with others now were the skinny watchers and gruff work-masters' orders.

Once she had heard and remembered one of the women say to another, "These are the abominations from England." Berta did not know what an England was or an abomination. She later ask another woman what abomination meant, and was told, "It means monster." After that she lost all hope, and just tried to survived.

Initially, there were over a hundred of them, at least that is what the work-masters told them. Over time Berta watched as that numbered dwindled. Many starved from lack of food, accidents or abuse. They worked hard and were never fed enough. They were always hungry. Berta watched her friends die one by one, some in her arms. They were few now, she heard the work-masters complain that there were only twenty of them left to do a job.

She and the others lived simply, because they had no other choice or any hope. After her last friend died she began to wish the next one to die would be her. That's when she began to hear the voices, but they had no meaning to her. Was her mind going first? Maybe the voices came before death.

Berta jumped up when she heard a new voice, but this time she could understand it. The voice said her name was Jane. It was a friendly and caring voice that told her about telepathy and ask her questions.

She asked Berta her age and she knew the answer. Due to a task once given to her, she was taught to count up to one hundred. From that knowledge and reconstruction of her history, she calculated that she was around seventeen years old. What that meant she had no idea, but from listening to other people, age seemed to be important to them.

This information now provided seemed to please Jane.

Sadly, Jane's other questions had little meaning. Jane asked where she was, and that had no meaning. She was here, where she always was. Where else would she be? Stranger was the next question about if she liked it there. No, she didn't like it, but she had no choice. That answer. Some of Jane's comments began to give her hope, something long forgotten.

The others began to gather around her. They said they were hearing the conversation between Jane and her and were as excited at something new as she herself was. But they waited for more and nothing came for many hours.

*** 

Jane pinged, *"Berta, are you there?"*

Immediately, Berta transmitted, *"Yes, we are here. We were afraid you would not speak to us again."*

Jane pinged, *"Who is we?"*

*"I couldn't keep it a secret. It seems the others also heard me talking with you, and they wanted to know what was happening. I told them, and they are excited both with this new ability to hear my thoughts and to know more about you."*

*"We have been looking for you, and we finally found you. We are here now to get you and take you to our home. Will you come with us? We are your family. We will take care of you and teach you many new things."*

*"This is exciting. We will come with you. We want to learn these things."*

*"Great. Come to the open area in your complex. We will meet you."*

All three saucers landed and waited for the Star Children to come, which they soon did. Tom had pinged and suggested that only the girls should go out. He was afraid the size of John and himself might intimidate them.

Jane was horrified to see them. The poor retched things were so skinny and clearly malnourished and were filthy. Their clothing was hardly more than rags, but from their features they were obviously Star Children. Jane was heartbroken and had to force a smile as she went out to meet them. Sue and Mary showed similar reactions as they came out from the other saucers.

When they got close, Jane said, "Berta? I am Jane. We are family." Berta smiled and came to her and they embraced. Jane quickly recovered and said to the group in German, "We must hurry before the Greys see us. Trust us. We will not harm you. We want to help you. We will talk more once we are safe.

The first thing the girls did was scan the Star Children for implants and found none. Jane then separated them into three groups and sent them off toward the invisible saucers.

Sue pinged Jane, *"The man in the back is not a Star Child. He is a secret spy for this group. He looks like one of us, but he is not. Bring him along so he can't report us."*

222

Jane noticed the man was not malnourished like the others and was also sensing the man's hostility. Jane led them to the ramp and sent them up one at a time. She timed it so the man was the last one. When his time came he bolted in the other direction. Jane immediately paralyzed him and sent him up the stairs in zombie-like movements. Once she was on board, the ramp lifted as did the saucer. Jane pinged in English, *"This man is not a Star Child. He has been monitoring these children and spying on them. Maybe he is a NAZI and we can learn secrets from him."*

Jane noticed a combination of pure fear, astonishment and excitement plastered on the faces of the German Star Children. In German Jane said, "Don't be afraid. We will be out of here soon, and you will be safe."

Berta said, "What did you do to Otis?"

"Otis is not your friend. He was working against you and meant you harm. I have simply frozen his body until we get back and find out more about him."

"We know he is not our friend. He has been mean to us. Do what you wish with him." Others of the German Star Children nodded agreement.

At first John was shocked that he understood the German being spoken but quickly realized he had just learned German on the way here. John said in German, much to Jane's surprise, "Put Berta in one of the seats and slip one of the head belts on. She will know English before we get back."

223

Jane did as he asked, and he instructed the Arcadian archive to teach Berta English and whatever else she needed to know. From time to time he would look at her for a reaction. Initially he only noticed a blank unintelligent stare, but it seemed each time he looked, her face seemed to register a higher level of understanding. He knew it was working.

Tom led them straight to the hole and up. It was comforting to see the hole disappear below them. Being inside seemed claustrophobic to Tom, not to mention the press of danger inside. But, they were relatively safe now as they streaked toward the open sea. Pure panic shown on the petrified faces of the new Star Children as they plunged into the water and under the ice shelf. They were almost back to the state of amazement when they floated up through the iris door and parked in their slot. When they had all disembarked and entered through the second iris door, the shock and awe returned, even to Tom. He never tired of the marvels of the Sanctuary.

No one spoke until Jerry said, "Let's go eat. I'm hungry as hell."

All turned in amazement when Berta said, "So am I."

John laughed at the shocked reaction and said, "The ship taught her English on the way back, and I learned German on the way there." The other English speaking Star Children nodded in understanding.

They rode the moving sidewalk all the way to the cafeteria and entered to a wonderful smell of aromatic food. Jane detoured with her zombie when she saw Major Burns and asked him to lock him up somewhere.

Major Burns said, "We found a perfect place for securing prisons and interrogating them." She released her freeze on his body and two Marines escorted him away.

Berta, John, and now Jane, the only interpreters, joined a churning group trying to introduce everyone. The nineteen new children were extremely excited to be here and relishing the food, like they hadn't eaten in quite some time, probably they hadn't. The children weren't exactly children. They all appeared to be at least sixteen, possibly even more, but they all looked like children in a toy store for the first time.

Berta said, "Jane, after we eat can we go to the library and learn more, especially English? Oh, and thank you all for getting us out of there. They were working us to death and starving us. Many of us have already died. Thank you so very much."

"Berta, we are all family or friends here. You guys are our family, and we are your family. You will soon discover that we are Star Children, and you have many dormant powers. That will all come soon enough, but first things first. I will ask Mary to take you to the library, since she found it, so your group can learn English and basic knowledge of the world. Afterwards, I will take you to meet Mr. Mum, our benefactor. He will explain who you are.

Once that's done we need to get you settled in housing so you can get cleaned up and into new clothing."

Dir. Setliff was again writing a report to the president and was going over the pictures of the German base. The implication presented a very sad outlook for the world. The other two saucers had found small towns of humans and other Grey villages but nothing like the military base John had found. John's information and pictures were bad enough, and the capture of a potential NAZI very interesting.

Dir. Setliff said, "I think we should interrogate him before I send the report. Jane, you caught him. Want to conduct the interrogation?" Jane nodded, and they followed Major Burns to his holding location.

# Chapter 9
## (Knowing is Preparing)

The Arcadians must have watched a lot of TV, especially NCIS; because they had constructed a complete interrogation room. There was even a two-way mirror to observe. In the seized mind interrogation method this was complete unnecessary. They entered the interrogation room and Otis jumped to his feet … obviously angry by his expression.

One look at Otis and it was obvious he was not a Star Child. He was big, as big as Tom or John. He had blond hair, but he had blue eyes instead of the characteristic green eyes of a Star Child. The obvious difference was his age. Otis was young but not young enough to be a Star Child, but of course the children didn't know that. He was obviously a plant by someone wanting the children watched.

Jane said, "Hello Otis. We need to talk."

Otis obviously understood English, since she spoke to him in English, but he had no intentions of cooperating and immediately sat down again and stared at the mirrored wall.

Jane said, "OK, I guess we will do this the hard way, for you anyway."

Jane tried to seize his mind, but this time Otis fought it. She was amazed that he could resist, he hadn't been able to earlier. They hadn't found any human so far that had been able to resist. Something was different about him. She concentrated harder and felt his will finally breaking. Sweat broke out on his brow from the effort, but he broke and relaxed in Zombie submission.

Jane said, "Who are you, Otis? Why were you monitoring the Star Children?"

Otis shook his head in defiance, but spoke in the monotone voice, "I am Otis Blitz. I am an Aryan descendant of the Lebensborn SS."

"What is the Lebensborn SS?"

"We are the true Master Race, descendants from the pureblood Aryan Race and loyal SS."

Dr. Wisscroff said, "Oh, I know who they are. Hitler initiated a program to selective breed blond haired blue eyed babies to build his Master Race. Rumor has it some genetic engineering was also employed. This race was to rule the world after Germany won the war."

Otis energetically added, "We *are* the superior race on Earth, and we *will* soon rule the world."

Jane asked again, "Why were you monitoring the Star Children?"

Otis resisted again but eventually said, "They have some powers we have not yet mastered. Until we do we remain cautious of them. My purpose for being with them was to watch and see how they control the elements, but these so-called Star Children have not demonstrated any powers. They are stupid and scheduled for termination, like the rest of them."

"How do you know they have powers?

"Many years ago we captured an injured Arcadian and experimented on him and used drugs to extract the information we needed to know. That's how we learned about the genetic engineering they were doing to put themselves into human bodies. We learned about their powers when they came to our underground world to get their comrade. The powers they demonstrated and used on us was devastating. We won't allow the Star Children to grow and assimilate into the human population."

"Do you fear them?"

"No, the 4th Reich is concerned, but we fear no one. We are strong of mind and body."

"Why have you left the Arcadians alone?"

"We leave them alone because they are few in numbers, and they have not returned to our world. Most of their abomination Star Children have been eliminated already. We know where the Arcadians live, but their residence is protected by a protection shield we cannot penetrate. Therefore, we leave them alone."

"How many of you are there?"

"We number 250,000, but the Greys number three times that. They obey us and are loyal. We guarantee their loyalty by keeping their families under our control."

"Do you all live there in your underground world?"

"All but a few of my race live here. The Greys live here and in other places."

"Where else do the Greys live?"

"They live many places. Area 51 in Nevada; Dulce, NM; China Lake, CA; near Phoenix, AZ and at strange places in MO, TX, NC, CO. The Greys pilot our saucers and must live near where they are stored."

The interrogation continued for some time more, but Otis' resistance increased to the point he was avoiding answering more or providing additional information. They finally ended the interrogation and returned to the cafeteria.

Jane said, "You know that Otis has a strong mind. He certainly wasn't typical for a standard human." She laughed and continued, "That sounded weird. I just haven't run up against much resistance before, but then I haven't seized that many human minds before."

Sue said, "I haven't encountered any resistance before. I wonder what the doctors did in their genetic engineering and selective breeding program. I mean, they might have done some strange things, trying to create their Master Race. Could it be possible that they spliced in some DNA from the Arcadians? I would hate to think they might be cousins."

Dr. Wisscroff said, "I wouldn't put anything past that group, but I seriously doubt their genetic engineering technology would come anywhere near that of the Arcadians. I don't think we need worry much about it."

\*\*\*

President Thompson called the special meeting to attention, "Now that we have reviewed Mr.

Canton's report on Operation High Jump and Dir. Setliff's latest report from Antarctica, I would like to hear your comments."

Air Force General Ron Warner, Chairman of the Joint Chiefs of Staff, spoke up for the first time in any of these meetings and said, "Mr. President, I have also been doing some research with some surprising results. The U.S. Air Force has been designing, building and stockpiling fleets of flying saucers in secret since 1950. I really don't know why it has been so Top Secret, but it has been. My guess is that after the disaster of Operation High Jump our government recognized the potential threat from Antarctica. Luckily, in 1947 a crash of one of what must have been a NAZI flying saucers at Roswell, NM, gave us our first opportunity to get our hands on the anti-gravity technology. I can initially understand the need to keep it secret from the world, especially the Germans in Antarctica and even Russia; but the Russians recovered a crashed saucer and the same technology in 1963. Since our recovery, our scientists have been very successful in reverse engineering the anti-gravity and weapons technology at Area 51, and I'm sure the Russians have as well. Under our blanket of secrecy, controlled by the NSA, we more than duplicated their technology, with the help of the Greys, and manufactured a large fleet of advanced flying saucers and weapons for our defense. Apparently, the Russians have done likewise under the same secrecy.

As the size of this project expanded, maintaining this secret has become a massive and complicated undertaking. To keep it secret we had to build deep underground bases all over the country to hide them. This also included an interconnecting tunnel system for transporting them. The expansion of the tunnel network as it stands today, we are finding out, has been kept secret even from us. The bottom line, Sir, is that we have the technology, equipment, personnel and ability to defend against their attack."

"The bad news is that we may not control our own fleet. The latest report from Dir. Setliff was disturbing in that the captured, self-proclaimed, NAZI reports the locations of the Greys' saucer inventory matches the list of our own flying saucer bases. We don't think this is a coincident. The NAZI said the Greys were their pilots and living near their fleets, which ironically seems to match ours. It seems fairly obvious that when this war begins they intend to take over our saucer fleet, a masterful plan. They help us with the technology and we build them at our expense. When they take over our fleet, assuming their plan works, they would also have eliminated our ability to fight back.

Now, for them to be able to take over our fleet they would have to already be in control or have the strong ability to take control of our bases, at least the underground ones. I think we now understand the purpose of the implants. If the soldiers and or pilots at those bases are taken out by detonating the implants, no one is left to resist them. The Greys could simply enter the base from underground, get in the saucers and use them to kill the rest of us. That is actually an act of genius in planning. The Greys must have been planted to monitor and guide our development. They let us spend our money to build the fleet so they could take it over. I hate to say it again, but it's actually a brilliant long-term plan on the part of the NAZIs."

President Thompson had listened intensely without interruption, but he finally bellowed, "Just when the hell were you going to tell me about our saucer fleet?"

General Warner calmly said, "Mr. President, remember, the existence of our flying saucers and anything to do with them was tagged above 'Top Secret' and strictly controlled and monitored by NSA. All the people that knew were under strict orders to maintain secrecy and subject to severe penalties for violation. I could have been executed as a traitor for this violation of those orders."

The president calmed and said, "I'm curious. Why can you tell me now?"

"Well Sir, several things have changed. You fired the corrupted NSA Dir. Jones that was controlling me and the others and replaced him with Dir. Hawkins, who has released me. Also, until Mr. Canton's and Dir. Setliff's latest reports about Operation High Jump and the discoveries at Antarctica, we had no concern in this committee about flying saucers. Up until then our concerns were the corruption of military personnel via the implants, the tunnel network and the death and future protection of the Star Children. There was no need at that point to be concerned about our secret weapons. Once I realized all these issues were tied together, there was a need to know. The main reason, however, is that I love my country, and I'm a patriot. For my country I'm willing to break my vows."

"Thank you, general. You know, I'm concerned. You are too young to have been around during all this past history we are finding out about. Are there any high ranking, retired generals or admirals still around that would be able to remember and talk about this history? Maybe advise us."

"We will come up with someone and let you know."

President Thompson said, "So, now I think we see their plan. How do we foil those plans?"

The Sec. of Defense said, "As far as Antarctica, we can simply nuke it. Problem solved."

President Thompson bellowed, "Shut the fuck up you idiot. You are a politician. Be smart or keep your mouth shut. Do you even know what would happen if you nuked Antarctica? The environmentalist have been preaching about that for years. The ice cap would melt from a nuclear detonation at 100,000,000 degrees Celsius, and the sea level would rise 230 feet and flood all of the coastal cities, including here in Washington. It would create a world disaster. Forget about nuking Antarctica!"

"Are there any sensible ideas?"

General Warner said, "Well, Sir, we, the Joint Chiefs of Staff, have been discussing the problem, and I have been chosen to speak for this military group. With the addition of the information learned today I have altered our plan somewhat. I no longer believe the implants were installed just to force allegiance to the Greys will. Of course some are compromised for just that purpose, but I now believe most of those with implants, especially at the saucer bases, are to be executed at the onset of the war. I believe that is how they plan to take over. I'm assuming, and I think I'm correct, all our AF saucer pilots have received implants, maybe through dental appointment. They probably don't even know they have them. It just makes sense. Our saucers would be useless to us if the pilots were all dead. Also, we don't believe all those bases could be totally compromised. We know from the very first forced interview by a Star Child that the Greys have one main base, probably in Antarctica, and two other bases where the Greys work with compromised humans. We believe those areas to be Area 51 in Nevada and Dulce AFB in New Mexico. We believe there may be a third location somewhere near Luke AFB in the Phoenix, Arizona area, also identified from the same interview. We think these three location are interconnected via tunnels, which presents additional problems, since the tunnel system must also be closed down too, or at least controlled. We believe all the other bases only have secret Grey forces that do not interface with our military. They are probably staged to

235

invade those only after the onset of war. These bases should be easier to control."

Our plan of attack must be simultaneous at all bases. Our priority must be the pilots. We can start by completely shutting down all the saucer bases and concentrating on the barracks and living quarters, identifying those with implants and removing them as we go. We then systematically canvas the entire base, doing the same. Then we move underground and do the same thing. We have entire battalions cleared for this work, both Marine and Army. Since they have concentrated on compromising Air Force personnel, we plan to keep this an Army/Marine operation. When we launch our plan we will need presidential orders to overrule any NSA or CIA standing security orders. We don't want a gun battle among branches of service. We may, however, have to engage the Greys. They might fight back."

Dir. Hawkins asked, "What do we do with the Greys?

"If they don't surrender we kill them. If they do I'm not sure."

President Thompson said, "We take them back to Antarctica. That's where they came from, and from what I hear, they belong here on Earth. They seem only to be controlled by the NAZIs. Once we take care of the NAZIs the Greys would be free to resume their lives in their underground world."

"By the way, general, that sounds like an excellent plan. I will support and give you whatever you need. You have my approval."

Dir. Hawkins said, "General, as a former veteran myself, I'm wondering about all those veterans, pilots and soldiers, that are no longer in the service or retired that may have implants. What do we do about them?"

"My guess is that the implants are coded with a personal ID number in a database somewhere. I'm saying the Greys would have to know our personnel records to be effective, and they would know who is active duty and who is not. They had the ability to execute only those AF soldiers at the gym without killing all those with implants. So, I don't think the inactive vets have much of a risk. All those additional deaths in the general public would cause a media stir and would bring too much attention. Still, it's a good question. We can produce a printout of those in question and work through the Veterans Administration to bring them in for a medical check-up. Since you brought it up, I'm thinking it is something we should do first and immediately for all ex-pilots of the flying saucers. We can clear them just in case we fail in our other plan. At least we would have some pilots.

***

Jane saw Jerry and Mary steer the German Star Children back into the cafeteria, and the new ones looked far different from when they left. She noticed a spark of intelligence in their eyes and said, "Do you kids understand English now?"

Berta said, "We all do, and we learned far more than just English. We also went to see and hear Mr. Mum, and we know who we are. The Arcadian

237

archives taught us much. Those NAZIs starved us in many ways. As it turns out, food was the lesser of our needs. They starved us of our life by depriving us of education. Several of us are soaking up knowledge from the archive like a sponge. Being starved, then suddenly fed knowledge has created a strong hunger for more. I'm going back to the library as often as I can. The NAZIs called us stupid, but I am discovering that we are highly intelligent, just deprived of knowledge. We intend to remedy that."

Sue said, "Berta, you even sound different. I think you and the others are ready to begin learning about your powers. I suggest you do that before you delve back into the archives. You may need those powers soon. One thing for sure, we need you guys to establish your communication matrix before telepathic communications becomes so garbled it can't be used. Any of the Star Children can teach you about your dormant powers."

"What dormant powers?"

Tom laughed and said, "Ask Tina to teach you how to fly. That should get your interest quick enough."

Tina giggled and leaped into the air and floated, catching the awed attention of all the new ones. Tina said, "Follow me outside if you want to learn how to fly." The new Star Children followed her like she was the Pied Piper.

The rest laughed, knowing what Tina was going to do and how their interest would be captured by the powers. Many of the Marines followed too, wanting to see Tina fly. The other children followed, knowing they would be needed soon to teach the others. Tom knew that since they all now spoke English they would assimilate much quicker and become family.

Tom also noticed that many more of the group had found the silver suit warehouse, even Mrs. Wilks and Tina were sporting their new silver suits, and he noticed Dr. Wisscroff looking at Mrs. Wilks' exposed figure through the tight silver suit. His reduced age must be being felt in an increased libido. Tom wondered if he would have to push them together.

John said, "Mrs. Wilks, have you assigned quarters to the new German Star Children?"

"I was about to take them over before Tina started showing off." Laughter broke out.

John said, "I might suggest you run them through the silver suit warehouse. Their clothing is quite scrubby."

"Yeah, I agree. Those poor children have been so deprived, but they sure seem happy now. I'll take them shopping for toothbrushes and toiletries as well, plus Major Burns said he had a barber in his group. Now that they know what those things are, thanks to intense knowledge downloads. I wish that archive worked on me. It took years to educate me. It took them about ten minutes. It worked so well with them, I'm going to cycle the others through the library. You might want to try it, too."

"Well, I did learn German in about ten minutes. It's amazing, and I will try it again. I'm anxious to

239

learn about some of this Arcadian technology, but I'm kind of tired right now. I think I need a nap. Want a nap, Jane?"

Jane laughed, stretched out her arms in an exaggerated manner and said, "Yeah, it's nap time."

Sue animated a huge yawn, winked at Jane and said, "Tom, you up for a nap, too?" He just took Sue's offered hand and followed her out.

Jack and Janet weren't far behind the exiting pairs, but they said nothing, just followed.

The Combat Cooks were establishing a routine for the meals, which all were getting used to. When the evening meal time came, the cafeteria was again full with all hands. They had just finished their meal and having a second cup of coffee when Jack's phone chimed. John watched Jack's reaction. It wasn't happy or sad, just a look of understanding.

Since all were staring at him he said, "It's a report from Mr. Canton about the president's meeting today. They think they now understand the plan the Greys are following and have come up with our own plan. It seems realistic." He read the entire report to a very silent and attentive audience.

Dr. Wisscroff said, "The NAZI take over plan sounds feasible and workable. It definitely would work if we don't interfere with their plan. I like that general. He is a calm one and smart. I like his plan, too."

Berta shocked everyone when she said, "Just in case the general's plan doesn't work we should quickly and secretly install a disabling network in all the saucers, something the Greys don't know

240

about. That way if they do make it to the saucers they can't fly them off. Think of it as a safe combination code or key to a lock. If they are worried about the code or key being leaked to the Greys, we might even go so far as installing a defective necessary part in the saucers, but give our pilot the working part to replace it."

Dir. Setliff looked shocked but said, "That my dear is an excellent idea. I will pass it on as soon as we finish our discussion. Any other ideas?"

John said, "Well, I think they are right about the implants being coded and controlled, and there would have to be a control center. Maybe we should interrogate that NAZI again and find out where they are controlled from and take it out. If we can do that we change the dynamics of their whole plan and remove much of the risk for our counter-attack."

Jane said, "Oh, hell yeah. I want another crack at his mind."

Fred popped up and said, "Another thing I would suggest. Instead of trying to launch our attacks on all the bases simultaneously, I would suggest doing a dry run on one of the more remote and isolated bases first. That way we could confirm their assumptions and discover anything we might not have thought of. Some of us can go and help. We would pick up on thoughts that might disclose their secrets. Another thing that I'm concerned about is the possible existence of a hidden Grey colony near the bases. Maybe we could find it with our enhanced vision."

241

Dir. Setliff said, "All damn good ideas. Let's go talk to the NAZI now before I make my report."

Otis was as defiant as before, maybe more so. He had obviously been practicing blocking his mind from being seized, but Jane was ready and doubled her pressure. She had learned to improve her mental focus, plus John helped her with the seizing. When she grabbed his mind he resisted, but his mental brick wall quickly began to crumble and he finally fell into the full zombie zone.

Jane said, "Otis, how many implants has your group installed and into whom?

Otis said, "Many thousands in guards, soldiers, pilots, military officers, politicians, manufacturing executives, bankers, FBI, NSA, CIA. Oh, we put some in Star Children."

"How are they detonated?"

"Each one is coded and can be triggered individually or by groups."

"How are they triggered?"

"Our computer network can sort and execute by name, location, job or any combination of tags we wish. We send a data pulse with codes out over our own satellites."

"How do you maintain the accuracy of your information?"

"We are tied into the military networks through a link through your NSA."

"Where do you control the implants from?"

"Our main base in the Underworld."

Jane placed the picture on the table of the underground base she had taken and asked him to point out where the control center was. Otis just pointed and said nothing.

John looked at the "X" on the picture and said, "Damn, that looks like a very secure location. It's right in the center of their base and probably underground surrounded by lots of troops. To get it will take a major combat force on our side. We are talking about war here.

Jane said, "We have powers."

"That's true, but the one thing we had better not do is underestimate them. Remember, they have had over 70 years exposure to advanced technology. That's a lot of time to develop advanced technology, and let's not forget about all those saucers we saw. I'm just saying it might be difficult to take it out."

Berta said, "That may be true, but our saucers are far better than theirs."

Dr. Wisscroff said, "How do you know that, Berta?"

"Coming in in a saucer fascinated me, and I wanted to know more about them. When the Arcadian archive kept asking me if I wanted to know more, each time I said yes. I now know the technology involved, and our technology is far more advanced than the original Resis technology they reverse engineered. I've seen many of the NAZI saucers fly. They do have anti-gravity perfected, but it only creates zero gravity to make it weightless. They use magnetic drive for propulsion, unlike ours. That limits their speed and keeps them confined to Earth's atmosphere and gravitational pull. Our saucers actually use a gravity drive for both, which can achieve multiple light wave speeds. They can't manipulate gravity like we do."

Doc said, "Damn, I wish I could hook up to one of those machines. Can you teach me the math behind gravity drive?"

Berta said, "Yes, I now understand the language of mathematics. I can try to teach you, but the math is highly advanced beyond the human level of understanding. You may not be able to follow the math."

Doc laughed and said, "It's been a very long time since anyone has talked down to me like that when it came to science and math. I kind of like it. It means I'm going back to school. Learning new things has always stimulated my mind. We need to find a blackboard."

Dir. Setliff said, "What are we going to do about the implant control? I need to let the president know in my report I need to write. We could save a lot of lives if we can take it out."

Tom said, "Well, we need to go back in with our saucers and blast it to pieces. We also need to identify their satellites and go up and take them out, just in case they have a backup control somewhere else. Jack, can we get them identified?"

"I'll make that request in my report."

Tom said, "Let's go back to the cafeteria, eat and talk about our assault on the, what did Otis call it, the Underworld? At this point that seems like the most important action we can take."

Major Burns said, "If it is going to be an assault, let me show you what we found at the armory. One of my men found it yesterday, and it is quite impressive. It's on the way back."

Major Burns led them to an off-street and into a large building. The first thing Tom noticed when they entered was an indoor firing range. It was indeed impressive. Major Burns took them into a back room that was full of strange looking weapons, one of which was a hand-held pistol. It had several circular glass rings surrounding a longish octagon crystal. It looked alien, which it was, but was made to fit a human size hand.

Major Burns picked one up and went back to the firing range. He said, "This shoots out a focused beam of light in pulses of about two foot long. It is quite accurate, devastating, and almost instantaneous."

To accent his description he pointed and fired. The crystal and glass rings flared red and a short bolt of red shot from the end of the crystal. Tom couldn't see the light bolt moving, but the brick backstop instantly exploded.

Tom said, "Wow! That is impressive."

Fred laughed and said, "That's not so impressive. I think I can do that with my finger." Everyone laughed, but Fred said, "No, really. let me think about it for a second. I think I can. Watch."

Fred thought for a moment, pointed his finger like it was a gun and pretended to fire. He even said, "Bang!" Everyone would have laughed if the backstop hadn't exploded. Fred said, "Gravity and light controls is all it takes." Fred blew on the end of his finger, at which point the room exploded in laughter.

When the laughter died down Major Burns said, "Obviously the Star Children don't need these pistols, so we can assume they were made for your human protectors … us. With your permission I will disperse them to my Marines." Tom nodded.

Jack was still full from the large lunch he had eaten late, but he was in need of coffee. He got his coffee and sat down to write his report. The information he had could be useful, and it needed to get it to the president as soon as possible. Things were beginning to come together. They had targets and a plan, and if the NAZIs continued to delay their war, they had a chance. Jack was actually surprised they hadn't launched their war. If the enemy waited much longer they would lose the element of surprise. Well, they had already lost that, but they didn't really know it yet.

Jack finished his report and sent it off. He then joined in the planning for the attack in the Underworld. They were just finishing up. The plan was simple: they would enter invisible like they did before with three saucers and attack the building with the saucer lasers. They would take some Marines just in case, but they didn't plan on landing.

The trip was identical to the last one, and Tom led the way. They began their descent into the black hole. Everything was going as smoothly as the last time until the saucer stopped suddenly and alarms flashed. The flashing writing said, "Force Field Ahead."

"Tom said, "What the hell is a Force Field?

Dr. Wisscroff said, "It means they were expecting us. It means we aren't going any farther. We better get the hell out of this confining hole and quickly."

Tom pinged the others, *"Force Field evacuate! This plan is an abort."*

They immediately shot back up out of the hole and headed back to the Sanctuary.

Dr. Wisscroff said, "This is a smart saucer. If we would have actually hit the Force Field we probably would have triggered another one at the top. We would have been trapped, and who knows what else we might have set off. That was close. I think the first time we went in there we just got lucky. They must have been lax with their security after decades of no attempts, but after we took the Star Children they knew their security had been breached. We'll have to find another way in. We need to talk to Mr. Mum again."

Once they returned and discussed it they realized how lucky they had been … both times.

Major Burns said, "Now that I think about what happened, it scares the hell out of me. We came so close to being trapped in that hole. If the trap had succeeded, well for one thing we wouldn't have been able to get out of the hole, and they could have taken their time firing at us with who knows what weapons they have. I know the saucers and the kids have defenses, but they can't last forever. Thank God for the warning."

Dir. Setliff sent out an immediate message to the president, notifying him that their failed attempt to take out the control center. He received an immediate response from Mr. Canton notifying him that the recommended strike on our base in North Carolina was still on for in the morning. He said the general consensus of the group was that they can't wait, and that they had located where the pilots were stationed, some at military sites distant from the actual underground facility housing the saucers. Because of this they felt safe in securing the area base and pilots. The actual securing of the underground facility would be a separate assault. He provided the coordinates of the base and time to meet to the director, and requested help from the Star Children for the saucer facility.

Thirty minutes later Dir Hawkins messaged him with the coordinates of three satellites he suspected were the NAZI satellites in question. He said there was no way of knowing for sure, because the NSA agent in charge of that department had had an implant and was sent to the CIA holding area. He had sent word to the CIA interrogators to verify this information, but since they couldn't find the owner or purpose of the three satellites, they strongly suspected these are the ones they were looking for.

Dir. Setliff read both messages to the group and asked for comments.

John said, "They aren't giving us much time, are they? But, since the satellites could be an important factor in this assault, Jane and I can go take out the satellites. Berta, you did say we could take a saucer out of our atmosphere? I assume the saucer can provide oxygen to us at that altitude?"

Berta said, "That is correct. The saucer is quite capable of interplanetary travel, and the saucer constantly cleans, refreshes and alters the breathing air inside. There should be no problem, and I'll go with you."

"That's nice to know. OK, we volunteer to do that job. You OK with that, Jane?"

Jane smiled and said, "Just try and go without me."

Dr. Wisscroff said, "I've been an astrophysics for many years. I'm not about to miss an opportunity to go into space. I'm going with you."

Dir. Setliff said, "One problem solved. We need someone to talk to Mr. Mum and find another way into the Underworld."

Mary looked at Jerry, received an affirmative nod and said, "Jerry and I can take care of that."

Dir. Setliff said, "Another problem may be solved. Tom, I assume you and Sue will take Janet and I to the meeting?"

"You bet your ass we will. I think we will take two saucers, because most of us Star Children want to get involved. Of course we can't all go, and it shouldn't need that many."

Major Burns said, "I want myself and a few of my Marines to go also. We can take the new weapons we discovered."

Tom said, "We need a third saucer pilot team, then."

Before anyone could say anything, the ten year old Tina blurted, "I want to fly it. You know I love flying. Fred can be my copilot." A startled Fred nodded agreement. He wasn't about to be left out.

Tom looked at Sue, shrugged and said, "Well, I know you will make a great pilot, just don't show off in the saucer like you do in free flight." Tina grinned and others laughed.

Gary said, "If we need a fourth pilot crew, Bridget and I would love to fly it. We can take Don and Karen with us and some Marines."

These four were all from the second group of twelve. They had witnessed and survived the alien's attempt to kill them and how the Star Children had saved them. Their fear turned to amazement of the powers then dormant within them and were thus dedicated to learn and use their powers to join with the others of their kind. They had been watching and learning since their arrival and wanted to be involved, and this was their opportunity.

Sue said, "Well, why not. Let's get some experience. Don, you and Karen might as well take your own saucer and get the experience, too."

Dr. Wisscroff said, "I've been thinking about the potential conflict underground. I think a few of the Star Children should visit the library and learn how to speak the Resis language, assuming it's there and can be spoken by humans. It might be nice to be able to talk to them and understand what they are saying to each other and to us."

Bridget said, "The four of us can visit the library and learn the Resis language. From what Mr. Mum said about visiting them, I think they must have been able to communicate with them. We can stop by and ask Mr. Mum on the way to the library."

Tom said, "Well, I guess we will take four saucers. Get it done guys. Anything else?" They all looked around but nothing was said. "Ok group, let's get some sleep and leave early."

# Chapter 10
## (First Engagement)

Gary, Bridget, Don and Karen left the planning meeting immediately for the Arcadian podium and Mr. Mum. Mr. Mum was still standing there looking around at no one in general, but when they arrived he looked directly at them and waited.

Bridget seemed to be the strong-willed person of the group and said, "Mr. Mum, is the Resis language available in the library, and can we speak it?"

Mr. Mum said, "Yes, it is available, and you are capable of voicing all their vocal tones. The language can be difficult but achievable. When you connect to the archive ask for Underworld languages, then Resis. The archive will download the data into your sub-conscience along with any moral values and traits recorded by our research team."

"Thank you, Mr. Mum. We truly appreciate your assistance and wish you were still alive to see the result of all your work and help us in this conflict."

"I wish the same, and we hope to help you in any way we can. We tried to prepare you for any eventuality, but I'm sure there will be situations we may have missed. Still, you Star Children have been given our race's intelligence, and we are confident you will keep our race alive. Good luck, children."

Mary and Jerry had followed Bridget's group and had heard Mr. Mum's response and Mary said, "Mr. Mum, we all appreciate all you have done for us. We will do everything in our power not to let you down." Mary then proceeded to explain in detail what had happened in the shaft to the Underworld and why they were attempting to return and what they hoped to accomplish. She then asked about an alternate route into the Underworld.

Mr. Mum said, "Yes, I understand the problem and need to accomplish the destruction of the Control Center. I will say that you were lucky that the saucer detected the force field. It could have been disastrous for the team. We have several force fields installed to protect the Sanctuary. Ours are smart force fields in that they scan and detect threats logically. Our scans would have detected Star Children and allowed you through, therefore the others of your group were not repelled. I would imagine theirs are far more crude in design, but they must also have an override, probably in their saucers or a device they carry to trigger the override for their force field. Possibly, if you capture one of their saucers you might find that device. It would still be risky, however. They did not have force fields when we entered into the Underworld. This must be a later development of their stolen technology from the ancient ones."

"There are underwater entrances for the submarines and saucers, but they are likely also protected by force fields. We know of no confirmed, alternate route into the Underworld, but there may be interconnecting small tunnels between our cavern and theirs. Their cavern is massive and spreads out somewhat close to our, but we never had the need to search out any interconnect. We do have extensive data mapping of both caverns, however, that can be compared and searched. Possibly, you might find an interconnecting shaft. I suggest you go to the archive and retrieve the mapping data. Request Sanctuary mapping, then Underworld mapping. Between the two you might be able to find something, if it exists. Our research did not include the smaller shafts, which are numerous. By smaller I mean, too small for a saucer to enter. That search would have to be accomplished by free flying."

"Thank you, Mr. Mum."

Jerry and Mary joined the others in the Arcadian Archive (library). By the time they got there the other four were happily communicating in what sounded like grunts, growls, yaps and squeals, with a few added wobbling, deep tones here and there. It sounded completely alien, which of course it was; but they seemed completely comfortable in the language.

They followed Mr. Mum's instructions and received the archive mapping for both areas. Jerry was amazed with the information and how it presented itself in his mind. The information was there as a visual in his mind, which he could zoom in for details. He pulled both maps together and

254

was easily able to see them referenced together. Once compared, it was simple to see the closest areas that offered the best opportunity for a potential connection. Unfortunately, there was at least a mile at the closest point separating the two cavern areas and spread out over several miles horizontally along the lower level Sanctuary wall, not to mention the vertical area. The maps showed full digital representation of the walls and openings of smaller caves leading off into the blank area, which were many. Telemetry showed the depth and shape as far as the telemetry from outside could reveal, but past that the map was blank. That was their job now, and it wasn't going to be easy.

As they were about to leave the archive Mary said, "Maybe we should learn Resis also, just in case we run into some." Jerry nodded.

Since the importance was so high, Mary and Jerry decided to go straight to work. From their comparison they knew the closest and most likely place to start was the fourth and fifth levels under the iris door below the saucer storage. They floated down and began searching.

The wall was craggy with many rocks jutting out and many indentions and caves. They quickly discovered that by pinging and connecting their minds they combined each other's discoveries, which registered into their common data map. Each telemetry search through their enhanced vision registered on their main joint data map, and the blank areas began to fill in. They quickly eliminated most of those searched, but some caves they had to float into, some hundreds of feet before they ended in a dead end or narrowed path. Separately they covered much more area. Jerry and Mary could follow each other's progress by watching the map filling in. After hours of searching they had hardly made a dent in the search area.

When they were both outside together Mary said, "We are never going to get anywhere using this method. It will take us weeks at this rate. We've certainly recorded a lot of additional mapping, but really, who cares about mapping. Let's try something different."

Jerry said, "Well, I guess we could concentrate only on the bigger entrances. I guess we could do a less detailed quick scan by flying over the entire wall to look for the larger ones."

"That's a good idea, but I've also noticed some with more water flowing out of them. That could mean they are deeper, more chance of seepage. Let's look for both."

They began flying back and forth across the entire planed search area scanning the wall and recording the data. After a couple of hours they had a fairly detailed surface area map identifying only ten potential larger caves with water flowing out. They each took one of the caves and floated deeper and deeper. Jerry ran into a dead end at about a half mile, and noticed Mary's ended a little sooner. They met outside and started again. Jerry noticed this cave split at several locations, but he always followed the largest branch with the most water

256

flowing. He got in almost a mile and hit another branch. Both branches were about the same size and very little water flowing in either one. As he floated, trying to decide which way to go, he noticed a dim glow in one of them and decided to check it out. Jerry smiled when he identified the glow. It was algae generating light, the same kind of light they had seen in the Underworld. The algae would have spread into this cave only if it was connected to the Underworld. He pinged Mary, *"I think I've found something. Come to me."*

Mary's cave had run into another dead end, and she was returning when she got Jerry's ping. She quickly viewed the map and saw Jerry's cave was surprisingly close to the Underworld, and she followed the contour of the map. She saw Jerry as she raced toward him. He was smiling and pointed to the glowing algae, and she knew immediately what that meant. They followed the cave about another thousand feet and saw a small opening full of light. When they approached the opening they were both smiling hugely. The exit was high on the Underworld's inside wall, and they could clearly see the Underworld below. They had succeeded in their search for an alternate entrance to the Underworld.

They had worked through the sleeping time and knew everyone would be awake and already on their way to the first engagement and sent out a general ping to all, letting everyone know that they had been successful in finding an alternate route into the Underworld. Now they had to go to the library to figure out how to upload their updated mapping data, then get something to eat and some well-deserved sleep ... together. Few knew that they were already paired together, but Jerry and Mary weren't trying to hide their feelings and really didn't care who knew. They just knew they were paired together for life.

***

As Tina promised, she had returned to Tom and Sue's quarters, but she took over the other bedroom. Tom was very comfortable sleeping with Sue, especially since they had become lovers as well. The two of them had been inseparable since they met, and they both liked it that way, but Tina was like their little sister and was very welcome.

Tina woke them up early saying, "The Army guys know we are going into battle and prepared breakfast. You guys need to stop kissing and come eat. We need to go soon."

They were actually sleeping and not kissing, but they found it funny. But, Tina was right, they did need to go soon. They dressed into clean silver suits and joined the others in the cafeteria. As they went through the buffet line, Tom thanked the Combat Cooks for their kind consideration for an early meal. Smiles greeted him through the line.

Tom was shocked and said, "Where the heck did you find bacon and eggs?"

The chief cook laughed and said, "That forest down below has hogs and chickens. We just harvested some."

"I'm glad you did. I love bacon and eggs. Good job!"

After a good, hardy meal and coffee the saucer assault team was ready. The teams proceeded to their saucers and flew out under the ice shelf and zoomed out and high in the sky and streaked toward the coordinates at the Air National Guard in Charlotte, NC. Tom felt comfortable flying now. It was simply an extension of himself. Now knowing the saucers were capable of multi light-speeds, he felt like pushing his comfort envelope and flew exhilaratingly fast. They approached the coordinates faster than he expected and had to slow quickly. Down they went until he saw a group of men standing outside the open door of a large hanger. His saucer floated above them, and they had no idea he was there. Tom slipped his saucer into the hanger and settled in a wide open spot and waited for the other three to settle. He lowered the ramp and allowed the saucers to become visible, surprising the group. Tom said, "It's your show now, Jack."

Dir. Setliff exited followed by Agent Welch, then him and Sue, Major Burns and four Marines. Those from the other two saucers quickly joined them.

Mr. Canton came to meet him along with the Sec. of the Air Force, Air Force Joint Chief and an Air Force colonel, Jack assumed to be the base commander of the Air National Guard base at Charlotte, NC. Standing to the side and stiffly at attention was an Army colonel in combat fatigues, Jack assumed was commanding the Army forces.

Dir. Setliff spoke first and said, "You do realize that we may be a little premature with this action, since we failed to take out their Control Center? We do have a team taking out the satellites, but it hasn't been accomplished yet. Additionally, we can't be sure there aren't alternate downlinks available."

Mr. Canton said, "This might be true, but President Thompson ordered it. He said it's a coin toss as to who starts first, and letting them start first could be devastating to our side. He wants to save what we can, that it can only get worse by waiting. He's angry."

"Colonel Smith is fully briefed and is cooperating completely. Once he saw the order from the president and saw who delivered it he was on board. We called ahead for a personal meeting with the colonel. After we met, the colonel ordered security and base personnel to stand down both here and at the underground base. Army Special Forces and Airborne Rangers out of Fort Bragg entered this base quickly and identified those with implants, especially the off duty pilots, and herded them into the large hanger next door. A team is in there now removing the implants. There are a lot. The Star Children would be a big help."

"Marine Special Operation Forces out of Camp Lejeune are dispatched to the underground base in the Black Mountains NE of Asheville, but we haven't heard any news yet."

Dir. Setliff asked, "How did you know where the underground base was and where the pilots were?"

NSA Canton laughed and said, "We knew where the secret base was all the time, we just didn't know its purpose. As it happens, saucer pilots have a special identifying job code number. We just identified where they were being housed. It got easy then."

Out of habit Tom checked those present for implants, especially the two colonels, and they were clear. The AF colonel did not radiate any hostility or fear, well maybe nervousness from the high ranking level of those present. But he wanted to test him and said, "Colonel Smith, where is the entrance to the tunnel network?"

Everyone turned to stare at the colonel, and he felt the colonel's sudden panic. Tom knew now that there was a tunnel system and the colonel knew where it was, but there was still no hostility.

Mr. Canton said, "Colonel Smith, we all know the orders and threats issued to you by the NSA. Many of us received the same, but these presidential orders supersede any previous orders. Those previous orders have been canceled by order of the president. In fact, most of those issuing those orders have been arrested as traitors."

The colonel stood silent for a moment then said, "Very well. I stand relieved of those orders. I would, however, like to get something in writing. I will take you to the entrance. It's close in the next big hanger and connects to the Black Mountain complex."

The Sec. of the Air Force said, "Thank you colonel. I will see that you get something in writing."

Dir. Setliff was shocked and said, "Tom, how did you know there was a tunnel system here? We didn't."

Tom said, "I didn't, but I assumed there might be, since the pilots live here. The colonel confirmed it and also his allegiance. I trust him now."

As soon as Sue heard the request for help she ushered the other Star Children to the hanger. Surprisingly, there were about one hundred and fifty pilots and soldiers in there. Some were on cots being worked on by the medical team, but she could tell it was a slow process for them. Sue yelled out, "Pilots and soldiers, form up in six lines, pilots first. You have implants that must be removed quickly. If not they will kill you. We can remove them for you quickly, but it will hurt. But the pain is far less than dying. Hurry up."

The fifty pilots were scared but quickly lined up in six lines. Sue pinged, *"Fred, Bridget, Karen, Don, Gary and myself will remove the implants. Tina, you watch for any hostile vibes. I hope you all know how to do it. Seize their mind, find it at the back of the nose under the brain, pull it out, and don't forget to cauterize the wound and stop the bleeding. We'll do the pilots first then the soldiers. Everyone cool with this?"* She received six affirmative pings in return.

Sue had done it before, but the others hadn't, so she watched to see if there were any problems. It went well on their first ones. Satisfied, she started on her line. They all began to float and stack the implants against the wall, just in case they went off. It began to get easier and after about twenty minutes they had cleared all the pilots. The pilots were uncomfortable but relieved, even smiling afterwards. They then started on the soldiers and got about halfway finished when the stack of removed implants exploded. One even exploded in front of one of the soldiers she had just removed it from. Sadly, over forty of the soldiers collapsed to the floor, dead.

Sue immediately pinged Tom, *"It's started, here anyway, they just detonated the implants, but we saved all the pilots here and about half of the soldiers."*

Sue, immediately went to the pilots and said, "OK, you saw what happened. That could have been you. Sorry to be so blunt, but I need answers, and I need them now. Are there Greys at the saucer base?" She detected confusion. They didn't know what she was talking about and therefore assumed there were no Greys there. That meant they had a little time before the Grey assault.

"How many saucers are stationed there?"

One captain said, "There are a hundred and two."

"How long is the trip to the saucer base from here in the tunnel, and are there other tunnels to other places?"

The same captain said, "The trip takes about fifteen minutes, and there are two other tunnels from here. They don't tell us where they go, but one goes north and one goes south. The one to Asheville goes west and continues."

Sue thanked the captain and meant to ping Tom, but pinged all with the information she just collected and waited.

Outside, Tom blurted, "Damn! They just detonated the implants here and forty of our soldiers are dead, probably all those at Asheville too. We were able to save the pilots that we had in the hanger and about half the soldiers. We have to move fast now, or we will lose the saucers we have at Asheville. The Greys will deploy their forces and pilots now. We have to get troops there before they do.

Colonel Smith said, "My God. This is real! Hurry, get your forces into the hanger. We can take the magnetic train. It's very fast."

The Army colonel, previously silent through the discussion, came alive and began barking orders into his communication net, ordering commands, troops and equipment on the double to the designated hanger.

Colonel Smith, now extremely motivated, took off running toward the larger hanger, leaving the rest running to catch up. Tom could already see trucks full of Special Forces or Rangers speeding toward them.

As soon as the colonel entered, he bellowed, "Open the wall ... now!"

There must have been someone constantly at the controls, because Tom heard a clank and what previously appeared to be an outside, solid wall began to separate, showing a wide-open space with a huge elevator platform large enough for several trucks. The colonel waved the entering trucks on to the platform. Tom and his group, now including the other Star Children, followed quickly.

Tom said, "You non-combatants should stay here."

Almost in unison they said, "We're going!" Tom shrugged.

The surviving soldiers and pilots came running. The pilot captain that spoke to Sue said, "We're going too. We know our way around down there and we can fly the saucers out if needed, some of them anyway."

The Army combat colonel said, "You soldiers don't have weapons. Stay to the rear."

One of the ranking AF soldiers said, "No Sir, but we have weapons at the other end, and it's our responsibility to defend the area. Plus, we know the environment and layout. You will need that when we get there."

"Very well. You stay close to me and follow my commands."

When all were on the platform Colonel Smith said, "Hold on to something, we are going down about a mile and will be dropping fast." He then pushed a button setting off alarm bells and sirens. The descent began slow at first then built up speed. Tom was thankful for the warning, because it began to feel like a free fall, then he felt more weight as the platform began to slow. By the time they came to the bottom it was normal speed, and once it stopped the Special Forces and Rangers poured out with weapons ready.

Colonel Smith said, "This part should be safe. Let's transfer over to the magnetic train. Drive your vehicles on to the flat cars."

The front and rear cars looked like a bullet with a flat bottom. Inside was hollow with benches. Tom suspected the pointed front and rear, pointing the other way, was to protect against wind resistance in either directions, since he also suspected the speed would be quite excessive to make the trip in fifteen minutes. There were no tracks or even wheels on the train. There were two continuous bars, like a rail, on the floor of the tunnel. The colonel had called it a magnetic train, which made sense. The bars must be for guiding and magnetic lift.

Everyone found a place and the colonel pushed another button and off they went. The trip was very similar to the elevator, it started off at a reasonable speed but escalated to a super-fast and blinding speed. Toward the other end the magnetic train slowed long before it ended.

Combat soldiers had their weapons up and ready as they jumped from the train and took guarding positions on the terminal, but there was no resistance. The AF troopers pushed passed the guards and entered into a locked warehouse. When they emerged they were heavily armed and took position at a new line. Both lines of soldiers moved forward into the complex. Soon they began seeing dead men laying on the floor as they progressed, many of them. They entered the saucer cavern to find more of the same. There were no live personnel of any kind, nor any enemy. The Special Forces continued their canvas of the complex to confirm. The full force dispersed to maintain total surveillance, while they established a command and communication center in one of the lower fortified rooms.

The Army colonel said, "It looks like we beat the insurgence here. Post monitors at all levels and on the tunnel. Mr. Canton, how do you expect them to enter?"

Tom answered instead, "From what the pilots said, they aren't aware of any Greys. So I expect they live hidden outside of this complex but reasonably close. I would expect them to either come by train or through the tunnel from their hiding place. It's possible, but unlikely, they may plan on breaking in a wall within the complex. Their goal is to obtain the saucers."

The AF colonel said, "They can't come by train. There are safety protocols that prevent trains from colliding, and when we launched our train any other coming here would have been prevented."

The Army colonel said, "If their goal is the saucers, get your pilots to get them the hell out of here and disable those you have to leave behind. Send your train back so the track is clear. We need to control our engagement location by letting them

267

bring their train in. Also, get someone to open the upstairs door for our troop access."

Colonel Smith said, "I can move the train to a side area and clear the main track. That will allow the Grey's train access." He pointed to one of his pilots and then the track. The pilot nodded and ran to do so. "Make what the colonel said happen. Disable those other saucers you aren't able to fly out of here. I don't know how, maybe pull a wire or something, then launch and go to the saucer base in Alpine, Texas. Be careful, you may have a battle there, since the same thing is going on there."

Tom said, "Wait! Send them to the main base, fuck secrecy. If they go to the saucer base our ground forces won't be able to tell friend from foe."

Colonel Smith said, "Belay my previous order. Fly to Laughlin AFB at Del Rio, Texas. We'll send you the coordinates."

***

John knew taking out the satellites would take some time, so he decided to get some sleep and embark when the others left in the morning. His team loaded and left under the ice shelf when the others left, but headed toward the stars instead. He had decided to start in the west and pointed toward those western coordinates over Asia and the Pacific. Berta said he could go a lot faster, but Dr. Wisscroff was enjoying the adventure and was soaking in the sites, so John didn't push the speed.

John said, "Jane, have you communicated with President Pramin since you left? He probably should be kept informed. I mean you are a Star

Child, but you are Russian, too. They have the same problems that we do."

Jane looked at John and said, "I hadn't even thought about it since I discovered I was a Star Child. I guess you are right, though. Russia does have the same problem. Still, I don't want to complicate political relations with the U.S. and Russia. I really don't want to get in the middle of politics."

Dr. Wisscroff said, "I can understand that. Just tell him enough to Force President Pramin and President Thompson to communicate, and let them worry about the politics."

"Great idea." Jane structured a short e-mail: Ask President Thompson about the real reason for the implants, about the Underworld, flying saucers and the NAZIs. "That should stoke his curiosity and get him to call." They all laughed.

John turned to Berta and said, "You said these saucers are capable of interplanetary flight. Are you saying the Arcadians came in these saucers?"

"The Arcadians came in a mothership. What I meant by that statement is they are powered the same, but once they came here they had no need for the mothership and hid it in the ice shelf. It is very large."

Jane said, "While we are traveling and have access to the Arcadian archive, I think we should learn the Resis language." Berta nodded and slipped on her headset.

John's team approached the geostationary distance for satellites, the distance where a satellite in orbit turns the same speed as the earth and becomes essentially stationary to a spot on Earth. There is nothing magical about it. It is just math, but all geostationary satellites line up in this belt above the equator. Since there are many satellites in this belt it gets a little crowded, especially at high speeds. John kept well under this belt until they got close to the provided coordinates, which were lit in red on the dome. John eased closer until he actually saw the satellite and focused. He mentally projected a bolt of laser light at it, and it instantly exploded. One down.

They then turned back, descended below the satellite belt and headed east again. Their target now was a satellite stationed over Central America that covered most of the US. There was no trouble finding it and it exploded. Only one more to go.

They continued east at a high rate of speed, which pleased Berta greatly. Before they got there, John received Sue's accidental ping, notifying every one of the detonation of implants in North Carolina. Now he felt badly, thinking it might have been his fault, that he should have flown faster or started last night. John felt that all those deaths were his fault. His emotions flooded him, and his shoulders heaved with heavy sobs.

Jane saw and felt his ruptured emotions and took control of the saucer. Jane located the third satellite and destroyed it. In the background she heard Berta telling Dr. Wisscroff what had happened.

Dr. Wisscroff slipped his arm around John's huge shoulders and said, "John, it's not your fault. The blame is on the NAZIs. They killed those people. Hell, we aren't even sure if these satellites controlled the implants. Remember the ones we save, because they want them all dead. This is war, John. People are going to die. Our job is to save as many as we can."

John sobbed, "I should have been faster."

"You can't know the future. Hell, if President Kennedy had known the future he wouldn't have gone to Dallas. Now suck it up, John. We need you."

Jane said, "I love you, John, and I need you. We need you. What do we do now?

John registered the words of Dr. Wisscroff and Jane. He forced his mind to calm, shook his head to shed the emotional cobwebs and did what Doc said, he sucked it up. He reengaged his intellect and said, "Well, there is obviously a war going on. Let's find out where we are needed."

***

Tom was impressed with the Rangers and Special Forces. They knew exactly what to do and did it. He, on the other hand, didn't have a clue, but he figured he would learn as they went along. The magnetic train was moved and the main track was cleared, the combat forces were fully deployed and ready for an assault, and he had heard that the Marines topside had entered the complex, the saucers without pilots had been disabled and those with pilots were taking off through a hole in the side of the mountain. All they could do was wait, so that is what they did.

While he waited Tom received a ping from John, *"All three satellites are destroyed. I'm very sorry if I was a little late. I received Sue's ping about the implants being detonated. We are finished here. Where do you need us?"*

Tom pinged, *"We are waiting at the tunnel entrance at the saucer base for a Grey assault. We were able to save fifty of the saucer pilots, and they are flying some of the saucers out to save them. They are going to Laughlin AFB in Del Rio, Texas. We have another Army assault team at Laughlin AFB and at the Saucer base hidden near Alpine. I have no idea if they were able to save any of the pilots there or if they were successful in preventing the Greys from taking over. It looks like the Greys are using the tunnel network, so there is probably a tunnel between the two facilities there. I think the best place you can go is Del Rio. You'll know how to engage once you get there. I'm sending both coordinates."*

Dir. Setliff shot off a message to President Thompson letting him know the war had begun and what had occurred at Charlotte, NC."

CIA Dir. Martinez must have been with the president, because he sent a response, "Thanks for notifying us. Let us know what you need us to do. The president also wanted me to inform you that the VA had jumped on our request to pull in ex-saucer pilots and identify and remove implants from those pilots. The VA reports that they have identified and

272

cleared about three hundred pilots from all over the country, and the president reactivated them to active duty. So, where do you need them?"

Dir. Setliff messaged back, "Send about fifty or so to Charlotte to fly those saucers to safety. Send the rest to the AFB in Del Rio, TX. Also, check your implant captives at Langley to see if there are any deaths. The enemy detonated some implants, but we need to know if they detonated all areas."

Tom heard the Army colonel's com report that a train was coming. He then heard the colonel announce to the troops to stand ready to repel an attack. Tom could now hear the train coming through his enhanced hearing. He motioned for Dir. Setliff and his D.C. associates to move behind a wall, but he, Sue and the other Star Children remained in the open. With their shields they remained relatively safe. The train came to a sudden stop and literally hundreds of tall, skinny Greys leaped to the terminal floor, firing lasers as they came. The troops began firing back, some falling on both sides. Bolts of light and smoke filled the terminal. Many of the Greys in front held a clear shield that seemed to repel the troops' bullets. Tom mentally seized a shield and yanked it out of a Grey's hand. He floated it toward Major Burns, who grabbed it and held it in front of him. The shield repelled the laser blasts as Tom had hoped. Tom immediately pinged, "Take the shields and give them to our Marines." The shields began to be seized and floated toward our side. Without the shield line Greys began falling faster, but there were many charging in reckless abandonment of fear toward our lines, firing as they came. They didn't seem to care if they were hit. Their onslaught began taking a toll on our troops. Tom projected a shield to protect our forces, but the shield worked both ways. His shield repelled the laser blast, but bullets wouldn't pass either. He had to pull it back, but replaced it with bolts of heavy gravity that knocked the Greys down. Other Star Children yanked laser pistols out of Grey's hands, launched gravity bolts or lifted whole groups into the air and left them hanging there to be shot, but still they came en mass, threatening to overrun our line of defense.

Tom heard noise behind him and turned to see Marines pouring off of the elevator platform that had just arrived. The Marine Special Operations forces had finally arrived from topside and joined the ranks of the Army defenders, turning the tide of battle. The Greys began falling like dominoes. The Greys were defeated but still they came, almost to the last combatant. They would have all died if Bridget hadn't yelled in Resis, "Stop charging, lay down your weapons, hold your hands high and we will stop killing."

Those few Greys remaining alive froze at the sound of their own language. They looked at each other, dropped their weapons, raised their arms and stood still.

The Army colonel bellowed, "Cease fire!"

A squad of Special Forces ran forward to seize weapons and lead the remaining nine live Greys at gunpoint to a holding area.

Bridget came forward and said to them, "I'm pleased you listened to me. You were defeated and there was no need for further deaths. You will not be killed if you remain calm and cooperate."

One of the Greys said, "Who are you? How is it that you speak our language?"

Bridget said, "I am an Arcadian. We know your language."

The Grey said, "Why didn't you kill us? We were told humans wanted us dead and will kill us all."

"Well, that is simply not true. Who told you that lie? We killed here because you attacked us. We stopped killing when you gave up. We mean you no harm … never have.

"Our home is in the Underworld. The humans there told us that. They conquered us and control us. They told us they are your enemy and will prevent you from killing us if we remain loyal. They are keeping you out of the Underworld so you can't kill us."

"Another lie. Most humans don't even know about the Underworld and that you live there. The Arcadians knew but kept it a secret."

Gary had come up beside Tom, Sue and Dir. Setliff and interpreted what was being said. Tom found it strange that Bridget would call herself an Arcadian, but after he thought about it, he realized she was right. They were Arcadians.

Tom said, "Bridget, find out if there are any more of them here and where they came from in the tunnel."

The Greys must have been accustomed to answering questions from humans, because when she asked the Grey said, "We all came from our cave to attack and get the saucers. We have failed to do so, and we will be killed, our families back in the Underworld, too. Our cave is not far from the next stop. It is not a terminal used much, mostly for clearing the track if necessary. We walked to get to the terminal and called for the train."

Bridget said, "Thank you. I'm not sure what we are going to do with you, but you will not be killed unless you force us to. Those you call Underworld humans are our enemies. It may be that we can help each other."

As Gary finished interpreting Bridget and the Greys' conversation, the Army colonel relaxed and said to his captains, "There is no longer a threat here. This engagement is over. Maintain security, but load up the dead and wounded on the train for the trip back to the main base. Gather up the Grey's weapons and shields. We will use them and steal the technology. Colonel Smith, please notify your base hospital that we have incoming wounded, and be ready. Another thing you better do is get your saucers immediately identified with some kind of logo or marking, so they can be identified from any foe."

Colonel Smith said, "I'll see to it immediately."

The Army colonel called the senior general, directors and other top decision makers together and said, "Any ideas how we proceed from here?"

Dir. Setliff said, "I think we are at the center of the war by reaching the tunnel network. I think we should follow the tunnel network, cleaning as we go. I mean, why go back up and worry about trying to reenter to the deep underground base when we are already here, and we can get to the next one by this magnetic train. We have the high chain of command already with us to pull rank."

Mr. Canton said, "Interesting idea, but we don't know where the tunnels go or what we will find there."

"Well, that's kind of the point isn't it? We need to know where they go and where the enemy is. What do you think, general?"

"I like the idea. The Sec. and I can issue a general order informing all commands that we are conducting a surprise inspection of Top Secret facilities on order of the president, and they are to cooperate fully. That should do it, but we need troops to go with us in case we run into more Greys."

The Army colonel said, "Yes, for sure. We will go with you."

The Marine colonel had joined them and said, "We will go also. We don't want the Army to have all the fun." Surprisingly, in the middle of all the deaths, laughter rang out.

Tom said, "I'm headed for Texas with Major Burns, a few of his Marines, Dir. Setliff, Sue and

277

Janet. We may need our saucers there. We'll take the train back when it goes. Bridget, you Gary and the Marines you brought in your saucer follow me to Texas. Tina, you and Fred come too. Don, you and Karen stay with the team here. It may be necessary to help them, especially if you run across any more Greys. Maybe you can talk them into surrendering." Tom expected compliance and turned to go.

Dir. Setliff received the message from Dir. Martinez he had been expecting. "Sorry, Dir. Setliff, I can't give you a definitive answer to the implants detonated. Unfortunately or fortunately, all the detainees at Langley had their implants removed, so we can't determine what implants exploded, but evidently at least some did. Unfortunately, we had the implants all together and they all exploded, but an explosion of some would set them all off. We just can't offer a guess."

"The activated ex-pilots are already en route. I might add, they are thankful to be saved and are motivated and hungry for action. We have already heard about the battle and your success. We hope the losses weren't too great. As always, let us know what we can do to help."

# Chapter 11
## (Second Engagement)

Now emotionally recovered, John resumed control of the saucer and streaked toward the coordinates given him for the AFB at Del Rio, Texas. John said, "Dr. Wisscroff, please message Dir. Hawkins and let him know we are on our way. Also, ask him the status there and find out if they saved any of the saucer pilots at the base." Dr. Wisscroff immediately pulled out his phone and began typing."

Before they reached Del Rio Dr. Wisscroff's phone chimed. He read the response out loud: "Yes, we saved most of the off duty pilots and soldiers but not all. We lost about ten and probably all at the underground base. We have a regiment of Military Police out of Fort Hood ready at the underground terminal waiting on a train to come so we can go to the saucer base. They are having difficulty at the saucer location. We have a regiment of Fort Hood's Stryker Infantry at the remote saucer base trying to gain access."

John said, "Good and bad news. Tell him to have two of the pilots meet us somewhere and send landing coordinates. Also, tell him we obtained information on the battle in North Carolina, hell he might not be aware of the battle, but let him know that the train has protocol to prevent two trains active on a track. If they can't get a train that probably means one is active delivering the Greys to the terminal, and that's how the Greys attacked at the other underground base. Tell him it sounds like the Greys might be waiting to ambush them when they come, but I may have a way to help. We can discuss it when we land soon."

The coordinates came to Dr. Wisscroff's phone as they were descending but in time to alter their landing site. As they slowly lowered they could see Dir. Hawkins and several others standing in a group, one he recognized as the Sec. of Defense and another was the Chairman of the Joint Chiefs of Staff, the big dog himself, General Warner. John settled his saucer beside the group completely unobserved and undetected. His saucer began to pulse visibly and the group jerked their attention toward the saucer as he lowered the bottom ramp.

Most recognized John from the president's briefing and came to greet him, Jane, and the others of his group, but John wasted no time in idle talk and said, "Warn your troops at the train that they will be going into an ambush. We are going to the saucer base and try to prevent the Greys from taking over the saucers, which they will definitely use against your troops at that end. We will get the doors opened from the inside so your forces can enter. Together I hope we can disrupt their attack on the train. Where are the pilots? I need them to go with us and show us the hidden saucer opening to the base."

The two pilots saluted him and one said, "Capt. James and Capt. McDaniel, Sir. We can show you the opening"

"Great! Go ahead and get in our saucer. We leave immediately. Dr. Wisscroff, please remain with this group. Explain what we have been doing and learn the same from them." John and his group turned to go, but he stopped and said, "Dir. Hawkins, grab a com unit from someone and go with us. We need to keep these guys informed." Dir. Hawkins turned to receive a com unit handed to him and followed John.

En Route John asked, "Berta, how are your powers? Have you learned how to use them all?"

Berta jerked alert at her name and said, "I still have some to learn, but I'm proficient enough. You know how hungry I am to learn. I practiced hard with the older Star Children."

"I need you to get the front door open if Jane and I get tied up. You will need to fly and use your invisibility shield. Can you do it?"

"Yes, I can do it."

As they approached the saucer base, Capt. McDaniel said, "See that cliff to the left up ahead? Underneath it is an opening. Fly under the cliff and up into the hole, then into the mountain. The saucer storage is below several hundred feet. Your next questions I'm sure is, 'Where is the outside door and how do you open it from inside?' The base external doors enters from the bottom of the mountain, which is roughly adjacent to the floor of the saucer storage area and horizontal for about five hundred feet. The floor also is adjacent to the train terminal. The outside, steel doors are activated and controlled by a control panel inside. It requires a code number (4952) then push the open button. This facility is mostly for storage, since we are so close to the AFB, most of the personnel stay on base."

John said, "How many saucers are stored there?"

"Typically, there are around three hundred at any given time, but this is not an active ready station. So, pilots and security personnel here is usually light. We take delivery here directly from contractors and distribute them as needed through the tunnel system."

John said, "Jane, I need you to stay with the saucer and down any saucers that come out. Berta and I will free-fly in invisible."

Dir. Hawkins said, "I just heard on the com net that their train has arrive at the AFB, and they are loading up."

"Crap." John said, "That means the Greys have probably already arrived here and unloaded. I will try to disrupt the Grey's ambush, while Berta gets the front door open. Are you ready, Berta?" Her face was ashen and stretched but nodded.

John turned over control of their saucer and opened the bottom hatch. He and Berta invoked their shield and invisibility bubble and drifted out of the hatch. They flew directly under the cliff and up into the hole and then down the shaft. The Greys were pouring into the chamber and building an attack line like had worked so well for the Special Forces in N. C.. There were many of them, but he didn't see a separate group headed for the saucers or the outside door. They were obviously relying on their successful assault using the pilots, something our forces would never do. This made Berta and his' jobs easier. Berta saw the side tunnel and disappeared down it, as he tried to figure out what to do to help.

Suddenly, John heard on the com-net that the train was slowing for the terminal, and on a sudden inspiration, pushed a line of gravity against the backs of the Greys, pushing many of the front line off the terminal and into the path of the oncoming train. Many Greys died as the train crushed them before it stopped. The confusion slowed the reaction time of the Grey assault forces, and the soldiers began firing before the train stopped. The Greys quickly recovered and were firing those deadly laser guns. Fortunately, many on the Greys front line had been carrying some kind of portable force shield. With most of those lost, many were falling on both sides, but the Greys had far more troops. John estimated there must have been over a thousand Greys. John continued to lob gravity grenades and light laser blasts into the Greys' line, but the battle remained mostly even. That's when the outside Marines came pouring out of the tunnel like a tidal-wave into the flank of the Greys, firing a barrage of bullets. Hundreds of Greys fell from the unexpected onslaught of bullets, and the Greys panicked, knowing they had lost the advantage and had nowhere to run. Even so, they continued to fight.

The battle was over, senseless to continue. John bellowed in Resis, "Surrender and live! If you continue to fight you will all die."

The Greys were shocked to hear their own language spoken and the meaning. Many froze and raised their hands high in the universal indication of surrender, and the remainder quickly followed their lead. Ceasefire was ordered, but all weapons remained at the ready, while soldiers went forward to seize weapons and herd the remaining fifty or so Greys away.

John settled to the floor before he became visible, shocking several of the soldiers near him. He walked directly to the commanding colonel and said, "Hello, colonel. I'm John Meeker. General Warner can vouch for us."

The colonel spoke into his com-net for a moment then listened and said, "You are a Star Child?" John nodded. "I suppose you are the one that warned us, opened the front door, performed that trick of pushing them into the route of our train, and spoke to the Greys?"

"Most of that." Berta visibly floated down beside him amid startled stares. "Berta here opened the doors."

The colonel said, "The general said give you anything you want, but I would have done that anyway. You, well both of you, saved a lot of soldiers today. Thank you."

John said, "What would you like us to tell the Greys?"

"Just tell them they will be taken to a holding area until we figure out what to do with them, but they won't be harmed unless they force us to. By the way, what do they eat?"

Berta said, "I will take care of that. I would like being on the controlling end this time. As far as food, you really don't want to know what they prefer, but they can eat most anything humans can eat. They can survive on MRE."

The colonel suddenly placed his hand against his com-net in his ear and listened intently. He said, "We are under attack by saucers outside." He then began barking orders to his troops.

John said, "We have someone outside that can help." He then pinged Jane, *"What's happening?"*

Jane pinged, *"Three saucers just appeared and began firing on troops outside. I'm on it."*

It happened so quickly. The saucers appeared without warning. Jane had been so intent on watching the cliff for emerging saucers that the other saucers appeared and began firing. It was actually Capt. McDaniel that noticed it first. When the pilot's warning came, Jane zoomed around the mountain. The saucers were doing major damage to the troops and equipment. Her immediate response was firing her own laser, exploding the closest saucer. The other two stopped firing on the ground troops and turned their attention in her direction, but they were unable to see her. It didn't stop them from firing blindly in her direction, but she had moved. Her next attack was with gravity. Jane's blast not only neutralized the saucer's gravity, but pulled it toward the ground. It hit hard and was immediately surrounded by troops. She did the same thing to the other one. The saucers would not be able to escape destruction, and the Resis knew it. The Greys reluctantly opened their hatch and came out and were immediately swarmed by troops.

Jane pinged, *"I destroyed one and grounded the other two. I want to land, but I don't want to get shot. Tell them I coming and friendly."*

John said, "Colonel, the saucers have been neutralized. No more immediate threat, and our saucer is landing. Tell those outside it is friendly." The colonel nodded and spoke into his com-net.

Jane landed and became visible, but maintained the shield, just in case. The reaction was mixed, but no firing. She opened the hatch and said, "Capt. McDaniel, I need you pilots to get into those downed saucers and try to find out where they came from. Afterwards, fly back to the base. I'll go ask the Grey pilots for information."

Jane walked to where the Grey pilots were being held and said in Resis, "Where are you based out of?"

The Greys were surprised, but only said, "We are based out of our cave."

Jane was instantly pissed and bellowed, "Don't play games with me you stupid lizards. You won't like the way I play. I want to know where you flew your saucer from. Tell me or I will hurt you badly." She had learned from the Arcadian download that the Greys had little respect for females of any race. They only respected power and force, but that they were easily intimidated. She had done both, plus they had killed a lot of soldiers to anger her. It really wouldn't take much pushing for her to kill them outright.

Both tactics worked. The Greys actually began to shake in fear and said, "You humans call the place Dulce, and we have many saucers and pilots there. We notified them of your attack, and they are coming. You will get yours soon, bitch."

She wasn't expecting that and immediately sent an open ping, *"I downed two Grey saucers and destroyed one. The two pilots are hostile and say they reported back and many saucers are en route. I only have one saucer to combat them. I need help!"*

***

Jerry and Mary got as much sleep as they could, but still woke up tired. It had been a very long day and stressful, but they had much to do. They made it to the cafeteria late and thankfully the Marine combat cooks immediately worked them up a meal, while they filled up on coffee. While they ate, several of the older Star Children came to sit with them. They were from the German group, although they all now spoke perfect English. Jerry had seen them, but hadn't been able to spend much time with them.

The one Jerry remembered was named Kurt said, "We want to help. We have been excluded so far, but we have now been educated and speak English, and we have learned the powers. We feel that we can help. We just need a chance. How can we help?

Mary said, "How many are there of you old enough?"

"Well, Hans and I, and there are about six others of us that are seventeen or older, but even the younger ones want to help. We want to belong and help you."

Mary said, "Oh, sweetie, you definitely belong. You are Arcadians and Star Children. You are family. Things have just been so hectic. So much is going on we haven't been able to help bring you along."

"We have been learning from the archive and practicing the powers with the other younger ones. They are quite proficient, also, you know. We all listen and watch, and we know more about what's going on than you might think. We also get the open pings, and we know that battles are going on. You guys need help, and we want to help."

Jerry said, "How do you suggest you help?"

Kurt said, "We want to man saucers and help in the battles. Also, we know you found a route into the Underworld and plan to infiltrate and destroy the Control Center. We know the Underworld, we can fight, and we want to go with you. You can't do it by yourself, and we can help."

Jerry looked at Mary, and Mary looked at Jerry. They both smiled and nodded. Mary said, "Go get your troops. Let's talk."

Kurt didn't hustle off. He only slightly cut his green eyes up, apparently pinging. Almost

288

immediately about twelve others came running. The group of older ones were Kurt, Hans, Max, Emma, Sophie, Mia and Hanna; but there were others younger by a couple of years.

Mary said, "How many of you have been through the archive training and are saucer knowledgeable?" She was shocked when they all raised their hands. "Wow! That's great."

One of the girls, Emma said, "We have all taken many downloads from the archive. We know much of the science used. We have had nothing else to do. Thank you for allowing us to help.

Mrs. Welks came with the others and said, "That's true. The kids are always at the library learning amazing things, even the young ones. Most of them are past doctorate level and into new science. When they aren't at the library they are at the gym or flying and exploring. You will find them very helpful in anything you wish them to do.

Jerry said, "We need saucer teams. I would say to you younger ones, become those teams, and do it now. The older ones, we need you to go with us and help us do the assault on the Control Center through the caves. We don't know what to expect against the NAZIs, and the assault will definitely be against them. It will be dangerous. Tell us what you know about the NAZI humans in the Underworld."

Hans said, "They are smart, big and mean. Most are as big as Tom or John, some bigger. Otis was a low-level NAZI assigned to us as a shitty job. Most are intelligent and can use mind control on the weaker ones. Their leaders are the strongest physically and with the best mind control, traits which they compete with in combat. I don't think we can seize their minds as easily as Otis. They are extremely strong and always carry laser weapons. Their favorite pastime is fighting among themselves in public arenas for sport and advancement. Sometimes they will fight multiple Greys at one time for sport. They always win and always kill the Greys."

"What do you know about the base"

Kurt said, "Some of us have been there on work details. The guards are mostly Greys with human supervision, but they do have entire military sections made up of only humans. They are used to keep the Greys in line. In their society only the NAZI humans are bosses or fill key roles. The Greys are trained to be the pilots. It has something to do with the UFO conspiracy theorist. If aliens are involved, the governments keep it secret, which the NAZI take advantage of, like they did with the saucer crash at Roswell and other places. They want Grey bodies found at crashes or downed saucers."

Jerry said, "That is very good information. We will take you seven with us. I suggest you go back to the library and download the maps we made. That way you will know the way back if we get separated or something happens to us."

Hanna said, "We already did. Like Mrs. Wilks said, we have been busy. We are ready to go now, and we know how important it is to take out that Control Center."

Jerry and Mary both laughed and Jerry said, "Well, let's go do it. You other kids go try out the saucers, get used to them and contact Tom and Sue or John and Jane to see where they might need you."

They were all smiles as they left to their tasks. The younger kids headed straight to the saucers, Jerry, Mary and the other older kids flew off to the lower chambers. The kids knew the route as well as he and Mary did. They shot through the winding and twisting tunnels until they reached the glowing algae, where they stopped for last minute planning.

Jerry said, "Kurt, take a look inside the Underworld and see if you can tell where we are in relationship to the base."

Kurt and Hans went forward and began a detailed study. After a while they called Emma and Hanna up to take a look. They seemed to agree and returned. Kurt said, "We think we see the lake where the base is. It's about six miles to our right."

"Well, let's invoke the invisible shield and take off."

Jerry and Mary led the way out of the opening and began flying. After a couple of miles the lake was clearly visible, right where they thought it was. After another three miles they could clearly identify their target. As they closed in they could see activity below. Grey's and blond humans mingled together performing some kind of work, but Jerry couldn't tell just what. Unfortunately, The work surrounded the target destination. They slipped closer and hovered, studying and searching for an entrance. He used his enhanced vision and looked through the building floor by floor. Finally, on the third level underground he saw what he believed to be a manned control room. He saw a data storage bank, computers, consoles and a transmitter. He could find no other entrance or exit. The only way into the complex was through the guarded door. It would be impossible to get by the guards undetected. While he hovered and pondered the problem one of the big, blond humans looked up, pointed directly at them, and shouted.

Kurt said, "That's one of the NAZI leaders, and he just saw us floating here and ordered an alert, something about troops and saucers."

Jerry thought quickly and remembered he had not gotten a download of the German language, and that was stupid. He looked down and saw the human staring directly at them. The man could definitely see them and began firing lasers at them. Luckily, they had shields, however. Jerry also felt a tingling in his mind, as if the man was trying to seize his mind, but Jerry forced it off. Jerry launched a gravity bolt at the man, but his bolt was diverted, evidently by the man. Jerry called for a withdrawal to a higher altitude.

Well, if they couldn't enter the building they would have to work from above. He and Mary and two others joined to send a joint and continuous shaft of intense temperature that melted through the roof and continued down, boring through the floors

292

into the third level. Once inside the room, they forced the heat shaft down hard into the room and released the heat into a thunderous explosion, demolishing the Control Room. To make doubly sure, they sent bolts of explosive, magnetic energy to fry any remaining electronics or traces of data. By the time they finished, the sky was full of red streaks of laser fire, all aimed at them, but the other children had built a solid force field bubble shield around all of them, and the lasers just bounced away.

With the job finished, they climbed to a safer height, and they all began launching gravity bolts and fireballs into those gathering below. Try as they did, the NAZI below repelled them all, but the Greys and some of the other humans didn't do so well. The Star Children raced away back toward their secret entrance. As they flew, remaining invisible, a saucer shot directly toward them, which Jerry found strange until it got close enough he could see a blond human at the controls.

The saucer didn't fire its laser. If it had, Jerry was ready to reflect it and destroy the saucer, but the NAZIs must have learned from their mistakes. Jerry tried launching gravity energy to force it down, but the energy was deflected. He said, "We have to put the saucer out of commission so he can't follow us to the cave entrance. I think that is what he is trying to do."

Emma said, "I will take care of that. I'll destroy its anti-gravity." Almost immediately the saucer began to wobble in the air and descended heavily to the ground trailing plumes of black smoke. It hit hard enough to send a fountain of dirt into the air to mix with the smoke billowing out of the saucer.

Jerry said, "How did you do that, Emma?"

"I saw him divert the energy you sent toward the saucer, so I sent my gravity energy wide and below the saucer and neutralized gravity under it. Anti-gravity generators require gravity to work. Without it, it overloads and implodes."

Jerry thought he should have learned about anti-gravity along with the German Star Children, something he would remedy soon.

They picked up speed and shot toward their cave entrance before another saucer could take off and locate them. They entered their cave without further incident, and felt far more secure once they were out of the Underworld.

Jerry wanted to report their progress immediately to Tom, but decided all the Star Children needed to know and sent an open ping, *"A team of Star Children entered the Underworld through the cave route we discovered and were successful in destroying the NAZI Control Center. Be aware, however, that the NAZIs have some mental powers, and the battle was not easy. The future battles in the Underworld will be difficult for human combatants, because of those powers. I believe the final battle here will come down to NAZIs vs Star Children. Tom, we are also sending four Arcadian saucer teams out to you. Please instruct them where to go. We can dispatch five more saucer teams if needed."*

***

Tom about half expected a counterattack, so he wasn't overly surprised to get Jane's ping for help. John and Jane had evidently separated, because he received a second ping from inside the mountain from John. Tom and his group had just returned to the main base on the magnetic train, and he was readying to leave when he got the pings. He called the executive group together and said, "Our forces just had a major battle in Texas, but we won the first engagement. We defeated the Greys' assault and saved three hundred stored saucers and most of the pilots. The implants were detonated in those at the saucer base, and many died. Unfortunately, there is a second battle coming. I've been told there are many saucers coming from the Dulce, NM base, and we only have one of our saucers there for defense. We will take our three saucers here to reinforce Jane. I think the gloves are off and we are at full out war. Someone needs to tell the president. Also tell him that the implant Control Center has just now been destroyed, so we don't have to worry about more death from implants … I hope."

The AF Joint Chief of Staff said, "I will take care of that. What do you recommend we do to confront them. Shouldn't we activate our own saucers? We have pilots en route here. Should we launch our fighter planes against the saucers?"

Tom said, "Don't launch any saucers until they are well identified. We wouldn't be able to distinguish between enemy or friend, and fighters wouldn't have a chance against saucers. Saucers move far too fast and erratic for a missile to track, plus there is no heat signature for an infrared missiles to lock on to. A radar lock missile stands a better chance, but it is still too slow. If the fighters had lasers they might get a hit, but it would still be a lucky shot. As far as a plan, I suggest you continue to check, clear and attack as necessary through the tunnel network, like you have started here. That's where the problem exists. I would suggest you pump a massive number of soldiers down into the tunnels ever place you can. Control of the tunnels is the key to winning this war. Sorry, but we must go. At this moment the Star Children are the only defense in the air."

Colonel Smith said, "Wait! I need to inform you. The base commander at Del Rio, where we transferred the fifty saucers to, notified me that none of the saucers had any markings at all, so he is marking our saucers with the standard AF Roudel Decals. That's the white star on a blue circle with twin red and white flags on each side. I have also ordered that done to the remaining saucers still in my storage base. So, these will be the good guys if you see any."

"Thank you for telling me. I'll notify my team." Tom pinged out the information to the Star Children. Tom also pinged to all, especially Jane, *"Hold on Jane. We are coming with three Arcadian saucers."*

***

296

President Thompson stood at the podium in total silence to address a full session of Congress. He had called for an emergency session. Only a very few had an inkling of what he was about to say, but all present knew it must be extremely important for him to call this immediate, emergency session.

President Thompson looked out upon the curious faces and said, "Ladies and gentlemen I stand before you today to inform you of several monumental facts most of you will find hard to believe. Two weeks ago I wouldn't have believed them myself, and I wish some weren't true." He stood in total silence in the House Chamber stacked full of lawmakers, the Supreme Court justices, media and onlookers.

"There is no easy way to tell you, but several facts must be revealed before I can get to the crux of the problem. Our government's propensity for secrecy has allowed many things to occur over time that were preventable. Of course some secrecy is necessary for National Security, but other secrets promote an atmosphere for corruption. Secrecy has become a cancer to our government."

"Far too many in government believe the general population is too uninformed or stupid to understand. I for one believe the population has a right to know in order to control their government. Hell, some things I, nor few presidents before me, knew. Yes, certain elements of our government keeps secrets from even the president, and certainly from the Senators and Congressmen. I have been fortunate to have some very honest and patriotic staff personnel that have discovered and presented to me startling information. For example: How many of you know that we did *not* win World War II, but that the NAZIs simply moved to an underground world with their scientist and SS, where they have continued to exploit alien technology with the goal of worldwide domination? Did you know they built flying saucers as early as the end of WWII? Did you know the Roswell crash, which was denied as ever happening, was actually a NAZI flying saucer? Did you know they discovered an alien race in their underground world and made them slaves? Did you know our government's secrecy allowed them to infiltrate our military and NSA? I bet you didn't know we have built fleets of our own flying saucers at taxpayer expense? I certainly didn't know. Did you know we have built many thousands of miles of underground tunnels crisscrossing America to hide and store these saucers at the cost of trillions of dollars? Did you know these aliens partially control these tunnels and plan to use our own saucers to defeat us and make us slaves for the NAZIs? I also bet you didn't know that they have launched their war already? All this has happened because of our crippling secrecy. We lost control of our government through this policy. Obviously I am destroying this policy by revealing the truth. I need your help and the people's help to take control back."

"Yesterday we fought two major battles with these aliens. These aliens attacked us to take control of our hidden saucers, but we won both battles. There have been many deaths, and there will be many more. But, these are battles we must win. I would normally ask the Chairman of the Joint Chiefs of Staff and the Sec. of Defense to speak, but they both are at the battle sites, along with several of my staff."

"I'll tell you another secret. We have help from another alien race. We call them Star Children, which was another secret our government kept from you until most of these children were murdered. That's when I got involved. Those remaining Star Children are helping us now. As I speak, they are fighting battles in our skies and in our tunnel networks. Without them we would have already lost this war, and it is a war we must win."

"My staff can give you more information, but know this, there will still be secrets. I can't tell you details about how we are fighting or where. That's still National Security. I *am* here today to reveal those secrets and ask Congress to Declare War on these NAZIs and their alien warriors."

After his address the president simply walked away leaving the congressional chambers in a roaring chaos. His staff took over and began showing slides of proof of the tunnel network, saucer storage areas, saucers, captured aliens and dead soldiers and aliens. Some slides even presented pictures of the crashed saucer at Roswell, and the saucer clearly showed a swastika on the body of the saucer. The news media fell into a feeding frenzy, and the Congressmen and Senators rushed out to cover their asses and get involved so they would appear to be part of the president's actions.

***

After the interview with the downed Greys, Jane immediately returned to her saucer and gained altitude and remained alert for the attack. John and Berta planned to fight from the ground, and she noticed that troops outside were positioning themselves to defend, while many others were taking refuge inside the underground base. She took a stationary position high, so she could see them coming.

Dir. Hawkins got her attention when he said, "What does this mean?"

Jane had not noticed before in the earlier saucer engagement but red dots were appearing on the inside of her dome. It had to indicate incoming saucers, and there were many red dots. Jane said and pinged, *"Oh my God. There are many incoming saucers, at least a hundred. I need help!"*

Jane received several open pings saying, *"We're on our way."* She didn't recognize some of them, but she could use all the help she could get. The ship's lasers began firing wherever she looked, and two incoming saucers blew apart. Her shield was up, but she continued to zig zag back and forth and up and down as she fired. There was no time to try and down them. Saucers were going down, but there were so many of them, and they were beginning to surround her. They couldn't see her, but they could see her laser shots. Laser fire shot toward her from every direction, some coming close and some deflected, but she continued to fire. Just as she was anticipating a lucky shot getting through to overwhelm her defenses, she noticed green dots on the dome. Yeah, help. She saw three dots zooming in from the east, then four more coming in from the south. The Greys' saucers began to fall around her. Twenty were falling from the incoming Arcadian saucers that had now surrounded them. Jane had blasted down at least fifteen herself, now many more were falling. Some of the enemy saucers were now trying to retreat, but they were caught in an ever tightening circle. Jane noticed that some were now being drawn down by gravity and settling to the ground. She switched her focus to gravity forces and began to push them down also. The battle was winding down to the point they could take more time and save some of the saucers, maybe half of them.

Capt. McDaniel wiped the sweat off his forehead and said, "Damn, that was intense."

Jane pulled her headset off momentarily to wipe the sweat from her brow. Yeah, it had been intense. She looked around and, in even with the heavy tension, had to laugh. Dir. Hawkins was wide-eyed and his mouth was gaping open, just like the other pilot. Jane said, "Hey guys, we won that one."

Dir. Hawkins snapped his mouth shut and said, "Damn, that was … was … intense. I've never been in a battle like that before, and I'm not sure if I ever want to do it again."

Jane pinged, *"Thanks guys. We all agree here that that battle was intense. I'm glad you showed up when you did. I was getting extremely busy. You saved my ass. Thanks."* She received acknowledging single pings in return.

As Jane landed she could see Berta and soldiers herding the downed Greys inside the complex, and she was extremely pleased to see John running toward her with his arms open wide. She fell into his embrace. That's when she realized how stressed she had been, because she broke down and cried on his huge shoulder. It had been far too eventful during the battle to allow herself any stress relief, but now in John's loving arms the damn burst with huge sobs.

Tom, Sue, Major Burns and Dir. Setliff came running up and Tom said, "Jane, you and John and your team did a fantastic job here. From what I hear you saved many people and saved, wow, three hundred saucers, and that doesn't count the fifty grounded from Dulce, NM."

Jane said, "I thought I was a goner. I was taking a lot of hits, and I didn't know how much longer my shield would hold. I'm glad you came when you did. Where did all the Arcadian saucers come from?"

"Well, we had three, and Jerry and Mary organized the other four using the German Star Children. They did good, and they're young. You'll see when they land."

John said, "What's the plan now?"

Dir. Setliff said, "General Warner thinks Dulce is crippled, losing that many saucers and thinks they might be weak now. I think he may be right, but Dulce is a long way away through the Tunnel Network, and it might take a while to get there."

"I can tell you that the president has asked Congress for a Declaration of War, but he is not waiting and has ordered the military to consider the Greys as hostiles. He wants our saucers protected, the Greys captured or destroyed and the Tunnel Network under military control." When he saw the startled looks he continued, "Yes, he told Congress and the general public and thus the world about the Greys, the saucers and about you Star Children, and I might add, you are being lauded as heroes. The president has definitely removed the veil of secrecy. We are hoping there will be no more conflict or resistance to our soldiers traveling the Tunnel Network, but we can't be assured. The Army and Marines in NC are doing that as we speak. They consider the tunnels on the east coast reasonably clear, since they are more commonly known about. Our forces are moving west, leaving a detachment of soldiers and FBI investigators at each terminal to make sure they are cleared and remain so. We don't expect trouble until we reach Missouri."

General Warden and Mr. Canton came up and heard the conversation and the general said, "Dir. Setliff, you must have heard from the president. That's new information for me."

"Yeah, actually Dir. Martinez is doing double duty with the president since so many of his executive team is in the field, and he is keeping me constantly informed. I'm glad you're here, so I can brief you all."

"As I said earlier, the president has gone public, and he is pissed. As soon as he heard the satellites were destroyed he cut loose and issued orders and spoke to Congress. He ordered troops out of Fort Riley in Kansas toward the hidden MO location, troops out of Ft. Sill, OK toward Dulce, NM, troops out of Fort Bliss to Luke AFB in Phoenix, and ordered Marines out of Camp Pendleton, CA to Edwards AFB. Lots of troops are en route with orders to find and secure the Tunnel Network, round up the Greys and protect our saucers."

General Warden said, "I understand the reasoning behind the troops selected, but why those target locations. What have you found out?"

"The agencies back in DC have been busy. They have had little success in finding information about the Tunnel Network, but from interrogations they believe there is a tunnel at least from China Lake, CA all the way across the country to NC. As it turns out, some of the locations were quite easy to find. They matched the concentration of the pilot job codes by location. Many, several hundred saucer pilots, are housed at Edwards AFB. The CIA suspects a tunnel exists there connecting to China Lake, like was the case here and in NC. There have been no further pilot deaths, so the satellite and control center destruction must have worked. They will still remove the implants, however. The plan at Edwards is to enter China Lake through the tunnel, take whatever action is required and follow the tunnels."

"There is a concentration of pilots at Luke AFB in Arizona, which suggests there is another saucer base somewhere near Phoenix. They suspect north east in the Black Mountains. The plan there is to do the same as in California. Since the guards are still alive, the hope is they can defend the saucers until reinforcements can arrive, and they have been put on alert. They are motivated since they realize they could have been killed."

"The facility in MO does not fit the arrangement set up for the other facility. There is a lack of pilots anywhere near the suspected hidden base location in southern MO. The train of thought in DC is the MO facility may be a totally Grey operation based upon the reports of NAZI flying saucers being manufactured in the Underworld. There are lots of caves in southern MO, enough to make it difficult to identify any exact location. They suspect it is located there and stocked with NAZI manufactured saucers and Grey pilots. Either way the plan is to find it through the tunnels from both directions."

"Dulce in NM and Area 51 in NV they feel are consolidated at the facility itself. Those two remain a big mystery. The intel from the NAZI, Otis, suggest the Greys are working with humans, so we don't know what to expect. We will surround the location and try to gain entry into the tunnels from both directions."

Dr. Wisscroff said, "I didn't hear you mention CO. That is one of the locations gotten from Janet's early interview."

Dir. Setliff said, "Due to the projected location of the Tunnel Network and the fact that Dulce is on the border of CO, they suspect the actual location of the base is in CO. on the Jicarella Apache Indian Reservation. UFO conspiracist have suspected that location for years. Maybe they were right all along."

Tom said, "If you still have pilots alive at the sights in question, why not order them to fly here or NC where the bases are already secure? That's one way to find out quickly if those bases are still in military control."

"Excellent idea. I'll inform the president immediately."

Tom continued, "You know the NAZIs and the Greys aren't stupid. They have to know by now that their master plans have been disrupted. Anyone have any idea how they will react? I mean, they have saucers. What if they attack by air, like they did here? I haven't heard anything about air defense. We can help, but we can't be everywhere."

General Warner said, "Since we can't use fighters or count on missiles for defense, and since President Thompson told the world we have saucers, I will activate those saucers and pilots we have saved and dispatch them to fly cover for the advancing ground troops. Our fleet of saucers being seen would only reinforce the president's statement. I would imagine the activated pilots have arrived in NC, and the others should be arriving soon at Laughlin AFB, TX. The saucers should be marked by now, so they are ready to go. That's about five hundred plus saucers to launch for air defense, and if they can't handle it they can call on the Star Children."

Tom had learned to be cynical when it came to the NAZIs and Greys. They had devised an almost perfect plan for taking over control, and they have had decades to plot it out and make it happen. It was only by sheer luck that the Grey's plan was discovered and hopefully disrupted, but they would have a backup plan, maybe several. They had been lucky so far, but Tom felt there would be other Chess pieces in play. It's unfolding too quickly and the mistakes would all be on our side. The other side had their plans in play far too long and would have considered every option. So, what was bothering him? What was he missing?

# Chapter 12
## (The War Continues)

It had been a very long and stressful day, and Tom was tired and hungry. He knew the other Star Children were also, but he felt exposed and vulnerable outside of the Sanctuary. Tom said and pinged, "During this lull in activity, we will return to the Sanctuary for food and try to get some rest before it starts up again."

General Warden said, "That's a long way to go just to get food. We can feed you here."

"Thank you general, but traveling great distances for us is but a few moments in an Arcadian saucer. Besides, we are exposing our saucers to danger when they are unattended and unprotected. They will be safe, us too, at the Sanctuary, and if needed, we can return just as quickly."

"Of course. I understand."

Tom was so tired from the stress of the day his mind was no longer alert and thinking well. His team evidently felt the same, because they too loaded themselves in their saucers. They took off together, all except Don and Karen, who were still in the tunnels at NC with the Marines. The seven saucers flew in formation, much like ducks flying south, and were soon back safely docked in the Sanctuary. Sue had flown their saucer leading the ducks, which had proved to be an even faster trip for all.

They were all famished, most hadn't eaten since their early morning meal, which seemed like a week ago. Thankfully, someone must have called ahead, because the Combat Cooks had hot and steaming meals ready for them when they entered the cafeteria. Tom and the others gratefully accepted the meals and, thankfully, hot coffee. Tom couldn't even remember taking in any water during the day. No wonder he was so exhausted. It must have been evident to all, since they were left alone to eat and drink.

Each team seemed to be in their own separate little world. As soon as he and Sue finished, they took off for their quarters for much-needed rests, and he didn't even remember going to sleep. He must have crashed as soon as they got in the room.

It seemed like he had just gone to sleep when Tina burst into their bedroom and said, "The Army guys have breakfast ready. It's time to get up and start another day. I think we will have a lot more battles today."

Surprisingly, Tom felt refreshed, and he thought Tina was probably right, but she didn't need to be so jubilant about it. Obviously, she found it exciting and was looking forward to more. Tom said, "Ok. Thanks Tina. We'll be over as soon as we shower and dress." Oh, the benefits of youth.

Tom and Sue quickly showered and slipped into a clean silver suit. Thank God for the Combat Cooks. As with most armies, his new army ran on its stomach, and the cooks were taking care of them extremely well. They got their food and coffee and joined the others already gathered at the main table.

As soon as they sat, Jerry said, "You were exhausted when you came back, so I'm assuming you didn't receive Don's open ping. As you know Don and Karen are traveling with the troops in the Tunnel Network from NC. Those forces have cleared all the terminals going west without incident all the way to MO. Don said the colonel had expected a major battle there, but they found the Grey's secret cavern, and it's completely evacuated. Don said there were docking slots for over three hundred saucers but no Greys or saucers. Don said it looked like they left in a hurry."

Sue said, "Damn, I wonder where they went?"

Dir. Setliff was listening intently to the information when his communicator chimed. He quickly thumbed it open and read. Dir. Setliff said, "Crap!" All looked at him, and he continued, "President Thompson was contacted by President Pramin, and the Russian president actually asked for our help."

"It seems that someone contacted President Pramin claiming to be a representative of the NAZI 4th Reich and demanded their immediate surrender." He chuckled and continued, "To the Russian president's credit, he told them to stuff it."

"The Russians lost their battle with the Greys, and all their saucers were taken from them, over four hundred, and the Greys are now using them to wipe out their fighters and destroying their air force bases. They have already lost most of their top-of-

310

the-line fighters. They can't stop them and want our help."

Tom thought quickly and said, "John, you and Jane pick a team and take six saucers to Russia. Try to down as many as you can, but stop the killing and destruction any way you can. It would be nice to give the Russian's back a fleet to fight them back. If the Greys win in Russia they will take over Europe and eventually come here. So, we must fight them there."

"I think what's happening in Russia is what's going to happen here, also. Dir. Setliff, pass the warning, and get your pilots and saucers up to protect your bases and intercept them. We will also launch our Arcadian saucers and teams to take the Greys on in America. Sue and I will lead this team, and we will disperse five for the US and recall Don and Karen to have their saucer join us. I don't like having one of our saucers sitting on the ground and unprotected anyway. Jerry and Mary, before you ask, I need you to remain here with the remaining three saucers to protect the Sanctuary. They know we are here and they have saucers stored in the Underworld. I don't trust them. They haven't made a move yet, but they may try to take advantage of the situation. Hell, what they are doing may just be a ploy to draw our saucers away. They are beginning to realize that the Star Children can and will severely disrupt their plans. We already have. I'm sure they will try to take us out if they can. So, I need you to observe and protect our Sanctuary." Jerry and Mary both nodded agreement.

Jane said, "We will take the German Star Children as saucer teams."

Berta said, "Hans and I will be one of the teams, and I suggest the teams of younger ones that helped defeat the Greys in Texas. They did well in combat and now have experience. That will leave the older ones to help Jerry and Mary if needed."

Jane nodded and said, "Good suggestion, and I agree. Those kids did very well and helped save my ass."

It was the always thinking and planning Dr. Wisscroff that grabbed everyone's attention when he said, "Before everyone runs off to battle I think we need to come up with plans. My first question to all of you is: How is the best way to down the saucers? The last battle destroyed almost half of the saucers. Of course we had to in our own defense, but possibly there is a better way. You were able to eventually down many of them, but there were plenty of soldiers below to quickly capture the pilots. We might not have soldiers available in this next battle, especially in Russia. Berta, you seem to be the resident expert on saucers, since most of the original Star Children group haven't bothered to learn the science of the saucers. Any thoughts?"

Before Berta could respond Mary said, "Emma downed the NAZI saucer in the Underworld by neutralizing gravity beneath it, causing its gravity drive to fail."

Emma said, "That's true, but my actions permanently disabled it. I caused it to implode. I don't think we want to do that in this situation, not

312

if we want to reuse them. I was also thinking we could mentally launch a focused Electro Magnetic Pulse (EMP) to fry the saucer's electronics, but that too would be permanent damage. We can probably come up with another method."

Berta thought for a moment and said, "Well, our Arcadian saucers are controlled by Arcadian minds and thoughts. The NAZIs apparently have been unable to reverse engineer any significant mind control technology from the ancient technology recovered, if it existed. At best it's certainly nothing like Arcadian technology. This is probably due to the physical and genetic sophistication of Arcadian mental power. In short, the human and Grey mental powers of telepathy are simply not strong enough. Still, according to the pilots we talked to, the American saucers, and probably the Russian, are partially controlled by thought, but only for basic control functions. The pilots mostly depend on manual physical control, and use thought control for anti-gravity instructions such as speed, intensity, instant engagement. This is what gives the saucers its unpredictable and instant change in direction. Physical controls are far too slow and predictable to achieve these abstract results, but mental instruction are relatively easy and basic. I guess what I'm saying is that a Star Child with our advanced telepathic abilities may be able to take over control of those instructions and drive it to the ground or even shut their anti-gravity off. I'm hoping we can land the saucer safely and turn it off until one of us turns it back on. This, of course, is only a theory but worth a try."

Emma said, "That might work with Grey controlled saucers, but we have seen the NAZI pilots at the controls in the Underworld, and they apparently do have some telepathic abilities, certainly mind controls. I've witnessed a NAZI divert our gravity blasts. I'm not sure we can override *their* mental controls. I think they would be able to turn it back on."

Tom said, "Well, there appears to be a lot of ifs, but it's worth a try. What are your other concerns, Dr. Wisscroff?"

"The stealth of the saucers. They don't show up on any Earth radars, but I heard Jane and Dir. Setliff mention green dots and red dots on the dome of her saucer. Evidently the Arcadian technology can see both the good guys and the bad guys, but Jane didn't see the incoming saucers until they were almost upon her."

Berta said, "Oh, that's easy. It's basic. Just mentally tell the ship to expand or focus the monitoring."

Jane laughed and said, "I must have missed that. I'll learn the technology en route to Russia, and speaking of that, we had better go. While I learn the science the other team members will have to learn Russian, if they haven't already."

John said, "Jane, we will need a high ranking Russian military officer with us to interface with the Russian military and government. Can you call President Pramin directly?

Jane said, "Yes, of course." She pulled her tablet out and dialed."

Tom said, "Dir. Setliff, there is little help you can provide in Russia. I think you better go with our group and stay here in America. Dr. Wisscroff, I suggest you go with John and Jane and help Berta with the science concerns. Berta, I think you would better help the Russian team in John's saucer so you and Dr. Wisscroff can discuss uses of technology. Let one of the others take your saucer. I think it is time to launch. Any other thought before we leave?"

None spoke, so the teams headed off to the docking area, and all were off toward their assigned areas.

As soon as the teams left, Jerry said, "I think Tom may be correct, and we need to be concerned about the NAZI's potential attack on our Sanctuary. I believe we need to keep a saucer up at all time to observe for any activity coming from the Underworld. Mary and I can take the first watch.

As they sped toward Russia Jane received a call from President Pramin. She had not reached him when she called previously and had to leave a message asking him to call Jane Turret immediately. His voice was strained.

Jane said, "Mr. President, we are en route to help with six of the Arcadian saucers. Please give me a status on your situation."

President Pramin bellowed, "What do you expect to do with six saucers? The Grey bastards commandeered four hundred of our saucers, and they are wreaking havoc on our military. I can't believe it, even after President Thompson told us about the Grey's plan. Our saucer defense forces were not decimated by the implants as they had planned, but the damned Greys attacked suddenly in overwhelming numbers and took them anyway. The damn saucers have almost destroyed our air defense, and they are attacking us everywhere. We are losing the battle, and we are completely at their mercy. Is there anything you can do?"

"Yes, Mr. President, our saucers, Arcadian saucers, are far more advanced than yours … well there's now, plus us Star Children have other powers. At a minimum we can destroy the saucers, but we hope to save them for you. We will, however, need some things from you."

"Anything!"

"We need a high-level military commander with us with command authority and communication so we can interface with your forces. We will attempt to down as many of those saucers as possible so you can take back control of them. We need coordinates where we can pick up your military liaison. Mr. President, we also need to speak directly with your top scientists with your saucer program to work out an attack protocol to recover your saucers."

President Pramin said, "We will comply with your requests. I will issue the orders and they will be contacting you immediately. Thank you, Jane."

John asked, "Where is he now?"

President Pramin said without reservation or evasion, "I'm underground in my bunker."

John said, "Tell him that if it were I, I wouldn't want to be anywhere underground in a war with the Greys. Underground is their habitat." Jane simply relayed John's message.

Jane was in the process of learning the science of the saucers when she received the call. He introduced himself as General Sergey Gasimov, the Russian Minister of Defense, and he would be the Russian liaison and travel with them. He then gave her the coordinates where he could be picked up. Jane said, "Thank you general. We will be there in fifteen minutes, and please have your encrypted military communication with you. I am also providing Dr. Wisscroff's secure number for the Russian saucer scientists."

General Gasimov said, "Yes, I will relay the number, and thank you for your assistance."

Within only a few moments Dr. Wisscroff's phone chimed. Thankfully, it was a video conference call from a team of scientists. Dr. Wisscroff and Berta skipped over the introductions and launched into the interrogations of their Mind Controls. The scientists were not evasive at all and began answering the questions candidly and in detail. Surprisingly, Jane was beginning to understand the scientific jargon, but her attention was mainly on locating the general's coordinates and trying to identify the locations of the attacking saucers. She had expanded the search range until she found most of them. Of the four hundred

Russian saucers they had dispersed into eight groups canvasing all of Russia. Jane thought that would make it easier for them to combat, but 400 saucers were still a lot to tackle.

John homed in on the coordinates provided and descended over a tarmac area at what was obviously a military airbase. Below them they could see two uniformed officers, one with abundant decorations of gold and service ribbons. The other was only slightly less adorned. John landed unobserved within twenty feet of the pair. Both were obviously startled when his saucer materialized. John left Jane and the others inside in case a speedy liftoff was required and descended the stair ramp.

Both men came immediately toward him, and the heavily adorned man said, "I am General Sergey Gasimov and this is Colonel Ivan Letov, and you must be John Meeker. President Pramin told us about you."

"Yes, I'm John. May I suggest we board our saucer and launch immediately. I don't like being on the ground." They nodded and followed John into the saucer. They were still making introductions as he lifted off and rejoined the other saucers.

General Gasimov said, "We have been and are being decimated by our own saucers. We thought the implants being neutralized foiled their plans, but the devil Greys hit us unexpected and completely by surprise in large force. The took the saucers quickly and launched their attack. The underground battle is still ongoing to take back the facility, but the Greys are hampering our attempts with aerial attacks at the entry locations."

Jane thought she had met the general, at least he apparently knew of her, and she said, "General, we understand the situation. What we need to know is which group of saucers poses the most problem. We don't need to know all the details right now. Just point them out on the dome display. Secondly, we need to know if your pilots survived."

The general nodded his understanding and pointed to a group over Moscow and said, "We have plenty of pilots. They were not on duty at the time of the attack."

"That's great, general. Hopefully, we can save many of the saucers for them. We will try to down some, so inform your ground troops to be ready to capture the Grey pilots when they land." Then to Dr. Wisscroff and Berta Jane said, "We will be in contact with the first group of saucers soon. Have you worked out a plan to down them yet, or do we shoot them down?"

Jane could hear Dr. Wisscroff, Berta and the Russian scientists talking hard and fast about how the mind controls were configured. She was even understanding most of it, but with her distractions she couldn't concentrate on the conversation and couldn't tell if they had finalized a solution.

Berta said, "We are getting there, but we are not there yet. We can still try downing them with gravity like before. Just give us a little time to finalize our plan."

319

Jane said, "Unless you have a definitive plan we must attack to destroy. It takes too much time to down a saucer with gravity. Plus, there are just too many of them to take a chance with experimenting until we reduce the odds. Just tell me when you have a plan."

Jane coordinated the attack with ping instructions. The Arcadian saucers spread out to make their run, and on their first pass destroyed twenty saucers. With multiple Star Children firing, the sky lit up with red, flaming bolts of laser light and explosions. As they turned for another pass Berta said, "We have plan. I'm sending it out now."

Jane received Berta's open ping and download. Yes, she understood. As their dispersed formation attacked on their second run, Jane executed her data discharge and immediately saw two of the enemy saucers shut down. They ceased firing and dove toward the ground to land softly. Jane looked around to see the entire enemy fleet doing the same thing.

Jane said, "General Gasimov, contact your ground troops and have them capture all those Grey pilots. Keep them detained but safe. We will deal with them later. After we finish with the other saucer groups we will return and activate these saucers for your pilots."

General Gasimov immediately instructed Colonel Letov then said, "Thank you Jane. You have saved many lives and many saucers. We were beaten until you and your group joined the battle. We are incredibly thankful."

Jane said, "Well, the battle isn't over yet. Point out the next group for us to tackle." He did, and they were off again.

En route John heard Dr. Wisscroff still talking to the Russian scientists and reported success. Cheers rang out on the conference call, but Dr. Wisscroff quickly came back and said, "It worked here, but we can't be assured it will work on the American saucers. What are your thoughts on those?"

The scientists laughed, and the lead scientist said, "I'm sure it will since we stole that technology from the Americans. Both countries reversed engineered crashed saucers and later received help with the technology from the Greys, thinking it was theirs. We both improved on the technology, but we copied the Americans. Didn't you notice that the mental thoughts required were thoughts in English? It was easier to teach our pilots to think in English than rewrite the entire program. Yes, we are positive they are the same program."

Berta said, "Your technology is still crude. When we get a chance to work with you we can suggest improvements."

Jane said, "What say we win this war first. We can talk about the science of the technology later."

John pinged, *"Berta, Dr. Wisscroff and the Russian scientist came up with a protocol that works on the saucers, the protocol Berta pinged earlier. In our first engagement we were able to save many of the saucers. We are going after the second group now. By the way, the Russian scientists claim to have stolen the mind control technology from America, so the same protocol should work."*

***

By the time Tom's saucer group crossed into U.S. territory Dir. Setliff received communication from General Warner. Dir. Setliff said, "Oh crap! Attacks have begun on several of our Air Force bases with major damage, but our saucers from Texas have been dispatched to engage them. They hit our F-22s at Tyndall AFB in the Florida panhandle and destroyed most of the F-22s and much of the base. They also hit our F-15Cs at Shaw AFB in South Carolina with much the same damage. The fighters tried to engage them in the air but never stood a chance, and the F-22 Raptor is the best we have. The U.S. saucers are en route to head them off at Eglin AFB Florida. That base is loaded with F-15Cs and our newest fighters, the F-35As. The general thinks they are trying to destroy all our fighter jets like they did in Russia."

Tom said, "Something is wrong. This doesn't feel right, but I can't put my finger on exactly what. Why are they taking out the fighters? They aren't afraid of them since they pose no threat. But, the pings from John and Berta said the new protocol works, so we will proceed with our attacks."

Tom called up the Arcadian radar and expanded the search radius until he located a large formation moving toward Eglin AFB. There were about a hundred of them. Tom led his group to intercept them, which was almost immediate at the speed he

322

set. The Arcadian formation spread out and shot over the mass of saucers aiming the mind control as they went. Nothing happened!

Tina pinged, *"Their saucers are shielded. I can see them shimmering."*

Tom immediately realized his mistake. These weren't the American or Russian built saucers. These were the NAZI saucers missing from the caves of Missouri. The sneaky bastards didn't allow the Greys to share that technology to make sure they maintained the advantage. Tom pinged, *"We aren't going to be able to down these saucers with shields. Take them out anyway you can."* He also said, "Dir. Setliff, tell the general to call off those American saucers. These NAZIs saucers have advanced technology, and they won't have much of a chance against them."

On their next pass their lasers refracted off the saucer's shields. Gravity pulses were also reflected and had little effect. Tom was about to panic when he received an open ping from Emma, *"Implode their anti-gravity generators by neutralizing gravity below them and below their shields. Their anti-gravity generator requires natural gravity to work. Your neutralizing beam must be held in place long enough to start a chain reaction, so make your beam wide, and the generator will implode."* Yes, now he remembered the conversation about the NAZI saucer she destroyed in that way. There was no need to explain to the others, since they had heard the same discussion.

The enemy saucers knew they were under attack and began firing blindly at the invisible Arcadian saucers, but Tom's group slid under them and generated a sweeping neutralizing layer of gravity under the enemies fleet. Soon the saucers began to wobble in the air, then some exploded in a plume of smoke. Others just bellowed smoke and fell from the sky. Soon the sky was clear of NAZI saucers.

Tom pinged, *"Well done. Follow me to the next group."* The next large group, most of them actually, seemed to be headed toward Arizona, probably for Luke AFB, where there were many fighters. Don and Karen's saucer had just rejoined Tom's group, and they were almost there when Dir. Setliff got the call.

Dir. Setliff said, "Crap! There is a formation of NAZI saucers over Washington D.C. firing on the White House and the Capital. They demanded the immediate surrender of the United States. Of course President Thompson told them to go to hell." After a moment of thought he said, "You know, this doesn't make sense. Why would they do that? They know by now that your saucers will attack them, and they will lose."

Suddenly it clicked in Tom's mind. He knew precisely what was going on. Tom asked, "What is the protocol for the president when there is a threat like this?"

"Well, the president is immediately taken to his underground bunker."

Tom said, "That's what I thought. The president is going to exactly where the Greys and the NAZIs want him. This whole attack ploy is an elaborate scheme to get the president underground. They thrive in the underground, and have had years to prepare. By the way, I would imagine that the Russian President Pramin is also underground. Director, if it isn't too late, get them the hell out of there. Do it *now*! They need to be somewhere else where they can be protected better. Tom said out loud and open ping, *"John, Jane, this whole attack affair in Russia and here has been geared to get the presidents underground where the Greys can get their hands on them. Why, I don't know, but it is something sinister."*

Dir. Setliff was frantically punching his phone as he said, "Well I know why. If they can kill or capture the president it would totally disrupt our government and throw it into chaos. Hell, the vice president hasn't even been briefed. If they are able to capture the president it would be even worse. They could hold him for ransom and try to force him to surrender. President Thompson would never do that. He would die first, but who knows what those other politicians might do if he is not firmly in control of the government. Needless to say, most of our current plans and operations would be disrupted, and they win. This is some serious shit!"

Dir. Setliff then turned and focused on barking orders into his phone, while Tom processed what he just heard. It made total sense, and he agreed completely. Tom pinged, *"Tina, you and Fred come with me to D.C.. We need to try and save the president. The rest of you continue on to Arizona and engage the saucers."*

***

After the success with the first group of Russian saucers, John and Jane systematically engaged the other groups with similar success. It was almost no contest. Berta's protocol worked perfectly, and with only a few exceptions in the first engagement they downed all the saucers. General Gasimov was extremely happy with the outcome, since he retrieved almost all of his saucers for reuse. The Grey pilots had all been taken into custody, and John's group split up to reactivate the saucers. The hopeless situation had completely reversed itself, and General Gasimov was all smiles.

As they were finishing up, the group received the open ping from Tom explaining the purpose of the attack and warning for President Pramin. Jane repeated the warning to the general. The general's smile vanished and he was immediately on his communicator. He spoke, then listened, then said, "It's too late! The Greys stormed the tunnel network in massive force and destroyed our forces protecting the president. They captured him and immediately loaded him into a saucer and took off down the tunnels. Security surveillance shows them traveling south, but no one knows where the tunnel network goes. They could come out anywhere and be anywhere. They haven't a clue."

Jane immediately began searching the skies for saucers, while John sent an open ping to the Star

326

Children reporting the abduction of President Pramin. Jane continued to expand her radar search without success, but suddenly yelled her success. She said and pinged, *"There it is! It's going south. It's already past Argentina. It's going to the Underworld. It has to be. There is nothing else in that direction. Jerry, try to down it with Berta's protocol before it gets in the hole to the Underworld. We believe it is carrying the Russian President captive on board."*

***

Jerry and Mary were still on patrol outside the Sanctuary when they received Jane's ping. Mary expanded her radar search and soon found the saucer coming toward them. Jerry quickly flew up over the ice dome and positioned the saucer close to the hole to guarantee interception and waited. Both Jerry and Mary had taken the download from Berta and were ready to down the saucer, like had been done so successfully in Russia. They moved inward on the saucer's path to ensure additional distance to safely land the saucer. Then the saucer was suddenly there, and they transmitted the mind control instructions. Nothing happened! The saucer continued its fast approach toward the deep hole to the Underworld. They sped after it repeating the telepathy transmissions.

Mary said, "Look. That saucer has a swastika roundel on it. That is not a Russian saucer, it's a NAZI saucer. It obviously has shielding like they discovered in America. We can't stop it!"

They continued to follow it and watched it descend into the hole and into the Underworld and safety.

Jerry pinged, *"We failed to stop the saucer. It was a NAZI saucer with shielding, and we couldn't stop it."* Jerry said, "Mary, after what happened in Russia and information from Tom's open ping about saving our president, the next saucer could be carrying President Thompson. It has to be stopped. Let's go back and talk to Mr. Mum. There has to be a way to get through their shields."

*** 

Tom and Sue shot toward Washington with Tina close behind. Dir. Setliff couldn't make contact with any of the president's staff or NSA Canton and became frantic and frustrated. General Warner finally called. Dir. Setliff listened intently and made no comments other than "Thanks. Please keep me informed."

A very solemn Dir. Setliff slowly turned and said, "The Greys ambushed President Thompson in the tunnel network. They had hordes of warriors waiting and killed all the presidents Secret Service and staff that was with him."

Sue interrupted, "Did they kill the president?"

"No. Sorry I didn't mention that first. They kidnapped the president and Mr. Canton and flew them down the tunnel network in a saucer. I presume like they did with President Pramin in Russia."

Tom said, "When did this happen?"

"Just now. The general said it just happened."

Tom immediately turned south and said, "Sue, try to find the saucer on the radar. We will intercept it."

Sue said, "What can we do? You know the saucer is a NAZI saucer with shielding. We certainly can't shoot it down."

"Hell, I don't know, but we can't just do nothing. If you can find it we'll follow it and hope something happens." Tom pinged, *"Jerry, the president has been captured and we presume they will take him to the Underworld, too. I'm not sure what we can do with its shielding, but I'm just letting you know to watch out for it."*

*Jerry responded immediately, "Mary and I are talking to Mr. Mum right now about the situation to see if he has any ideas."*

Mr. Mum stared directly at them as if he were looking into their minds and said, "I understand the situation as you have explained it. What I am perceiving is that you children have not yet comprehended what it is to be Arcadian. Technology is simply a tool to be used no matter who wields it. Technology does not use an Arcadian. Know and understand the technology and what it truly is, then you can use it to serve you. The Arcadian mind is the real power, not technology. Use your minds children."

Jerry and Mary raced back to their saucer and once back inside Mary said, "I'm more confused now than before we talked to Mr. Mum. What the hell did he tell us?"

Jerry laughed and said, "He said for us to use our minds and make technology serve us, but he didn't say how. But, he seemed to be saying it could be done."

Mary thought for a moment and said, "Well, he said know and understand the technology then use it to serve us, or something like that. Maybe that's how. Let's learn the technology." She slipped the head ring on and called up the arcadian archives and began learning. Jerry did likewise as he steered the saucer out of the Sanctuary, but this time he took all three teams and saucers.

All the Star Children airborne at the entrance of the Underworld were learning the shield technology when they received Sue's ping. She had found the escaping saucer and confirmed it was headed directly for Antarctica. Sue said they wouldn't be able to catch it in time, and those at the Underworld end were the only line of defense. Nothing like putting pressure on them.

Mary had learned the technology of the Arcadian shields, which was probably far more advanced than the ancient technology the NAZIs reversed engineered for their shields. The technology was highly advanced and complicated, but she kept coming back to what Mr. Mum had told them, use the technology to serve them. What did the technology do? According to the archive, it formed an energy block, like putting a steel wall around them. It clicked, and Mary suddenly understood. The Star Children had learned how to penetrate steel walls. They could see through them, hear through them and manipulate gravity pulses from the other side by using the power of their minds. Tom had used that power to enter the Sanctuary. Why should this be any different? Why not? Why make it complicated. It was simple, use your mind and not the technology.

Mary's face split apart with a huge smile and said, "Bring them on. I can deal with their shield now. She then sent an open ping to all the Star Children, *"The shields are nothing. You can penetrate through them with your mind, like looking or hearing through steel. Their shields are only technology that we can manipulate. We will down the saucer and save the president."*

Jerry said, "Don't get cocky. We haven't done it yet, but I must admit it does looks easy."

"I'll penetrate the shield, but you need to protect the president while I do it."

Emma pinged, "I see the saucer on my radar. I also see two Arcadian saucers speeding to catch it, but they won't make it in time. It's up to us."

Mary was ready as it approached. Their saucers paced the NAZI saucer, and she enhanced her vision and saw the shield. Instead of blasting against it she formed her gravity force within it. The saucer immediately stopped. Her gravity force filled the inside of the shield and began to slowly lower it. Mary realized that she could actually turn the shield off from inside, but with it intact she could more easily focus the gravity energy within it. Jerry formed his own shield within their shield and placed it around the president and Mr. Canton. The other two Arcadian saucers descended to the ice and waited for the captured saucer to land. When it finally settled, the Star Children surrounded it, turned the shield off and forced it open. They seized the Grey pilots and soldiers and zombie walked them out into the freezing cold, where they were tie-wrapped and loaded into an Arcadian saucer. The president and Mr. Canton came out next, still protected in a shield and now a warmth bubble and were escorted into Jerry and Mary's saucer. Both still frozen in fear and shock and mechanically followed instruction.

As they began to ascend Tina open pinged, *"Jerry, they are coming, coming from the Underworld. Three NAZI saucers are coming."*

Jerry said, "I don't know where Tina is, but she must be close. Jerry pinged, *"Thanks Tina. We will be ready."*

They shot up and waited, and it wasn't long. The NAZI saucers dove toward their downed saucer and opened fire. The downed saucer exploded. Jerry pinged, *"Take them out. Don't bother trying to save them."* Immediately the invisible shields of the attacking NAZI's saucers filled with bright flames just before they exploded.

Mr. Canton remained petrified and simply stared into blank space, but President Thompson, having apparently somewhat recovered, bellowed, "Those SOBs just tried to kill me! If those bastards want war, we are going to give them a war, and they won't win this one. Get me back to the White House."

Jerry said, "Sorry, Mr. President, the safest place for you right now is our Sanctuary. We are close, and we can protect you there. Tom and Sue are on their way, and we need to make plans"

"Very well. The Sanctuary it is. I've wanted to see it anyway."

Mr. Canton, now also recovered, said, "Mr. President, you aren't going to believe the Sanctuary."

The president gasped when the saucer dove under the water and under the ice cap, and his eyes remained wide as they went into the underwater cave and up through the iris door into the docking area. Jerry noticed that Tom's saucer was already docked, and he and Sue were standing on the stairs smiling.

As Jerry and Mary reached the platform, Tom said, "We heard your success and didn't bother coming to your rescue. We just came straight here."

President Thompson and Mr. Canton then descended the ramp. The president was smiling and went to Tom and shook his hand firmly and said, "Thank you, Tom, and thanks to all the Star Children. Jerry and Mary caught us up on today's activities, Oh, and thanks for rescuing me. I'm very impressed. It's too bad you were unable to rescue President Pramin. We will have to do something about that."

"We will come up with a plan, Mr. President."

# Chapter 13
## (Aftermath)

The president's surprises continued as they entered the Sanctuary, traveled the moving street and eventually settling into the cafeteria. The Marines greeted the president with stiff salutes, and the Star Children greeted him with cheers. After all the greetings and introduction they all settled in and had a good meal and strong Marine coffee.

After the coffee and meal, President Thompson got on Dir. Setliff's phone and reported his rescue and resumption of control of the government. Then he began giving out orders. President Thompson called General Warner and after a brief interchange said, "It's about time Congress declared war! I wasn't going to wait on them, anyway. General Warner, I want those tunnels cleared, and I want you to pump all the warriors you need into them to get the job done. I want all those Greys either dead or captured. I also want all our saucers back in our control. I also want an invasion fleet and force headed to Antarctica. We need to finish that war with the NAZIs. Do you hear me? These are my orders. You are in charge of all the military in this war. Now get it done."

President Thompson put the Dir Setliff's phone on speaker in time to hear General Warner say, "Sir, we have never stopped. The Star Children have destroyed all the attacking NAZI saucers. With the skies clear we have pumped thousands of Marines into the Tunnel Network and many, many are already cleared. It's amazing how cooperative those compromised traitors are since the NAZI control center was destroyed. They are coming back to our side and fighting with us. Of course they still want the implants out, however. One of the Star Children, Karen I think, recorded a message in the Grey's language. I'm not sure what it says, but something to the effect, surrender and live or fight and die. Anyway, we are playing it and most are surrendering. We are gathering up quite a large number of them and putting them in a quickly arranged detention camp at Edwards AFB, California."

"Most of California is cleared and even Area 51 in Nevada. The Marines went in through a tunnel near Camp Pendleton and, with help from the local in-station military, the Greys went down or surrendered. China Lake went down first, and it was easy. They are cleaning it out now, and the saucers are intact and operational. There were two hundred there. Per your orders the in-station personnel had disabled the saucers, and there was no way the Greys could have gotten them."

The president interrupted, "What about those skinny, green lizards that attacked me and killed my people?"

"Well Sir, they are going down as we speak. We believe those Greys came from the hidden base in Missouri that our forces found abandoned, we're positive the saucers did. They followed a different tunnel route to Washington. It was a suicide attack, but it was planned to work … and did. I guess the NAZIs figured the Greys were expendable.

Unfortunately for the Greys, we found a tunnel base near Camp Lejeune, North Carolina. The Marines in massive force poured into it after you were captured, and they have been crushing the Greys up the east coast tunnels ever since. Most of the Greys are dead or retreating, but they won't get far. We have forces coming up the tunnel from the Missouri side. The Greys are cornered, and the Marines are pissed."

The president smiled and said, "Thank them for me, and keep up the good work."

General Warner said, "Mr. President, Washington is going ape shit since your kidnapping. They want you back at the White House where you can be protected."

"Yeah, right. They did a great job protecting me before. You just tell them I'm with friends and safe now, and I'm well protected here with the Star Children in their fortress. I'll come back when the threat has been neutralized there and as soon as President Pramin has been rescued … not before. You tell Congress and the world that I'm bringing him back with me."

"Yes, Mr. President. I will take charge and deliver your message to the world."

President Thompson disconnected the call, looked around the cafeteria at all the faces and said, "Well, you all heard me and my promise. How are we going to do it?"

\*\*\*

John and Jane could do nothing. The saucer had far too much lead on them, so they waited anxiously. When the pings began coming in of the existence of a force field protecting an apparent NAZI saucer and Jerry and Mary's failure to rescue to rescue President Pramin, John informed General Gasimov and Colonel Letov of these facts.

General Gasimov was shaking in distress and said, "What can we do."

Berta yelled, "Get me and Dr. Wisscroff to the Russian scientists' location before you take off to Antarctica, like I know you will. We need to teach them how to build a force field for their saucers."

Dr. Wisscroff blurted out, "Berta, we can't just teach the Russians. That wouldn't be right or even fair. We can't give the Russians the technical advantage."

"We will teach both at the same time. They both need shields to go against the NAZI saucers. General Gasimov, does that sound fair? Can you set it up?"

"Yes, young one. That sounds very fair, and I will set it up immediately." After a few moments on his communicator he gave Jane the coordinates.

When they landed there were some very excited scientists gathered and waiting, many of which they had met in the teleconference. They surrounded Dr. Wisscroff and Berta and were pumping their hands in warm greeting. Soon they escorted the Dr. and Berta toward a lab apparently hastily set up, complete with video teleconferencing. Dr. Wisscroff had no idea how they were able to set it

337

up so quickly, but on the other end were an equal number of excited American scientists itching to meet them and learn new technology. Dr. Wisscroff felt that this must not be the first time these scientists had collaborated. So much for secrecy.

Emma remained with her saucer to give them a ride back, but also because she had learned the technology of the force field shield and wanted to help Berta teach the scientist.

Berta was the prime lecturer, and good at it, but Emma jumped in where she could. Berta stood at a blackboard writing formulas, sketching out designs and schematics and lecturing, while the scientists at both ends remained totally silent, writing and sketching frantically. Any outside observer would find the situation strange indeed, a young seventeen-year-old holding these older scientists in rapt attention. Many of the scientists could be seen nodding in sudden shock, understanding and agreement. Others looked lost in the vast depth of the knowledge being presented. But, it was also obvious that most of the scientists comprehended the ultimate objective and goals of the technology and how to get there, or at least some part of it.

The whole lecture had only taken an hour, but all of it had been recorded and would be replayed many times as required. Berta and Emma felt confident that the scientists would be able to quickly develop the technology and implement it soon. They quickly dismissed themselves, leaving the scientists already engrossed in the project. The Star Children and Dr. Wisscroff immediately boarded their saucer and zoomed up and toward the Sanctuary.

Once they were en route Dr. Wisscroff said, "Damn, Berta, I felt like a high school student in an Introduction to Science class. That was amazing."

Berta said, "Sorry, Dr. Wisscroff. I tried to keep it simple, but it is a very complex technology. The thing is, did you understand the technology?"

"Oh, yes. We all did the way you explained it and presented it. I dare say they will have the technology mastered in no time. After all, those groups of scientist are some of the smartest in the world. They may feel somewhat overwhelmed and their dignity may be injured, but they will get over it quickly with the project at hand. In short, they got it, at least some parts of it and will be able to piece it all together collaboratively."

***

John and Jane's team, less Emma, returned immediately to the Sanctuary and arrived in time for them to hear President Thompson tell the world he would bring back Russian President Pramin with him. Cheers rang out in the cafeteria.

General Gasimov said, "Mr. President, I can't tell you how happy I am to hear your promise. Russia stands with you on that, and we appreciate your support. I will tell the Russian people how you and the Star Children have helped save our country and how you are trying to obtain the release of our president."

President Thompson said, "Hello general. I wasn't expecting to see you here, but under the circumstances, I am pleased you are here. We certainly have a common enemy, an old enemy, and a common goal. We must rescue the Russian president. Having said that, how do we do that?" With that last statement he searched the room for answers.

Tom said, "Well, Mr. President, the NAZIs are full of surprises, and they have advanced technology of their own. We believe they also developed some mental powers similar to our own. We have seen some demonstrated, but we don't believe they are as powerful as ours. Still, we can't know for sure until we get in combat. Jerry, Mary and some other Star Children have met them in battle, and Jerry believes a human mind will not be able to engage them in battle. They would be overwhelmed and mentally controlled. I think that limits the battle to NAZI versus Star Children. Our technology is far better than theirs, and we have recently learned how to defeat their force fields. Still, they could surprise us with unexpected technology. We believe we can defeat their security shields now and simply fly into the Underworld and defeat them, but that is not the real problem. They have the Russian president as a hostage. I mean they must have kidnapped him for a reason. They might kill him if they face defeat, and Jerry says we aren't able to seize their minds to stop them, not all of them anyway."

Jerry said, "We might sneak back in through the cave entrance we discovered and try to locate where they are keeping the president, but the genetically modified NAZIs can see through our invisibility shields. I'm not sure what other mental powers they might possess. I know that some can mentally deflect our attacks. We've seen it, and I'm sure they will be watching for us. We learned that their hierarchy is established by their mental and physical powers in combat. So, all their leaders will possess mental powers and exceptional physical abilities."

Berta, having just arrived, said, "The NAZI leaders are all genetically altered and have powers. Their leadership positions are decided by combat. The strongest and most powerful fill their hierarchy, and they take pride in their contests. The contests are a public event. If someone challenges the current leader or ruler for any powerful position they must accept. It's the law and the way things are done in the Underworld, but I can assure you it wouldn't be easy. The current ruler is Otto Heinrich, and he has been in control for about ten years. He easily defeated the last ruler and every challenge since. He hasn't even been challenged in the last few years."

"It's possible that the kidnapping of both presidents was to force just such a combat challenge. I see no other result, since he now knows they can't defeat us in battle. Otto would feel highly confident of winning. For him it would be a sure thing."

Tom said, "Maybe I should challenge him. Is he required to accept?" Sue gasped out loud but remained silent otherwise.

Berta said, "Yes, the ruler must accept, but a challenge is not just a contest. It is combat in a locked cage using mind control powers and physical fighting skills, and there is no yielding, it's a battle to the death. If you are seriously considering a challenge, you should know you are huge, but Otto is very big, far bigger than you and very powerful and extremely skilled at killing. He will be able to resist your mental powers used against him. You better think hard about challenging him."

"Well, I don't see any other choice. We either fight a losing battle, for President Pramin, in the Underworld or we fight one-on-one with Otto. I don't see we have another choice."

Berta said, "Tom, you are very powerful with your mental powers. I've seen them, but remember your skills in combat would most likely come down to your physical fighting abilities, because Otto can resist and deflect your powers directed at him. Those of us that lived in captivity in the Underworld were allowed, even required, to witness those battles. I know you are mentally very powerful and you are large and strong, but I have never seen you actually fight a physical battle. We have seen Otto fight, and he is formidable. Once the powers are neutralized on both sides, the battle will come down to martial arts, boxing, wrestling and pure meanness, and Otto is ruthless. There are no rules, and we have seen him kill quickly. To be cruelly honest, I don't think you can win, and I don't recommend a challenge."

Tom said, "Well, thanks for the support, Berta."

"Sorry, Tom, I'm just being realistic."

Dr. Wisscroff said, "I wasn't going to openly express this thought before, but now it seems necessary. I have given this a lot of thought since Otis mentioned the capture of an injured Arcadian in the past, and the fact that the NAZI scientists had done genetic experiments to create their 'Master Race'". It is very possible that their scientists incorporated some of the Arcadian DNA in their experiments. In short, these genetically engineered NAZIs may have some of the Arcadian powers. To battle this Otto Heinrich might be like fighting another Star Child, which could be extremely dangerous."

President Thompson said, "I think we must challenge the NAZIs in this manner if we hope to save President Pramin, and we must save him for the stability of the world. Unless we can guarantee we can save him another way, we must challenge. Does anyone have a better idea?" The cafeteria remained totally silent for many long moments.

John got everyone's attention when he said, "I agree with Berta, Tom. I don't think you are prepared to take this Ottis Heinrich on in caged combat. You are just too young and inexperienced in his kind of ruthless fighting. Oh, your Arcadian powers are strong, very strong, but this battle will most likely come down to physical fighting skill, which you don't have."

"I, on the other hand, grew up not being aware of my dormant powers. As a result I grew up differently. I had to learn early in the orphanage how to take care of myself, and I've been doing it ever since. I joined the Marines at seventeen to get out of the orphanage. I learned Marine fighting skills and saw action in Iraq. Afterwards, I worked my way through college on a wrestling and boxing scholarship. Not only am I skilled in wrestling and boxing, but I'm well versed in martial arts. I learned physical fighting skills the hard way, but I learned the same way Otto has learned. If anyone challenges Otto it should be me. I think I stand a better chance of survival." Jane looked seriously concerned, but to her credit, she said nothing, and Tom lowered his head slightly and reluctantly seem to accept John explanation.

Dr. Wisscroff said, "Well so much for who. Of course it should be you, John, but I need to ask a single question. Why the hell would this Otto accept a challenge? I mean, what's in it for him? Maybe, like Berta says, it's the law of the Underworld, and he must accept a challenge, but why would he? What are the stakes? They will need a motivator. If John wins he then rules the Underworld, and we get whatever we want, but what if he loses? Sorry, John, but we must decide what we are prepared to gamble to save President Pramin? We are relatively sure we can win an all-out war with them now, but that would almost surely guarantee his death. What incentive can we offer to get Otto to accept a challenge. I certainly wouldn't count on the NAZIs following their laws if it benefited us."

A cloud of silence floated over the cafeteria for many long moments until General Gasimov broke the spell and spoke. "Thank you for what you are trying to do. The Russian people will appreciate your efforts to save our president, but we can't let you take all the risks. I would be willing to challenge this Otto myself, but without mental powers like yours, I wouldn't stand a chance against him. Still, the risk should be ours. Mr. Pramin is our president. I agree that the NAZIs would demand a substantial motivation to risk combat. Since they have already demanded our surrender, I suggest that this should be our risk. Hell, without the Star Children we would have already lost the war. If Otto wins, Russia will formally surrender to the NAZIs and honor the agreement. To strengthen the offer I suggest, Mr. President, that you offer to formally witness and sign the Russian surrender. I think this might provide the incentive for Otto to accept the challenge."

President Thompson said, "Great suggestion, General Gasimov, and a formal witnessed surrender is far better than one obtained by coercion, which the NAZIs no doubt have or intend to soon have. These ideas are brilliant. Anyone wish to disagree or comment further?"

Major Burns said, "I only have one problem, Sir. As my Commander in Chief and absent your Secret Service, I will not allow you to enter the Underworld. It's far too dangerous. If it comes to that we will have to find another way for you to witness the surrender. Let's face it. If Otto happens to win, which I don't think he will, what's to stop him from demanding your surrender also?"

President Thompson said, "Well said, major. My dead Secret Service agents would be proud of you for protecting me, and I will honor them and you. I will heed your instructions."

"Do we all agree this plan to be our recommended course of action? How about you, Mr. Canton and Dir. Setliff? You represent the U.S. government." They both nodded and no one else spoke out and seemed to be in agreement. The president continued, "Very well. Let's set up communications with the Underworld, as it's called. Let's make it video as well, if possible. I can judge his reactions better if I can see his eyes. I will make the first contact and negotiate the deal, and I am very good at negotiations."

As it turned out both the Russian government and the United States government had identified the frequency of the NAZI communication from downed saucers and were in the process of establishing communication when Dir. Setliff contacted them. They escorted the president to the Sanctuary communication center equipped with massive holographic presentation viewing. General Gasimov communicated with the Russian government and explained the situation, and Dir. Setliff briefed those on the American side.

All were ready when President Thompson entered. He said to those linked on the Sanctuary side, "All of you. I want to establish some rules before we establish the communication link with the NAZIs. I will do *all*, I repeat *all*, the talking." It is necessary to present a single front." He then said to

Jane, "When you interpret, try to be as precise as possible. I want my words and meaning exactly presented. If it becomes necessary to get anyone else involved I will let you know, and you must keep your responses short and simple. I will not hesitate to disconnect any of you from the negotiations if I feel it necessary. Is this understood?" The president didn't wait for an acknowledgement, he just pointed and said, "Connect."

The main holograph platform filled suddenly with a huge man in his early forties, heavy with muscles. He had blonde hair, almost as white at the Star Children's, but his eyes were blue as a deep pool of clear water. This man was dressed in a heavily adored NAZI uniform, complete with the dreaded SS insignia. This had to be Otto. He was sitting at a plain metal table with his hands laying loosely on the table in front of him like sledgehammers too heavy for his lap. The cheeks and brows were heavy and scared, but he looked calm, almost amused.

Otto said in perfect English, "I am Master Otto Heinrich, Supreme Commander of NAZI Germany's 4th Reich. We will not need the Russian interpreter bitch at your side, because, as you can hear I speak perfect English. I have lived among you and was educated in England, holding degrees from both Oxford and Cambridge. Many of us know your ways and lived among you. I have introduced myself. Now, who are you?"

President Thompson laughed loudly and said, "Well, Mr. Full of Yourself. Don't ask stupid questions. If you don't know who I am, then you are not as well educated as you think, and this conversation is a waste of time."

The smile on Otto's face vanished and he bellowed, "I know who the fuck you are. You contacted me. What do you want?"

"I want to see you in my courts where you can answer for your crimes, or I want to see you as a casualty of war. But, we can talk about that later. Right now I want the release of President Pramin."

It was Otto's turn to smile, then he said, "I'll bet you do, but that release won't come easy. You are just lucky we don't have you here, also. We certainly tried, and we would have you if the Star Children didn't save you."

"What do you want?"

"We want Russia and America's surrender."

"That is a stupid request. First of all, you have lost your war already with Russia and America, and the only thing that prevents us from totally destroying your Underworld 4th Reich right now is the fact that you hold President Pramin hostage. If anything happens to him we will launch immediately and your 4th Reich will cease to exist. I repeat, what do you want?"

"We here in the Underworld follow old traditions. Like old England, we follow the code of the Knights of old. Countries once settled wars by allowing Champions to fight in combat with the winner winning the war. We want Russia, since we only have their president, to present a Champion for combat with our Champion. The winner takes all. Russia gets their president back alive if their Champion wins. If our Champion wins we get their unconditional surrender.

"Continue."

"We know how devious your countries are, so we will require full worldwide television distribution so the world will know of the contest, the stakes and witness the outcome. We will also require America, you Mr. Thompson, to publicly agree to honor the results before the beginning of the Champions' contest. If this is not agreed to, bring on your war, and we will record President Pramin's execution and broadcast it to the world. That should provide good television and embarrass your governments. You ask what I want. This is what I want."

"I will have to talk to those in charge in Russia to get their response, but I can tell you one damn thing. Russia and I will want a whole lot more than just the release of the president. We will want *your* unconditional surrender."

"We will agree to those conditions, since I am the Champion here, and if your Champion wins I will be dead. Did I mention the battle of Champions is to the death? This point is not negotiable. This is the way our society runs, and makes the combat outcome absolute."

President Thompson said, "I believe you failed to mention that fact. I will discuss your terms and challenge with all concerned and will get back to you." The president pointed to end the conversation, which abruptly ceased.

President Thompson said, "Well, that was easy. It seems we assumed right, but it's now obvious that was his goal from the start. Otto realized he wasn't going to win the war, so they exercised 'Plan B'. If they had been able to get me there they would be trying for America's surrender as well. Actually, it was a strategic and calculating move, trying to snatch victory out of the jaws of defeat. Well, it's time to calculate the odds and decide what our answer will be. Any thoughts?"

Of course the response from Russia was to accept the challenge. They wanted their president back … alive. But, it was the Star Children taking the physical risk.

John said, "I don't think we have a choice. I agree to be the Champion. I still think I am the best prepared to take Otto on, but I want some time to prepare. I want to work with anyone, especially the Star Children, that can sharpen my skills."

The president said, "At best we may be able to buy a few days to set up the distribution of the television transmissions, but much more than that would be hard. Otto seems to want this to happen soon."

General Gasimov said, "I know I'm much older now, but my hand-to-hand skills remain sharp. I can work with you, also Colonel Letov is very skilled.

Major Burns said, "I can also help."

Dr. Wisscroff said, "I'm sure everyone is willing to help, especially the Star Children.

Physical fighting skills may be very key and important in the battle, but we can't forget about the powers skills, since Otto may have some surprises in that area. These skills must be honed to defend himself and to find weaknesses in Otto's defenses. If he does, John can win this easily. I will supervise this exercise. In fact, most of us should go to the gym now and get started, while the politicians do their stalling and negotiations."

President Thompson accepted the challenge on behalf of the Russian government and managed to stall it off for four days, claiming it would take that long to set up all the communications networks necessary for worldwide distribution. In reality, however, the news media, once notified, went into a feeding frenzy to cover the event. They would have been satisfied with 24-hour notice.

A single team made up from CNN, FOX and MSNBC, along with their talking heads, were granted access to the Underworld to cover the event live in English. A Russian collaboration of elite broadcast teams were also allowed access to cover the event live in Russian. These teams quickly converged on the South Pole entrance in helicopters. NAZI saucers led them to descend into the Underworld. These news broadcast organizations were obviously allowed in in order to provide credibility of the event to the world. The world airwaves were already full of events in preparation for the Champion's combat in many languages. Every movie ever made involving

Knights in combat were being broadcast, even the very old ones.

Otto was also ready to present himself to the world. He allowed interviews with the networks as both the Supreme Commander of NAZI Germany's 4th Reich and also the designated Champion. He took the opportunity to present his version of history. He justified the kidnapping of President Pramin and the attempted kidnapping of President Thompson by claiming NAZI Germany, the real leaders, had never surrendered and were still at war with Russia and America. He told the world that they had simply regrouped in the Underworld and waited for a better time to resume the war. Amazingly, he was stirring up some support for his government. The news media, as typical, was anxious to promote the controversy and presented Otto's version, which some even supported.

There was also a lot of speculation as to who Russia's Champion would be, since neither government had released that information. They wanted it to be a surprise to Otto, although he probably figured it would be a Star Child. None other but a Star Child would stand any chance against him, and he knew it.

The combat was scheduled for tomorrow, and John hoped he was ready. Today was a day of rest for John. Even Jane would let him do nothing more than eat and rest, which was frustrating, because Jane had been vigilant about him maintaining his strength since he volunteered to be the Champion. That meant no sex.

Dr. Wisscroff had been relentless in his training, but he insisted on full head and hand gear. He didn't want to risk any injuries by accident. General Gasimov and Colonel Letov had proved to be quite proficient in fighting and taught him some new techniques. John felt refreshed and at the peak of his game. The Star Children, especially Tom and Jane, constantly bombarded him with mental powers. Together they tried to seize his mind, and it took all his will and strength to resist, but he did. They forced him to maintain his shield through continuous attacks. They even attacked while he was fighting the general to force his mind not to wander.

Dr. Wisscroff drilled John without mercy. He established many exercises using every power he could imagine. Dr. Wisscroff told him, "John, this Otto might surprise you in several ways. If he does have some Arcadian DNA he might possibly have all the powers you possess, and he has had years to perfect them. He may have some you don't yet know or have discovered. Expect the unexpected and be prepared to learn quickly. You might surprise him by using powers he does not have. Test him. Use all your powers and find his weakness. Everyone has weaknesses, and so does he. Hopefully, this will be easy for you, but don't expect it. Be prepared for a long battle and don't try to win quickly. Let him expend his energy and wait for your chance to strike."

# Chapter 14
## (Champions' Contest)

During the four days leading up to the challenge combat of the chosen Champions the world had been in total chaos. Hardly anyone on the planet had not heard about the contest and the stakes. All was in readiness as President Thompson took his chair in the Sanctuary's communication facility. The link had been prepared and the world anxiously watched and listened.

President Thompson said, "Per our agreement with the Russian government and the so-called NAZI 4th Reich, I have agreed to sanction the outcome of this confrontation of Champions. America will honor the outcome of this battle. We do this to help the Russian government try to save their president. I am sympathetic to their desire, because I too was almost captured. I was saved only by actions of our friends, the Star Children. The Star Children, which I have already spoken of, have already saved our countries and the world from the initial attacks by the NAZIs. They have been true friends to Earth, and they continue to be. The chosen Champion for Russia is a Star Child. His name is John Meeker and he is my friend and a friend to humanity. He has agreed to battle Otto Heinrich according to their customs, which I do not agree with, but I agreed to honor the outcome. This is all I have to say at this point." He then abruptly indicated to end their transmission.

Jane lowered their Arcadian saucer into the Underworld and toward the base. Barely enough space existed in the crowd of people for them to land. They exited together and she escorted John to the arena. She kept touching him all the way and encouraging him with her words. John had been so busy preparing and training for battle that he hadn't had time to worry. Now, looking at the huge crowd, cameras and knowing that the world was watching, he realized that the time had come. Now he began to worry. This was life or death, his life or death, but he forced that thought to the back of his mind, as he entered the cage. He must remain focused.

He didn't have to wait long before Otto entered the cage, where John got his first surprises. Otto was far bigger than him in height and weight. Otto was also dressed like a Roman gladiator in black thick breast leather, a metal helmet and black leather forearm and thigh protectors. But, the most intimidating aspect of his garb were the sharp, metal spikes protruding from his leather armor. John hadn't expected that and worn only loose gym shorts. That was his first mistake. He had been thinking like this was a sporting contest, but in reality this was a killing match.

Otto grinned hugely under his helmet and laughed and said, "You are so fucking stupid. I can't believe they talked you into being their Champion. I have been so wanting to get one of you Star Children in a cage. I will hurt you badly and punish you before I kill you for the world to see. I will enjoy this."

Otto strutted around in the cage like a rooster as he talked, flexing his huge muscles. He was performing for the audience, but he was also trying to get inside John's head and terrify him. Had John not been prepared mentally it might have worked, but John was not the least bit intimidated. Maybe he should have been.

Dr. Wisscroff had said watch for his weakness, and he had already seen it. He saw it in several ways. First he saw it in his own mind and then with his enhanced vision. Otto was far too arrogant and confident, a total narcissist. That was Otto's weakness. He was so full of himself that he hadn't yet generated a shield. John did not respond to Otto's goading with a verbal response. He immediately built up an intense heat pulse tuned and focused on the metal in Otto's wardrobe and launched it. Otto was totally unprepared for the sudden burst of energy. Instantly the heat bombarded the metal of Otto's helmet and spikes and turned them white hot. Otto's face contorted, and he screamed loudly in pain. He pawed insanely at his melting armor, but he had enough foresight to throw up his shield. The helmet bounced on the floor of the cage then the leather guards with their burning spikes. By the time Otto was shed of them he had red, angry blisters every place a metal spike had been, and most of his head was burnt, and his hair was smoking. John almost laughed when he smelled the burnt flesh and saw Otto's burnt head and singed, blond hair. Plus, Otto was standing there in nothing but a jock strap. Even the crowd laughed. Otto was obviously embarrassed, but it quickly turned to raging anger. Otto was soon only interested in revenge and murder, and it was all focused toward John.

John realized he probably missed his golden opportunity. His mind had been thinking about those spikes and the dangerous advantage they gave Otto, so when he saw his opportunity he took them out. What he should have done was kill Otto outright when he had the chance. Now he might not get another chance.

Otto bellowed, "You alien bastard. You will pay for that!"

For the first time John spoke, "Shut up you arrogant shit and fight, or are you all show and talk."

John's intent was to keep Otto angry in hopes he would get careless. He succeeded in making him angry enough to charge him. Their shields collided with visible sparks, but both shields held. With their shields engaged they couldn't actually make physical contact with each other, but Otto was able to force his mind through both of them and tried to seize his mind. John didn't understand how Otto was able to do that, but he had. Otto's mental power was extremely strong, and John felt his mind weakening, but he remembered Mary's recently discovered method of projecting through a shield and forming her power inside the others shield. Apparently Otto was doing that. John projected his own power and focused it to form inside Otto's shield, like Mary had done with the NAZI saucer's shield. Their minds continued to struggle for advantage but neither was able to take control. Eventually both ceased trying. Otto charged again using his massive bulk and momentum, which took John by surprise. The laws of physics prevailed, and John flew backwards hard against the cage wall. The sudden force stunned him, but he fought back quickly and began forming gravity energy inside Otto's shield. Otto sensed it and dissolved his shield and repelled the energy. John immediately understood the logic: eliminate the shield to prevent it from holding the energy within. That way he was free to push it away. John shut his down also to prevent Otto from using it. Now they were both without shields, and Otto charged again swinging those huge hammer fists. John jumped up and dodged to the left just in time, as one of those lightning fast fists grazed his cheek, leaving a painful burning along his right cheek. If his fist would have connected solidly the contest would have been over. That was too close for comfort. Otto quickly turned and fired another lightning swing, but John's fighting training kicked in. He ducked under the massive arm and drove his right fist hard into Otto's jaw. The leverage, angle and force behind it were perfectly calculated and precise. Unfortunately, John's fist encountered a tree trunk. He felt the painful jar all the way to his shoulder, and worse, it had no effect on Otto. Otto immediately swung with his second hammer fist, but he was off balance, and it went whizzing just barely over john's head. John knew he would lose the battle fighting hand-to-hand. Something had to change. He had to slow Otto down or he would die. John shot out time energy to slow Otto's movement, but again Otto pushed it aside, and it had no effect.

Dr. Wisscroff had told him to be prepared to learn quickly. John would have to do that to survive. He had hoped to be able to use his time altering energy to see Otto's movement in slow motion, but Otto could prevent time energy from sticking to him. But … but Otto could not repel energy applied to John himself. *"Yes, learn quickly."* John thought. If I can't slow his movements maybe I can do as Jerry had originally said. Jerry described the power as increasing his own reaction time. It had been Dr. Wisscroff that identified the power as time manipulation.

John projected his time energy on himself to increase his own time, speed himself up, increase his reaction time. The effect should be the same. Otto should still appear to him in slow motion.

Yes, Otto was moving slowly, very slowly. Otto crept toward him swinging slowly. John let the hammer fist pass as he dodged. Otto's chin pointed directly toward him, but Otto's chin had obviously been reinforced to take a blow. John altered his aim and pounded his fist directly into the end of Otto's flat nose once, twice, then three times. John heard the snap and felt the nose bone break. Otto fell to the floor holding his face. Otto no longer tried to speak, he couldn't, but his body shook with rage. Otto jumped back up and charged John, but he came slowly. John wanted to end this and timed his next punch directly into Otto's throat and felt it collapse. He then spun and connected with his elbow into Otto's neck and continued again into the temple, like a jackhammer. Even the expression of shock was slow coming. John rolled to the other side and spun another elbow strike into the other side of Otto's neck ... hard. John felt and heard the neck snap. Otto went down again in slow motion face first, and did not move. Otto's feet quivered for a moment, then stopped. Otto's head lay at an awkward and unnatural angle. John resumed normal time.

John waited, and after a few moments of no movement by Otto, a doctor and an official came into the cage. The crowd remained silent in anticipation as the doctor checked out Otto. Finally the doctor spoke to the official. The official nodded and announced, "Otto Heinrich's neck is broken, and he is dead. I officially declare the combat of Champions is over, and Champion John Meeker is the winner. Master John Meeker is now the Supreme Commander of the Underworld."

The visiting media were going crazy and cheering, but many of the NAZIs remained in stunned silence. They couldn't believe Otto had been defeated. Some, however, began cheering and jumping in excitement, obviously pleased.

John wasn't expecting that declaration. He didn't want to be the Supreme Commander. Hell, he never wanted to fight in the first place, and now he had killed a man in personal combat. Otto wasn't a good man and had caused the deaths of many good people, human and Resis; but he had been a human being. The combat was stress enough, but now he felt it was required that he speak. In this situation he thought the combat might be easier than speaking, but the world and the audience was waiting. John said, "As the new Supreme Commander I order the release of Russian President Pramin. Bring him to our saucer. Now!"

Most of the NAZIs remained in shock that Otto has lost his battle, but others scrambled to comply. A few moments later a confused President Pramin was led out toward the saucer, where Jane took him in tow and led him stumbling and confused up the ramp. As soon as he was aboard, the saucer took off for the exit and the safety of the Sanctuary.

John had won his battle, but that was mere fighting, which he knew how to do. Now, things had drastically changed. It was now time for politics. He had been educated in political science in college, but this was far above his head, and he knew he needed help. John pinged Tom, *"Have Jane bring Dr. Wisscroff and Dir. Setliff to the Underworld. Bring Berta also, since she knows the Underworld."* Tom acknowledged compliance.

Exhausted, John waited in the arena with the NAZI official as attendants carried the broken body of Otto out of the arena, just as the Arcadian saucer landed. Dr. Wisscroff, Dir. Setliff, Berta and Jane rushed to join him in the cage.

When they surrounded him, John privately said, "I was prepared to fight, maybe even die, but I wasn't prepared to become the Supreme

361

Commander. I now find myself in charge of this Underworld, and I have no idea what to do. I need advice."

Dr. Wisscroff said, "I take it this official is the government interface, and he is awaiting instructions?" John nodded. "We can advise you, but I recommend you go back to the Sanctuary and rest first and come back better informed and rested. They can wait for their orders for a couple of days." Looking at the official he said, "Can't you? By the way, what is your name and position?"

The official said, "Yes, we can wait. My name is Peter Petrov, and I function as the Assistant to the Supreme Commander ... I get the Supreme Commander's wishes done."

Dir. Setliff said, "Were you friends with Mr. Heinrich? How do you feel about his death?"

Peter laughed and said, "Otto had no friends. He was cruel and ruthless. He governed as a dictator and will not be missed. Many here were secretly hoping to see him replaced. Now it has happened. I will serve John Meeker now if he wishes."

John said, "Mr. Petrov, I'm still stressed and tired from the combat, and I can't think clearly. I think I will return to our Sanctuary and discuss all our futures with my advisors. Mr. Petrov, I want you to come with us for those discussions. Do you have others that should be involved?"

For the first time open surprise flashed across Peter's face, and after a moment said, "Really, you want me involved in those discussions? I would be honored. There is one other that could provide valuable information, but he poses potential hostility. General Simon Schuster is ... was in charge of our military. He might resist change, but he knows all the details of our history."

"Good. Bring him along."

Peter motioned for an attendant, who came immediately. Peter spoke and the attendant was instantly off to do his bidding. The general must have been close and soon came into the arena.

The general came to face John and said, "I am General Simon Schuster at your service, Sir."

John said, "General, you will come with us in our saucer. We will be gone a couple of days, so issue the orders now to your combatants to cease all hostilities and surrender immediately to the local military commands. Understood?" The general nodded and snapped to attention and saluted.

General Schuster said, "It will be done, Sir."

John said, "Berta, do you have any suggestions?"

"I think it might be time to get the Resis involved. They haven't had a voice of their own in decades."

John turned to the official and said, "We will also want a representative, leader if there is one, of the Resis Race." After a short conversation with the official, the attendant was off.

All the conversations within the arena had been kept low, so none of it reached outside of the arena. Mr. Petrov went to the center of the arena to the outside microphone to the world and announce, "Our new Supreme Commander, Star Child John

363

Meeker, is returning back to their Sanctuary to organize our future government. General Schuster and myself will be accompanying and assisting him. Our first command from our new ruler is to cease hostilities with the outside world. We will return in a few days with our new instructions."

As they waited to board their saucer, news teams were busy making predictions on the changes that would be made. Soon two nervously shaking Resis arrived. Berta greeted them in their own language and tried to calm them then escorted them on board.

John was exhausted from the stress of battle, but he welcomed Jane's hugs and kisses she had held back in public.

Dr. Wisscroff said, "John, I know you are exhausted and obviously still stressed, but I have *got* to know one thing. I watched the match intently, and could pretty much figure out what was happening right up to the end. I suddenly saw you moving at super-fast speed, but how did you do that when he was repelling your powers.

John gave him a weak smile and said, "He was repelling my burst, like you said, so I launched the time power on myself and speeded up my reaction time. That did the trick."

"Incredible, you learned and reacted. Amazing. I'm so proud of you."

Soon they entered the cafeteria, where he was greeted with cheers, especially from the Star Children. The now recovered President Pramin greeted him warmly followed by President Thompson.

President Thompson said, "John, we won! The Greys are surrendering all over the world in mass numbers. The Tunnel Networks are clear and we are in firm control again of the tunnels, all of our underground bases and our saucers. The scientists are marveling at Berta's shield technology and hard at work to implement it. We still have a lot of work to do within our own governments to weed out all the traitors, but that will happen. I've already thanked Tom and the others for the help of the Star Children, and now I/we want to thank you for what you did." John simply shook their hands. He was too tired for anything else.

After the initial congratulations slowed, the Combat Cooks presented John with several trays of food and fresh milk, which he readily accepted. Dr. Wisscroff and Dir. Setliff took charge of those he brought from the Underworld, both engaging in deep conversations, while Berta took charge of the Resis. Major Burns remained close with obviously assigned guards. John knew the visitors would be cared for and watched over until he was ready to meet with them.

Both presidents obviously wanted to also meet with him, but right now all he wanted to do was sleep, rest and make love with Jane, in the reverse order. John dismissed himself from the chaos in the cafeteria, and he and Jane headed for their quarters. The fight was over and he knew Jane would not say no tonight.

Tina woke them up the next morning later than was her custom. John assumed that even Tina knew he needed rest, or maybe Mrs. Wilks had kept her restrained. Tina burst into their room and said, "Everyone is waiting, and the Army cooks have breakfast ready."

John had to laugh and said, "Well Jane, it looks like everything is back to normal." They laughed and donned their silver shits, but when they entered, the cafeteria was far from normal. They did get their breakfast, but it was served to them at a group of abutted tables. Around the group of tables were all the major players ... waiting. It seemed that both presidents were already in intense discussions over how the Underworld continent would be distributed between Russia and America.

John was fresh mentally now and very much back in charge of himself and now the Underworld, also. John said, "Sorry gentlemen. The Underworld continent will not be divided up. It will remain intact and will be controlled by me. I am the new Supreme Commander. I'm the Champion that fought the battle, and I'm the one that won. Have you forgotten already?" The dejected and solemn looking Peter Petrov and General Schuster both perked up and smiled.

President Pramin said, "But you fought the battle for Russia, and we have sustained major losses. It was my understanding that there would be an unconditional surrender. This is what happens when you surrender." President Thompson was nodding in agreement.

John said, "No gentlemen. I fought to save you, Mr. President, and I have saved you. I almost died doing so. We, the Star Children, fought to save both countries, and we have. The war is now over and we won, but we didn't fight so you could gain a new continent. We fought so you wouldn't lose the ones you already have. The Star Children will decide how it will be governed. The Underworld will emerge as a democratic nation to join the rest of the world in peace."

"We have made many friends during the war, and we wish to listen to your advice. But, the decision is ours. We, the Star Children, must supervise the Underworld.

There is something you and the world must understand. With the existence of the genetic powers created in the race of humans in the Underworld, we are the only ones that can control them, but we do want to create a completely new constitution for the government in which all the inhabitants have a voice, including the Resis. We will want your help in developing this constitution."

"One of the first issues is the elimination of combat as the method of choosing the Supreme Commander. I want my battle of Champions to be the last. We want the new government to be a democratic form of government and not a dictatorship."

Berta had been translating John's comments, and the nervous Resis began to actually smile. John had never seen a Resis smile before and found it humorous.

John continued, "As the de facto leader of the Underworld, regardless if I want it or not, it is up to me to make the decisions for them … us. Please tell me your thoughts and recommendations."

General Schuster quickly spoke up, "You *are* our leader! We should remain our own independent country. We have ceased hostilities, but we can still defend ourselves in our own country. In fact, we are impregnable. As to the Resis, they are our slaves. They do our bidding. It has always been that way. They don't have a voice in our government and shouldn't. They are not intelligent enough."

John said, "No general, the Underworld is not impregnable. The Star Children can pass through all your defenses at will. As to the Resis, our new government will not tolerate slavery. We want to join the world, and slavery is not tolerated in the world society. The Resis will have a voice and their freedom. In time we will educate them. Don't forget the Resis were once intelligent enough to have created the original technology you found there and reversed engineered. From what I have seen, they are sentient and intelligent, and from what I understand, they inhabited the Underworld long before the NAZIs came. Any hostilities from them has been the forced NAZI's hostilities, and you said yourself that they are slaves and do your bidding. General, things will change, for sure; but there will still be a place for you and the others. It will just be a different society." The general said nothing further.

President Thompson said, "John, we can appreciate what you are trying to do, and I'm sympathetic to your cause. Still, there have been many deaths and massive property loss, and it is appropriate to expect compensation in the form of property, namely the Underworld."

Tom, previously quiet, allowing John to do the talking, said, "John, I think what you are planning is good. The Star Children are with you. Do what you think is right." The other Star Children either nodded in agreement or voiced their "Yes" in agreement.

John sighed, visibly relaxed and said, "Thank you, Tom and others for your support. I was worried about that and value it.

"There you have it, Mr. President. Your countries will have compensation in the form of technology and money obtained by the patents on technology we will file. You are already benefiting from our technology, with more to come. We will call it a balance of power. Nevertheless, the Star Children now control the Underworld. That is the only way it will work. Russia nor the United States would not be able to interface in the Underworld. Your agents would quickly be mentally crushed and controlled there, because of the genetic alteration of the Underworld human race. Since, in part anyway, they are partly Star Children. It would be like you trying to control us. Just ask General Schuster or Mr. Petrov. Gentlemen, am I correct?"

Peter said, "Yes, you are correct. I'm sure outsiders would eventually be manipulated mentally by the stronger of our race. This is why our race reverted to combat. A lesser man would be controlled, so we elevated the strongest. Otto was the strongest of our race, but Mr. Meeker was stronger. That is why he is now the Supreme Commander."

President Pramin said, "I think I understand now. So what do we do with all those Greys we captured?"

John said, "Ship them all here. We will introduce them back into the Underworld where they came from. President Thompson, please do likewise. We will protect them if they are not hostile."

Berta said, "The Resis are docile in their natural environment. I've been interpreting and they are far from hostile. In fact they are extremely pleased with what they have heard. They said they would be good."

Dir. Setliff said, "What about the NAZIs? What's to be done about them?"

John said, "Well the NAZIs must remain in the Underworld under Star Children supervision. Of course they won't be NAZIs anymore. They will become industrialists I suppose. They are great at building things. I suspect the world will be purchasing a lot of their goods, and they will be putting the Greys to work. They will have to figure out how to pay them with goods now. Life should become interesting in the Underworld. As far as the Star Children, most of us will remain in our Sanctuary, although we do have much technology

370

we can also share. We will be available if you need us, but I suspect we will mostly remain isolated here for the same reasons the Underworld will remain isolated. We don't want the temptation that comes with these powers, and I'm sure you don't want to see them as well."

Dr. Wisscroff said, "I don't suppose we have a choice in this matter? So, I for one accept your terms, but I intend to stay here with you. Perhaps I can learn and disperse some of this technology."

Tom said, "Yes, you, Mrs. Wilks and any others of our friends are welcome to stay here in the Sanctuary, but we will control what technology gets dispersed. The world is not yet ready for much of it. To the world the Sanctuary is and will remain a Star Children operation, which now includes the Underworld. But, as you have already seen, we are a benevolent race and intend to remain so. Trust me. It will all work out … I hope."

## The End
### or
## A New Beginning